THE DRUID'S DAGGER

DEREK FEE

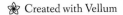 Created with Vellum

For my Family

PROLOGUE

His eyes flicked open. Above him, a full moon illuminated a clear sky. He tried to move but his muscles wouldn't obey the commands from his brain. He lay prone on his back. At college, he'd read Franz Kafka's *The Metamorphosis* and wondered whether he too had turned into a beetle in his sleep. That was ridiculous. But it was just as insane that he was lying powerless staring at the sky. His eyes tilted down, and he saw his naked chest. He tried to remember what he'd been doing before he found himself here. He was still trying to bring up memories when his heart jumped as a man wearing a long red robe and a goat-head mask entered the right side of his field of vision. He could feel the pounding in his chest, and he thought he could hear faint chanting in the distance. He had the sudden memory of a satanic ritual he should attend. He tried to clear his mind, but it appeared to be wrapped in an impenetrable fog. Nearby he heard the ocean crashing against the rocks. The goat head looked down at him. This had to be a joke, either that or a bad dream. He closed his eyes and willed himself to open them again. Nothing had changed, he remained prone, and the full moon still illuminated the sky above. The goat-head mask had moved closer and seemed to be observing him with interest. His eyes were concentrated on the figure as it threw off its cloak to reveal a man's ochre painted naked chest. His mind recoiled in terror. He could hear the chanting louder now and it appeared to be reaching a crescendo. He willed his arms to move but nothing happened. The man in the goat-head mask raised his right hand that clasped a large dagger that the prone man recognised as his. He screamed but no noise emanated from his mouth. The goat head was directly above him now. The dagger hovered above his chest and the man holding it said something he didn't understand. He let out a silent scream as the dagger was plunged into his heart.

DAY ONE

CHAPTER ONE

J oe Larkin sucked in the familiar smells of cow dung and sea air as he peddled the last few yards to the entrance gate at Dun Aengus, a Neolithic fort situated on the western side of Inis Mór, the largest island of the Aran Island group located off the west coast of Galway. It was mid-September, and the tourist season would soon be ending. But it had been a fine summer and the islanders depended on the tourists to augment the small income they made from fishing and farming. Larkin had been happy with his salary as one of the custodians of the principal touristic attraction of the island. He looked around the empty fields. By mid-morning, the area would be awash with all manner of people. The cycle from his home in Kilronan to the fort was getting more arduous every year. He couldn't fight time; he was getting on and he would soon have to hand over the job of opening the site to someone younger and fitter. He parked his bike beside a small ticket kiosk and turned towards the gate that barred the access to the path leading to the fort. He stopped and stared when he saw it hanging open. He sighed. Cider parties were a regular feature of life on the island but most of the young people contented themselves with cavorting on the beaches. He decided to head up to the fort in case the revellers had left detritus behind. Cleaning up the empty bottles and plastic cups didn't bother him but from time to time he'd be obliged to remove evidence of sexual activity. The American tourists wouldn't be reticent at penning a review on Tripadvisor about condoms littering the site and that would land him in trouble. He started climbing the rocky path that was the first impediment in reaching the Neolithic structure. The one-kilometre trek was over a gravel path and gradually ascends. He loved this short walk principally because the neighbouring fields were dotted with brilliantly coloured flowers. He stopped and admired the hardy gentian whose trumpet-shaped flowers were a striking lapis colour. They were interspersed with lilac wild orchids. Such an abundance of nature gladdened his heart. Continuing uphill he soon reached the second and more effective barrier to the fort, a so-called chevaux de frise, a series of vertical limestone pillars set into the ground to impede attackers. Larkin had his own route through the maze but even he had difficulty reaching the open area beyond. He made his way to the small door cut in the outer wall of the fort and squeezed through. He came out into the open area that constituted the fort's keep. He looked around the area and thankfully didn't see the tell-tale bottles that would have indicated a party. He moved towards the black stone platform that rises several feet above floor level. Something strange lay on it. As he approached, it became clear that it was a man and there was a black object sticking vertically out of his chest. 'Holy God.' Larkin made the sign of the cross. He moved slowly towards the platform. The figure resembled a snow-white alabaster statue. But already Larkin's nose picked up the sweet smell of death. He reached the edge of the platform, turned quickly and vomited onto the ground. He was no stranger to death, but the sight in front of him was something else. The man lying on the platform had been stabbed and eviscerated, his innards lying between his naked legs. Larkin staggered away from the rocky platform, pulled out his mobile phone and walked uncertainly towards the hole in the outer wall. There would be no visitors today.

CHAPTER TWO

Detective Sergeant Fiona Madden had already put in a two-hour practice session in a dojo before making her way to the CID office located in Mill Street Garda station in Galway city. Her short blonde hair was still wet as she slid into her ergonomic chair and turned on her computer. She and her partner, Detective Sean Tracy, had been investigating a series of muggings in the centre of Galway and had managed to apprehend the miscreant the previous day. Tracy had been tasked with completing the paperwork and she was concerned that there was no sign of him in the office. Tracy was a college graduate and, as such, had been weaned on paperwork. On the other hand, Fiona hated it, so the partners were compatible in that area. Fiona sighed with relief when she saw Tracy entering the office carrying a cardboard tray with two take-away coffee cups.

'Hard night?' she asked.

Tracy put a cup on her desk, slumped into his chair, and immediately ripped the lid off his cup and took a draught. 'Launch of a new book on the history of the Lynch family. Cliona gets invited to all these arty events and there's always an after-launch party. Wine and canapes at the launch and something a little stronger afterwards.'

Fiona sipped her coffee. 'Any drugs about?'

'Not that I saw. But everyone knows what I do for a living.'

'You don't have to go.'

'It'd be more than my life's worth. These people in the arts would turn up for the opening of an envelope.'

'Did you make much progress on the paperwork for the little mugging toerag?'

'I'm working on it.'

Fiona looked at her partner. His new girlfriend had certainly made changes. His dark locks hadn't been shorn in weeks, maybe months. They hadn't seen a comb in days and had the ruffled look associated with down-on-their-luck painters. His hair wasn't the only thing that had changed. He had been what people might have called a careful dresser, but he now sported open-necked grandfather shirts, jeans and loose-fitting linen jackets. Fiona wasn't one to talk. She normally arrived at work in jeans and a leather biker jacket. Tracy's new look was growing on her. When he arrived in Galway, he looked like he'd just graduated from university. Cliona had given him an altogether rougher look. Think Colin Farrell.

'I'd better get to it.' Tracy finished his coffee, dumped the cup and turned on his computer.

'I don't think your heart will be in it today.'

'Is there anything else on?'

'Not a thing. I was thinking of checking out the latest edicts from HQ.'

'You're kidding?'

'Yes, I am. The last thing I fancy is spending my day on a task that will leave me wanting to eat my head by five o'clock.'

Tracy began typing. He was normally a touch-typist, but his fingers appeared to have difficulty finding the right keys. 'What I wouldn't give to get outside in the fresh air. They say it's going to be a scorcher. Are you sure there's nothing on the wire?'

Fiona shook her head and despite her protestations to the contrary, she opened the email file that contained the latest administration decrees She delayed before opening the first notice which dealt with the inevitable problems with the over-time budget. Her phone rang and she grabbed the handset.

'You and Tracy in my office, pronto,' Detective Inspector Horgan said.

'On our way.' She put the phone back in its cradle and ruminated on her boss's definition of pronto. Horgan was old-school and she assumed he meant immediately.

'Horgan wants us upstairs, pronto,' she said to Tracy. 'So, we'd better get our skates on.'

Tracy smiled. 'We're going out. What's with the *pronto* and *get our skates on*? We're not back in the 1970s, are we? Remember that TV programme *Life on Mars*, a copper goes back in time to the 1960s. Maybe Horgan's gone back in time.'

'Chance would be a fine thing,' Fiona said. 'But the idea of Horgan disappearing into the past is attractive. Let's go and find out what's bothering him today.'

'I'M NOT KIDDING.' Horgan leaned forward in his chair to emphasise the fact. 'The caretaker found the body this morning when he opened the site. The man is naked as the day he was born, lying on a raised platform of rock with a knife planted in his chest and his innards covering his genitals.'

Fiona and Tracy looked at each other. 'Sounds like a stunt a group of medical students might get up to,' Fiona said.

'If it is something that students got up to,' Horgan said. 'I'll teach them that the Garda Síochána don't see the funny side of such shenanigans.'

'Or it could have been a prop for a horror movie, and someone left it on the platform for a joke,' Tracy said.

Horgan frowned. 'I have it on good authority that it's a real body.'

'You want us to look?' Fiona said.

'That's the plan. Given that you're detectives and all.'

'There's a small plane serving the big island,' Fiona said hopefully.

Horgan laughed. 'The ferry company are holding the boat until you and Tracy arrive. The local man, a Garda Clarke, will meet you on arrival and convey you to the crime scene which has already been cordoned off. The CSIs from the Technical Bureau are already on their way to Rossaveal so why the fuck are the two of you still sitting here with your thumbs up your arses.'

'Boss, there's a lady in the room, that sounds a bit sexist,' Tracy said

Horgan glanced theatrically around the room and finished by glaring at Tracy. 'Are you still here?'

CHAPTER THREE

Fiona and Tracy arrived outside the office of Aran Ferries at Rossaveal, a small port on the west coast of Ireland best known for its fishing fleet. The English name is a corruption of the Gaelic Ros a Mhil which translates as the peninsula of the great whale or sea monster. It has no touristic value except as the departure point for the ferries serving the Aran Islands. Tracy had managed to do the forty-kilometre trip along the coast road in forty-five minutes, but they were still responsible for delaying the ferry by fifteen minutes.

'Park here,' Fiona said.

'There's a no parking sign.'

Immediately they descended from their car they were approached by a large man wearing a high-vis jacket. 'You can't park there.'

'I told you so,' Tracy said.

Oh yes, we can.' Fiona held up her warrant card. 'Garda on duty.'

The man wandered off towards the ticket office mumbling to himself.

A middle-aged woman exited the office and accosted the high-vis man. 'It's okay, Cillian. They can leave the car there.

We need to get them on board as quickly as possible. The skipper is doing his nut because he missed the sailing time. The schedule for the day is going to be screwed up.' She looked at Fiona. 'You're Detective Sergeant Madden?'

'Yes, and this is Detective Garda Tracy.'

The woman held out her hand. 'I'm Maura Leavy.'

Fiona shook her hand. 'Are you in charge here?'

'God no, I just manage the ticket office.' A sharp whistle sounded and Leavy looked along the quay. 'They're waiting for you to board so that they can cast off. Your colleagues from the Technical Bureau are already on board.'

Fiona ignored the whistle. 'How many people will be leaving Aran on the return journey?'

'I'd have to check the manifest to be sure, but I'd guess there are at least a hundred. We're pretty busy what with the good weather and all.'

'Do you have the names of all the passengers?'

Leavy smiled. 'The trip costs thirteen euros. It's the equivalent of a bus journey from Galway to Furbo. We take the money and give you a ticket.'

'Does that mean you have no idea who the people that are about to leave the island are?'

'In a nutshell, yes.'

Fiona looked at Tracy. 'You're going to be a busy boy when we arrive on the island. I want the name and address of everyone who leaves Inis Mór today. And there will be no return sailings if I don't get them.'

'Maybe Maura could arrange with her colleagues on the island to at least start the process,' Tracy said. 'That might shorten the delay. We could get Garda Clarke involved as well.'

Fiona turned to Leavy. 'Garda Tracy is a real charmer, but he does have a point. Can you get on the phone and tell your office that I'll need the name and address of everyone leaving today verified by a photo ID?'

'You're kidding,' Leavy said.

'Tracy and I never kid. There's apparently been a murder on the island and you're lucky that we don't cordon off the whole island; no one in and no one out.'

'A lot of them are Americans who'll be moving on today.'

'Then the sooner we start taking the names and addresses the better.'

Leavy rushed off in the direction of the ticket office.

'Isn't that a bit draconian?' Tracy said.

'If that means what I think it does, the answer is no. If the man with the knife in his chest was murdered, and I think there's a good chance he was, we don't want the killer catching the next ferry and disappearing like a puff of wind. It's hard enough to find a murderer under ideal conditions but murder on a small island in the Atlantic packed with tourists from all corners of the world poses challenges. I can see a nightmare ahead.'

'Unless you're right and it was a student prank,' Tracy said.

'I don't subscribe to that theory.'

'But you came up with it.'

'Let's wait until we examine the body.'

'Then all the name taking might be a waste of time.'

'So be it.'

Leavy exited the office. 'They're hopping mad but they're going to check everyone's identity. The skipper wants you on board now. He's threatening to leave without you.'

'Just let him try,' Fiona said but her comment was drowned out by another blast of a ship's horn.

'Maybe we should board,' Tracy said.

'You brought the coveralls, overshoes and masks?'

'As directed.'

'Get them and follow me.'

Tracy went to the rear of the car and removed a rucksack.

Fiona sauntered along the quay. She ignored the stares of

the passengers arranged along the rails. The delay was cutting into their time on the island. She raised her eyes further and met the gaze of the heavily bearded man she assumed was the skipper. He didn't look happy. She and Tracy climbed the gangplank which was immediately hauled on board by a young crew member. Ropes were tossed to crew members at the bow and stern of the boat. The engines began to churn, and the ferry pulled away from the quay. They had missed the sailing time by twenty-five minutes.

Fiona and Tracy moved towards the saloon and were almost through the door when a member of the crew stopped them. 'Skipper wants to see you, ignore the sign on the stairs barring entry to the bridge.'

The two detectives looked at each other. 'Ready to face an angry seaman?' Tracy said.

'I've never been on the bridge of a ferry.' Fiona made for the stairs that led to the bridge. 'And I've taken more than one bollocking in my lifetime. Another one won't matter.'

As Fiona and Tracy entered the bridge, the skipper turned from the large window at the front. 'Fiona Madden, you always were a nuisance.'

'And who would you be?'

'Michael Coyne. I was two years ahead of you in Glenmore school. You probably don't remember me.'

'I don't. But it doesn't help that you're hiding your face behind that mask of hair. You look more like a pirate than a ferry captain.'

Tracy had drifted to the front of the bridge and was conversing with the helmsman.

Coyne handed her a cup of tea. 'The stuff they serve in the saloon is glorified cat's piss. You've screwed up my schedule for the day.'

She took the cup from him. 'Blame the poor guy with the knife in his chest in Dun Aengus.'

Coyne thought for a moment. 'I don't think there's ever been a murder on the island.'

'So, I hear.' Fiona sipped her tea; it was strong and sugared. Her mother would have said that you could trot a mouse on it.

Coyne laid his cup on a chart table. 'I live on the island myself and my wife's an islander. They're a close-knit lot. You'll have a job getting them to talk if it's a local issue. Any idea who he is?'

'No, the site's been cordoned off by the local Guard. How many passengers have you got?'

'Officially ninety, unofficially over a hundred.'

'And the same on the return?'

'The same. I hear you're taking names. I don't envy you.'

'A policeman's lot is not a happy one.'

'Neither is a ferry skipper's. That was a bad business with the young Joyce girl in Glenmore.'

Fiona finished her tea and handed the cup to Coyne. 'It was nice to meet you again, Michael. Thanks for the tea. I think my colleague and I should take our places on the deck. We need to find the CSIs and I want to take a good look at the mob that are leaving the island.'

'We'll see each other on the way back and exchange village gossip. Don't forget we sail at five o'clock.'

Only if I say so, Fiona thought.

CHAPTER FOUR

F iona and Tracy left the bridge and stood together at the rail looking at the islands rising before them. It was a sight that Fiona saw each day from her cottage in Furbo. Depending on the weather conditions, there were days that she felt she could reach out and touch the islands while on others they appeared hundreds of miles away. There was something bewitching about the Aran Islands; they appeared older than time itself. They headed inside and located Foley and his assistant O'Malley in the saloon having their breakfast and left them to it. The saloon was packed so they returned to the deck.

'Do you know everyone in Connemara?' Tracy asked.

'It's a small place.'

'You're frowning, what's the problem?'

Fiona shielded her eyes from the sun with her hand. 'That we're possibly screwed. We might have lucked out. The Joyce murder was local and Clifden involved a closed society. There are eight hundred and fifty residents on the island and there are probably two or three hundred visitors. As of this moment, we have more than a thousand suspects and one hundred of them are about to disappear back to the mainland. If I had my way, I'd close the island off for the duration of the investigation but that's out of the question. Too many people's livelihoods are at risk.'

Tracy looked out at the island. 'It looks so peaceful. I heard the skipper say that there's never been a murder there.'

'Not officially at least.'

'You're a true-born cynic.'

'So, they tell me.'

Tracy's phone rang. He looked at the caller ID, answered and moved along the deck.

They were approaching the end of their journey and the backpackers were gathering up their rucksacks and heading for the lower decks. The sailing had taken forty minutes and she assumed that should have given the island's ferry employees time to take the passengers' names. When she'd been a young girl, Fiona had visited Inis Mór many times. Her father had family there and the Madden family made an annual summer trip. It was in the days before the new quay was built and passengers had to be offloaded from the ferry onto a currach and rowed ashore. It was a delicate process that sometimes led to hilarious accidents. It was a pity that YouTube and TikTok were decades in the future. She watched the expectant crowd lining the quayside as the ferry cut speed and eased towards the mooring at Kilronan, the largest town on the island. This time the crew tossed the mooring ropes to the men waiting on the quay and the boat was tied up. Tracy returned and stood beside her, his private call terminated. He turned on his camera and panned along the line of tourists and locals waiting to return to the mainland.

'Try to get pictures of all of them.'

Tracy gave her a thumbs up.

Fiona looked up at the bridge where Michael Coyne stood staring down at her. He gave her a silent salute. She knew by his face that her arrival was known by every islander. The gangplank had already been run out onto the quay, but she didn't follow the crowd heading below. Instead, she concentrated her attention on the people waiting to board. They were a mixed bag of young backpackers, middle-aged tourists and islanders heading to Galway to shop in a supermarket for a change. None of them was kind enough to have murderer tattooed on their foreheads. The bard was right when he'd written *There's no way to find the mind's construction in the face.* She'd studied Macbeth during her last year at school and enjoyed Shakespeare. He knew people so well that she thought he would have made a good detective. The passengers on the quay made way for those descending on the gangplank. None of them seemed more anxious than the next person to be away quickly from the island. She moved off slowly and was one of the last people to leave the boat. She forced her way through the crowd and used the process to check for nervousness. She noticed none, just a desire to get the best seat on the boat.

Tracy had already reached the end of the quay and stood talking to a uniformed Garda who Fiona assumed was Dominic Clarke. Foley and O'Malley made it a foursome and the two steel cases at their feet contained their equipment. It was past eleven o'clock and the sun was warm. Fiona continued her slow progress through the waiting passengers. The locals were already hustling the tourists, promising tours of the island by minivan and open horse-drawn carriages. Fiona brushed away their entreaties by speaking to them in Gaelic. She finally joined Tracy and Clarke who tried a salute.

'No formalities, I assume you're Garda Clarke?'

'Yes, ma'am.'

'Yes, sergeant, will do. I don't see myself reaching the exalted level where I'll be addressed as ma'am.' Sweat ran down Clarke's face which was the colour of a ripe tomato.

'Loosen your tunic, for God's sake man,' Fiona said. 'In fact, you might think of dumping it altogether. We're rather light on information and I suppose you've already been up to the fort. You can give us a briefing on the way. Did you recognise the corpse?'

'I didn't get close enough to see him clearly.' Clarke opened the buttons on his tunic and the top button on his shirt before taking his tie off.

'Your first murder?' Fiona asked.

'Yes.'

'We'll need transport.'

'Our official vehicle is a bit of a banger, so I've requisitioned a minivan.' He waved at a group of men standing at the end of the quay. One of them detached from the group, walked to a white seven-seater minivan, started the engine and drove it to where they stood.

'*Failte go dí an Oileann,*' the driver said as he slid the rear doors open. '*An bfuill Gaelge agaibh.*'

'We're not tourists so you don't have to play up to us,' Fiona said. 'I'm a Gaelgeoir but my colleague prefers English.'

'Thomas O'Flaherty,' the driver said. 'You want to go to the fort.' He had a slight but noticeable American accent.

'If that's where the dead man can be found,' Fiona said. O'Flaherty looked to be in his early thirties with a head of black curly hair and a dark complexion that might have been inherited from a passing Spanish sailor.

'And you are?' O'Flaherty asked.

'In a hurry.' Fiona said.

O'Flaherty helped Foley and O'Malley load their cases into the luggage compartment before ushering them into the two rear seats. Fiona and Tracy sat in front of them while Clarke took the front passenger seat.

O'Flaherty closed the side door, took his seat and drove up the narrow road that led to the opposite side of the island and Dun Aengus. Their minivan manoeuvred through a throng of young people who had rented bicycles.

'The site has been cordoned off,' Clarke began. 'Visitors have been told that the fort is off limits. Of course, that might not stop the headcases, but the site manager has called in helpers to keep people away. It's a hell of a sight up there.'

'What about the doctor?'

'She's waiting for your arrival,' Clarke said. 'I've been busy with the ferry people taking the names of the departing passengers and checking their photo IDs.' He removed three A4 sheets from his inside pocket and handed them to Fiona who passed them to Tracy without examination. 'So, as of now, we know nothing.'

'Except that there's a body on the platform,' Clarke said

'That was an excellent briefing,' Fiona said. 'Now Mr O'Flaherty can forget about listening and concentrate on driving.'

CHAPTER FIVE

O'Flaherty parked his van beside the kiosk at the entrance to Dun Aengus. All five passengers descended and stood beside the van. The kiosk had a large handwritten sign above it indicating that the site would be closed for the day. Four men stood outside smoking.

Clarke looked over at the group. 'The man on the left is Joe Larkin. He's the one that found the body. He's worked on this site since Moses was a baby.'

Fiona followed Clarke's stare. 'Detective Garda Tracy and I will have a word with him.' The man who had been pointed out by Clarke appeared to be in his seventies. He was a large man dressed in a wax jacket and cord trousers.

'How far is it to the fort?' Foley asked looking away to his left where a narrow path ran uphill.

'A good twenty-minute walk,' O'Flaherty said. 'And uphill for most of it. Then you'll have to move through the standing stones before a second climb.'

'And who is going to lug our equipment up the hill?' Foley asked.

'Are we paying Mr O'Flaherty?' Fiona asked Clarke.

'We are.'

'Then he'll be able to assist Detective Garda Foley. I'm sure a strong young man wouldn't allow a young lady to carry a heavy case.'

Foley moved to the rear of the van and unloaded the steel cases. He had a face like thunder.

'I thought you were going to give me the packhorse job,' Tracy said.

Fiona walked toward the group of men Clarke had indicated, accompanied by Tracy. 'The Garda Síochána hired you for your nimble mind and not your broad back. I think our driver is more suitable for the role. I want to have a quick word with Larkin and then we'll be off after Foley's little band.'

The four men shuffled their feet as the detectives approached.

'Mr Larkin,' Fiona said.

Larkin absentmindedly twisted a flat cap in his hand. He stopped and put it on his head. 'That's me.'

Fiona introduced herself and Tracy then shook hands with Larkin. She could see that his normally tanned face had a tinge of pallor and there was a tremor in his hand. 'You discovered the body?'

'I did.'

'Tell us what happened from the time you arrived at the kiosk.'

'I open up the site every morning. I've been doing it since I was a young man. When I'd put my bicycle away, I noticed the gate was open. I close it in the evening but I'm getting on and I suppose I'm a bit forgetful. I thought I might have forgotten or that maybe a group of young people had broken in and had a party in the fort. It's happened before. I'm responsible for the site and if there was a party, I'd have to clean it up before the clients arrive. I wasn't too worried, I had plenty of time and I enjoyed the walk. When I got to the fort, I didn't see any of the rubbish that the kids usually leave lying around. That's when I saw the figure on the platform. It was as white as the driven snow and had a black knife planted in its chest. I thought it might have been a model but there was nobody about. Then when I got close, I saw the knife and the blood and the intestines. I threw up when I realised what I was looking at.' He took a packet of cigarettes from his pocket and offered it to Fiona who shook her head. He removed a cigarette and lit it.

Fiona noticed his hands shook. 'What did you do then?'

'I phoned it in straight away.'

'You called Garda Clarke?'

'No, I called the office, and they called the Guards.'

'Has anyone been to the site since?'

'Only Garda Clarke. He rigged up crime tape across the door in the outer wall and we posted a man there.'

'You did right. Has anything like this happened in the past?'

'A dead man? Never.'

'Did you recognise the victim?'

'Faith, I don't think his own mother would have recognised him.'

'He's not an islander?'

'I don't think so. I've lived on this island for the past seventy-two years and I've never run across him. But I don't get out as much as I did.'

'What time did you close last evening?'

'I did a final check at six o'clock. There wasn't a soul on the site.'

'Could people have hidden up there?'

Larkin pulled deeply on his cigarette. 'I suppose so. But I didn't see anyone on the way up or the way back.'

'And what time did you open up this morning.'

'I arrived on site at eight and I went straight up when I saw the gate open.'

'Anything strange or unusual?'

'Over the years we've had problems with groups that want to hold ceremonies in the fort. They say it was the site of human sacrifice and orgies and that kind of thing. The priests of the old religions ruled over it before Saint Patrick brought Christianity. Strange things have happened up there. I always get an eerie feeling inside the fort.'

'Why don't you go off home now and get Mrs Larkin to make you a cup of tea. Detective Garda Tracy will take a statement from you later.'

'You'll find me in Kilronan.' Larkin took his bike and cycled down the hill.

'The poor bloke is shocked.' Tracy had retrieved his rucksack from the rear of the van and had it slung over his shoulder.

'Remember the beach at Caladh Muinish?' Fiona said smiling.

'You promised to never speak of that.'

There was a shout from up ahead.

'I think Foley is having difficulty traversing the standing stones,' Fiona said. 'If I remember correctly from my visits here, it's a little tricky. Let's go see our murder victim.'

CHAPTER SIX

Fiona and Tracy accomplished the first part of the climb with ease, the second part wasn't so easy. As they entered the chevaux de fries the air around them was rent with Foley's expletives. Fiona didn't blame him, lugging a steel box full of scientific instruments was difficult at any time but doing so amid a field of raised jagged limestone pillars designed to impede upward progress was a trial worthy of a stream of curses. Beyond the standing stones, there was a relatively gentle grass-covered slope to the next hurdle: the outer wall of the fort which was constructed of large boulders laid in drywall fashion. They made their way to the small door in the wall and reached it just as Foley, O'Malley and O'Flaherty exited from the standing stones. They ducked through the outer wall and found themselves in another grassy area which served as an outer keep. Up ahead was another large thick stone wall with another small door that had been blocked off with yellow crime scene tape. A man of similar age to Larkin sat on a boulder beside the door.

'I'm Detective Sergeant Madden,' Fiona said. 'You can go down; we'll take care of keeping people away.'

Tracy pulled away the layers of tape and Fiona ducked

into the doorway. She found herself in the inner keep and the sound of crashing waves they'd heard on the way up intensified. A hundred yards in front of them the rock floor of the keep terminated in a sheer cliff that fell into the Atlantic Ocean. The site of the fort had been chosen well by the Neolithic tribe that had built it. The sheer cliff meant that they couldn't be attacked from the rear. She ignored the closeness of the drop into the ocean and turned towards the black stone platform that dominated the centre of the keep. On it lay the corpse they had come to see. They approached the rock structure together. The corpse lay spreadeagled on the platform. It was a male, and a dagger, decorated with a curved design, was buried almost to the hilt in his chest. She heard Tracy gasp beside her. The corpse's intestines lay across his genitals.

'I don't think it's a joke by medical students,' Fiona said. 'Neither do I think that it's a model from a horror film.'

Tracy handed her a pair of overshoes and gloves and bent to put on his own.

Fiona slipped on the overshoes and gloves and approached the platform. She'd seen weird murder scenes, but never anything like this. 'Take photos, lots of photos.'

The corpse had lost a lot of blood and rigor was well advanced. He'd been a big man, over six feet by at least a couple of inches. He had a reddish-coloured beard and had a full head of light brown hair. She fancied they might find that he regularly touched both up. He wasn't fit but he wasn't corpulent. He hadn't been a sportsman because what fat he had was loose. In life, she would have guessed that he wasn't bad looking. But his facial features didn't look so good in death. There was a rictus on his mouth that indicated he didn't die in peace, but she had seen much worse. His legs were open, but his arms hung by his side.

Tracy took out his mobile and took photos from every angle. 'Looks like it might have been a ritual killing.' He pointed to the ground on the other side of the platform from Fiona.

She joined him and found that a large pentagram had been painted in black on the ground beside the platform. 'Let's not jump to conclusions.' She knew that the diversity of forms of murder is only matched by the diversity of man himself. Very few people would believe that a murderer would lure victims by promising them sex and then proceed to murder and eat them. But that was precisely what Jeffrey Dahmer did. She returned to examining the body just as Foley and O'Malley entered the inner keep. 'Don't let O'Flaherty inside,' she said to Tracy who hurried off in the direction of the door. Fiona watched as O'Flaherty was escorted from the keep.

Foley and O'Malley joined Fiona.

Sweat rolled down Foley's face and he muttered curses under his breath.

'Going down is easier,' Fiona said.

'I'm quitting this job.' Foley kicked his steel box.

'We're all quitting but we all keep turning up even though it ruins our lives and our relationships.'

'Let's get on with it.' Foley flicked the locks on his case. 'The sooner I'm out of here the better.' Foley removed his Tyvek protective gear and suited up.

Fiona and Foley approached the corpse on the platform. 'No ligatures visible,' Fiona said.

Foley picked up the hands and examined the wrists then moved to the ankles. 'He wasn't restrained.'

Fiona bent to examine the wrists and ankles, 'So he just lay there while someone drove a dagger up to the hilt into his chest.'

'That's what it looks like.'

Tracy had returned from ejecting O'Flaherty. 'If he was a sacrifice, he would have willingly accepted his fate.'

Foley and Fiona were sniffing the air. 'Bleach,' Foley said. 'And lots of it.'

'Isn't Google a curse?' Fiona said. 'I suppose you can look up how to commit the perfect murder.'

'Don't give me ideas,' Foley said.

O'Malley circled the platform photographing the corpse from every angle.

'Processing this site will be a bitch,' Foley said. 'There must have been a herd of elephants through here yesterday by the look of the grass.'

'No, it was worse than a herd of elephants,' Fiona said. 'It was a couple of hundred tourists.'

Foley removed a UV light from the case and shone it on the platform. The site was covered in blood. 'The poor bastard has been almost totally exsanguinated. Why don't they just murder people in their homes and give us a chance of lifting useful evidence? I can tell you now, Madden, we're going to find fuck-all here. That doesn't mean that we won't do our best, but the scene is chaotic and what we do pick up will be ninety-eight per cent trash and we won't recognise the two per cent of valuable evidence.'

Fiona examined the body. 'There doesn't appear to be any bruising,' she said. 'It's looking like he wasn't coerced.'

'It's ritual murder or maybe we should call it human sacrifice,' Tracy said. 'Did you ever see the original version of that film *The Wickerman*? They burn this big effigy of a man made from wicker and the human sacrifice is inside. But they can't put him there, he has to go in of his own volition.'

Foley stared at Tracy.

'He's a horror buff,' Fiona said. 'And he's been to university so he can use big words instead of small ones.'

Tracy nodded and Fiona turned to see Clarke had entered the keep. She walked to meet him. He didn't need any more information on the corpse than necessary.

'What's up?' Fiona asked.

'You wanted the doctor, I have her outside.'

'Bring her in.'

Clarke disappeared through the door and returned several minutes later with a woman in her forties carrying a black satchel. The doctor was dressed in black slacks and a white blouse. Her fair hair was cut to the shoulder and her face was bland; she gave a new meaning to the word plain. Fiona extended her hand and introduced herself.

'Noelle Burke,' the woman said. 'Dr Noelle Burke, where's the corpse?'

'On the platform in the centre of the keep.'

Burke looked over Fiona's shoulder. 'Who are those people in the white suits?'

'They're CSI technicians from the Garda Technical Bureau.'

'Do I have to wait until they finish?'

'No, what we need from you is fairly simple. Just declare him dead. We know the cause and we have an idea of the time of death. There'll be a post-mortem in Galway, and we might be able to be more precise about the time of death. Shall we?' Fiona started walking towards the platform.

CHAPTER SEVEN

As she viewed the corpse, Noelle Burke's legs buckled, and she dropped her bag.

Tracy caught her by the shoulders and held her until she steadied herself.

Fiona stared into her face; it was ashen. 'What's the matter? Are you okay?'

'I know the victim. He's one of my patients.'

'Name?' Fiona said.

'Sebastian.' She made a choking sound. 'Sebastian Danger-field. He lives in a small cottage at the back of Kilmurvey Beach. Excuse me for reacting like that. It was most unprofes-sional; I've seen lots of dead bodies.'

'But I bet they all died of natural causes,' Fiona said. 'You'll remember this one. Most doctors remember their first murder victim.'

Burke nodded. She opened her bag and removed a ther-mometer. 'I suppose I'd better take his temperature.'

'Doctors usually do.' Fiona looked at Tracy and nodded in Burke's direction. She'd never seen a doctor react that way. There such a thing as first-time nerves, but Burke displayed a higher level of discomfort than usual.

Foley moved the body and Burke took the rectal temperature. She took out a pad and did a series of calculations.

'Time of death is difficult,' Burke said. 'He's been exposed for most of the night, and I have no idea what the outside temperature was.'

'An educated guess,' Fiona said.

'I know you won't be happy with this but it's the best I can do. The time of death was sometime between ten o'clock in the evening and two o'clock.'

Fiona watched her put away the thermometer and close her bag. 'You're right I'm not happy.' A four-hour window was larger than she'd hoped for. She prayed that the pathologist might have more experience than the local quack. She moved away from the platform and motioned for Burke to join her. 'Shall we let the CSIs get on with their job?'

They walked across the keep and stopped at the stone door. ''Does Mr Dangerfield live alone?' Fiona asked.

Burke took in a large breath. 'Yes, I think so.'

'Any relations on the island?'

'Not that I know of. He's only been on the island about a year. I've been treating him for eczema. I've been to his cottage for tea. Who in heaven's name could have killed him like that?'

Fiona ignored the question. 'Does he have any friends or enemies that you know of?'

'No, not that I know of.' The colour was gradually returning to Burke's face. 'He kept himself to himself as the locals say. He was a bit of a recluse. I think he spent a lot of time reading; his cottage is full of books.'

'Any idea where he came from?'

'Dublin, I think. I'm not sure. I suppose I never asked, and he never told me.'

'What age was he?'

'Late fifties I think. I probably have his date of birth on my file back at the office.'

'Make sure that Detective Garda Tracy gets it.'

'Do you have much experience with murders?' Burke asked.

'A little,' Fiona replied.

'Why kill someone like that? It would have been very painful, but I think the evisceration was post-mortem. At least I hope it was.'

'People kill in different ways. If it's not premeditated, then they usually use what's at hand. Since I doubt very much that such a distinctive dagger was close at hand, I assume this murder was premeditated.'

'What else could it have been?'

'As my colleague, Detective Tracy has pointed out it has all the hallmarks of a sacrificial killing. A special type of knife was used, the location appears to have been chosen and a pentagram has been painted on the keep floor.'

Burke's brow furrowed. 'I didn't think of that. You think the occult has something to do with it?'

'I'll be keeping an open mind and that may be one of many hypotheses.' Possibly the only one for the moment, she thought. Was it really murder if the victim accepted his death willingly? There had to be reasons for everything. There was no doubt that the platform on which the body lay had all the appearance of a sacrificial altar and the knife was special as was the location. Could there possibly be an occult group on the island? Of course, it was possible, one only had to look at the crowds that congregated at Newgrange for the summer and winter solstices.

Burke shifted from foot to foot. 'The lifeboat people are bringing up a stretcher. They should be here within the hour. Do you need anything else from me?'

Fiona could see that the doctor was anxious to be back in her comfort zone of bicycle accidents. 'Yes, please keep the identity of the victim to yourself. And please don't speak to anyone about human sacrifice. I may need to speak to you again.'

'I'm easy to find.' Burke took a card from a pocket in the side of her bag and handed it to Fiona, then turned and disappeared through the small doorway.

Fiona sauntered over to where Foley and O'Malley were working at the platform. 'How are you doing with the body? Someone from the lifeboat crew has arranged to bring a stretcher up and they should be here in an hour.'

'We're good to go as far as the corpse is concerned,' Foley said.

Foley and O'Malley had already encased the hands and feet in plastic bags. If there was any evidence there, it would be collected during the post-mortem.

'Whoever killed this poor bastard was careful enough to leave little or no evidence. But we'll keep at it.' Foley produced a body bag from his case and he and O'Malley rolled the body into it. 'There we go all packed up and ready to travel.'

'Anything for us?' Fiona asked.

'We've taken samples of the blood. There's a mass of fingerprints and handprints on the platform. Exclusion would be a nightmare but if you find someone, we might be able to match it. Other than that, you'll have to wait on the report.'

Fiona's phone rang. She saw Horgan's ID and took the call.

'Brophy outdid himself,' Horgan said. 'The army rescue helicopter is on the way. They should be here any minute and able to land in the fort and take the body directly to Galway Regional Hospital.'

'We have a name,' Fiona said. 'Sebastian Dangerfield.'

'That's a hell of a name but at least we're making progress. The media have already got wind of the murder. Probably from someone on the island. The chief is getting up a statement and will appear on the evening news. Watch out for a media circus on this one. It isn't every day that a man is murdered in a fashion that piques the interest of Joe Public. The only angle that we're missing is sex and I'm sure someone will add that somewhere along the line. Before the tabloids are finished there'll have been a coven of naked women dancing around the platform as the knife plunged into the victim's chest.'

'You watch too much television.'

'You think. Wait until you see what they come up with.'

Fiona had been looking out to sea and she heard a heavy drone behind her. She turned to see a bright orange helicopter heading in her direction. 'The helicopter has arrived. I'll be in touch.' She killed the call.

She turned to Tracy. 'You'd better cancel the stretcher.' He looked bemused. 'Is something bothering you?'

'It's the victim's name. I think I've heard it somewhere before but for the life of me. I can't remember where.'

'When it comes back to you be sure to let me know.'

CHAPTER EIGHT

Fiona and Tracy bent instinctively as the rotors of the helicopter whipped up the air over the keep at Dun Aengus. They watched as the machine whirled away and headed east over the island and on towards Galway. Fiona had heard that there was a helipad constructed on the roof of the Regional Hospital so the body would be delivered directly to the morgue. Foley and O'Malley were still sifting the area around the platform, but with the body gone Fiona's and Tracy's work was done. It was time to get on with the investigation and that meant being all over Sebastian Dangerfield's life. What kind of a man becomes a recluse on an island off a small country? Maybe he was running from something, perhaps a failed marriage or a relationship gone sour. There were probably a thousand reasons why someone should want to bury themselves in a remote location. The problem would be finding out which motive pertained to Dangerfield.

'Ever been in a helicopter?' Tracy asked.

They can never take the boy out of the man, she thought. Tracy was pissed that he didn't get a helicopter ride. Boys and their toys. 'No.' She looked at him and saw the desire on his handsome face.

'What's next?' he asked.

'Get on to Brophy and tell him to get me everything he can on Dangerfield.'

'Is he working with us?'

'Not officially, but neither he nor Horgan need to know that.'

She walked to where Foley was working. 'Tracy and I are heading back to Kilronan. Will you be here much longer?'

'An hour or two should see us out of here. You should consider carrying out a search of the surrounding area. Maybe even the area outside the keep. I don't think the victim was naked when he came up here. Any sign of his clothes?'

She shook her head. "Don't worry I was thinking the same thing. A man walking around nude might have attracted attention, especially among God-fearing islanders.' Foley had a point. She would have to ask Horgan to free up a group of officers to carry out a detailed search of the area. There would be plenty of takers provided the weather held up and the expenses covered a nice lunch and a couple of pints.

Foley stroked his chin. It was his thinking tell. 'It was a hell of a way to die. I've been around but this is one for the memoirs.'

'That thought also had occurred to me, if only I could write.'

'I'm a mad reader and I remember reading a book about a murder on an island that resembled a pagan ritual. It turned out to be the case, but it also turned out that everyone on the island was pagan. I found it farfetched.'

'I doubt everyone on Inis Mór is a pagan. But there may be one or two who worship an older God.'

'I don't envy you on this one. It's not your everyday murder. The hierarchy are going to take an interest in this one. A pretty devious mind was at work here.'

'There is nothing new under the sun. Everything you can

think of has already been thought about by someone else. I'll send the car back at one o'clock.'

'Okay as long as we're on the boat at five. What about you and Tracy?'

'We'll leave this evening, but we'll be back to stay tomorrow.'

'A stay on the island in weather like this. I think I might envy you.'

'I'll try to find something for you to do.' She left him to his work and walked back to the exit from the keep.

'Brophy is on it.' Tracy joined her. 'How are the techs doing?'

'They've taken their photos and collected their samples and now they're looking at the area around the platform. Given the fact that a cleaning crew doesn't come in every evening, I guess they won't find much of assistance to us. But we can live in hope.'

O'Flaherty sat on a rock talking with the man who had been guarding the entrance. Fiona saw a small crowd had gathered below at the ticket kiosk. They were going to be disappointed. There would be no visitors to the fort today or for the conceivable future.

'Where to?' O'Flaherty joined the two detectives.

'I'm hungry,' Fiona said.

'I know the very place.' O'Flaherty started down the hill.

'I'm sure you do.' Fiona followed along behind him.

The full vista of the island opened in front of them as they made their way down. The landscape was peaceful and serene in the bright sunlight. It was different from the atmosphere in the keep. Fiona could see why someone with a reclusive nature would be attracted to live here. Maybe Dangerfield might turn out to be simply someone who liked his own company. If that were the case, why did he have to die? They reached the standing stones and made their way through.

'Bad business,' O'Flaherty said when they got to the other

side. 'And bad for business. No visitors today means no revenue for those people who depend on what they make in the summer to tide them over. When will the site be open?'

'The day after tomorrow, maybe.' Fiona stumbled but regained her balance immediately.

Flaherty held out his hand, but she ignored it. 'I heard the poor man was naked and had a knife buried in his chest.'

'You've a great pair of ears,' Fiona said.

'Thanks be to God I have. Part of my patter for the tourists is the story that the Neolithic people who lived in the fort had a religion based on human sacrifice. But there's no basis for that story because they left no written record behind.'

'It looks like somebody believed the story.'

They had arrived at the entrance. Fiona gave the bad news to the lady selling the entrance tickets and she passed it on to the small crowd who dispersed.

THEY TOOK their seats in Tigh Watty. Although no invitation had been issued, O'Flaherty had joined them at their table and Clarke walked into the pub five minutes later. Every patron looked in their direction. It was a small island. A waitress passed around the menus. Fiona and Tracy settled on chowder while O'Flaherty and Clarke ordered sandwiches and Guinness. Fiona raised her eyes to heaven. 'I suppose the drink driving laws don't apply here.'

Clarke reddened. 'We tend to be a bit more liberal than on the mainland.'

The chowder arrived and the two Galway detectives were impressed by the amount of fish floating in the thick creamy soup.

'Do you know Sebastian Dangerfield?' Fiona had been toying with dropping the name and had decided that the bush telegraph probably already had it or would have it sooner rather than later. So, what was the harm?

O'Flaherty put down his drink. 'Old fella rents a cottage at the back of Kilmurvey Beach. Is he the naked man on the stone?'

'Yes, do you know him?'

O'Flaherty thought for a second. 'I couldn't say that I do. I've seen him about. He sometimes comes into the pub to listen to the music. Sits by himself in the corner drinking the odd pint of Guinness. Generally, has his head stuck in a book. I picked up one of his books when he was at the toilet. It was a fantasy I think, something about myth and magic.'

She turned to Clarke. 'What about you?'

Clarke put his pint of Guinness down. 'Never came across my radar as they say. I don't think that I've ever spoken to the man.'

'And yet someone plunged a knife into his heart and eviscerated him.'

'I know every local on this island,' O'Flaherty said. 'And I don't think any of them would be capable of murder.'

Fiona dropped her spoon into her chowder. 'You'd be surprised who is capable of murder. Do you know who owns the cottage Dangerfield is renting?'

'My cousin,' O'Flaherty said.

'Why didn't I guess.' Fiona stood up and walked towards the rear of the room.

'Your boss is a bit of a looker,' O'Flaherty said as soon as Fiona was out of sight.

'I suppose you're the local Lothario,' Tracy said.

'Would I be interfering in something?'

Tracy shook his head and smiled.

'What's so funny?' O'Flaherty said.

'Nothing.' Tracy concentrated on his chowder.

'She has a reputation for being a hard-arse,' Clarke contributed.

'She doesn't take too many prisoners alright.' Tracy looked at the back of the room and saw Fiona returning.

'We'll be needing accommodation from tomorrow evening until the foreseeable future,' Fiona said as she sat down. She looked at O'Flaherty. 'I suppose you know someone.'

'I'll fix you up with a bed and breakfast. Will that be a double or two singles?'

Fiona and Tracy both started laughing. 'Two singles,' Fiona said when she caught her breath.

'You're very chipper for coppers,' O'Flaherty said.

'Where did you get your American accent?' Fiona asked.

'I spent five years in Chicago working up the price of a house.'

'Ever meet a guy called Conor Madden.'

'The Irish community is very clannish. If he's a Gaelic speaker, I might have run across him, but I don't remember. Your brother?'

'My father. Are you finished?' she asked Tracy.

He picked up his bowl and drank the contents. 'I am now.'

'Then let's go and see how Dangerfield lived.'

CHAPTER NINE

Kilmurvey Beach sits on a horseshoe-shaped cove a five-minute car ride north of Kilronan. It wasn't the first time Fiona visited the beach, but she had forgotten how much the pristine white sand and the turquoise water reminded her of pictures of beaches on Pacific Islands. There were a series of sand dunes behind the beach and across the road was the small, thatched cottage that was home to Dangerfield.

O'Flaherty parked directly outside and was about to exit the van when Fiona tapped him on the shoulder. 'This is a police officer-only gig. You stay in the car.' She turned to Tracy. 'We'll need to suit up.'

Fiona, Tracy and Clarke exited and stood facing Dangerfield's residence. It was a picture-perfect cottage surrounded by a well-kept garden enclosed by a wild fuchsia border. For the second time, Fiona thought if you had to live somewhere remote this was the place to do it. They walked up the short path that led from the road to the cottage.

The three Guards stood in the porch and Tracy pushed the front door, but it remained closed. Fiona looked at her watch. It was two o'clock in the afternoon; they had three hours before the boat left. She turned to Tracy. 'Call Foley and tell him we're sending O'Flaherty back to fetch him and O'Malley. We need them down here to give Dangerfield's house the once over.'

Tracy immediately got on the phone.

She looked at Clarke. 'Tell O'Flaherty to call his cousin and get him here with a key. And tell him to get back to Dun Aengus and pick up Foley and O'Malley.'

Clarke walked back to the van.

She watched O'Flaherty make a phone call and then head off.

'They're on their way down,' Tracy said. 'Foley is spitting nails because they had to lug their gear. They've plastered the doorway to the keep with crime scene tape.'

'O'Flaherty's cousin is on the way, and O'Flaherty will be back in fifteen minutes,' Clarke announced as soon as he joined them.

Two minutes later a car pulled up outside the cottage and a man bearing a striking resemblance to their van driver exited. He marched up the short drive and produced a key from his pocket. He offered it to Fiona. 'I'm Michael O'Flaherty. Thomas said you'd be needing this. Is it true that it's Dangerfield you found up in the fort?'

Fiona took the key. 'It appears so. Doctor Burke recognised him. We'll have to do a formal identification at the Regional in Galway, but we'll probably need a relative for that. Maybe since you're here you'll answer a few questions.'

'If I can. I rented him the house, but I don't really know him.'

'When did he rent the cottage?'

'Almost a year to the day. He was regular with the rent and the electric was paid on the dot. You could say he was the perfect tenant.'

Fiona took the key and passed it to Tracy. 'I understand that he didn't mix much.'

'That would be an understatement. I never saw him with another human being.'

'Did he have any visitors? Maybe relations?' She watched Tracy open the front door of the cottage.

'I never saw any. He has a local woman that cleans for him, name of Bridget Heaney. She would probably know if he had anyone staying over at the cottage.'

'Do you have a number for her?'

'I don't, but she cleans for a local B and B, Kileany House. You can get her there.'

'We will.'

She nodded at Tracy. 'Let's look inside.'

Tracy handed her gear to her before suiting up himself.

Fiona pushed the door wide before stepping inside. She found herself in the living room of the cottage which originally had the three-room traditional structure. There was a door on the right that led to what should be a bedroom and a similar door on the left. The furnishings in the living room were sparse, consisting of an overstuffed three-seater couch facing a coffee table on which sat a chessboard with the white and black pieces set for a game, a wing-backed chair with a lamp perched directly behind it, a table supporting what looked like a thirty-two-inch television with a DVD beneath and an oak bureau. A small four-tier bookshelf unit whose shelves sagged from the weight of books stacked on them was flush against one wall. There were more books stacked on the floor beside the wing-backed chair. A DVD box set of Shakespeare's plays and another of Alfred Hitchcock movies stood beside the TV. There was a large potted plant in one of the corners. Fiona walked to a door at the rear of the living room which led to an extension containing a small galley kitchen and a bathroom. The whole place spoke of someone who was excessively neat and tidy. When she returned to the living room she found Tracy examining the bookshelves. 'Find anything interesting?'

'He must be the only person in the world who doesn't have

a dog-eared copy of a James Patterson novel on his shelf. His taste is a bit esoteric, there's a whole section on the occult and myths and magic. I think he might have been an interesting individual to talk to.'

'Somebody closed off that option. Since you've already started you can take the living room and I'll do the rest of the rooms.' She opened the door on the right of the living room and found herself in Dangerfield's bedroom. It contained a double bed that was made up but not slept in, a wardrobe and a chest of drawers. A bedside table, on which a reading lamp and four books sat, stood on the right of the bed. She examined the wardrobe first. It contained two suits showing light wear, a tweed jacket, a wax jacket, a winter coat and three pairs of dark trousers as well as two empty hangers. On a shelf at the bottom, there were two pairs of stout leather brogues and a pair of walking boots. There was a space between the brogues where another pair of shoes would have fit. Dangerfield was no slave to fashion. One drawer of the chest of drawers contained underwear and socks while the second was filled with similar recently ironed white shirts. Fiona was getting a picture of Dangerfield as someone who lived a regimented life. She wondered whether he had possibly been in the army. There was an unsigned and untitled painting on one of the walls of what looked like a Georgian mansion. She knew nothing about painting but to her eye, it was the work of an amateur. She exited the bedroom and walked across the living room. Tracy was rifling through the bureau. She opened the door on the left of the living room and found the spare room was used as a storeroom. There were two empty suitcases, an empty overnight bag and more books, a broken kitchen chair, a machine that she had seen an ad for on television that improved the circulation in the feet and a large, framed map of Ireland. She closed the door and went to the extension. The kitchen was spotlessly clean. Every utensil was stored in its place. There were no missing knives. She was hoping that

Tracy was having better luck in the living room. She moved on to the bathroom which again was spotless. The toothbrush was in its holder and the soap in its dish. A selection of men's toiletries stood on the glass shelf above the sink. She noted the absence of photographs and wondered whether Dangerfield had a family. She joined Tracy in the living room. 'Well?'

Tracy shrugged his shoulder. 'Nothing much I'm afraid. If I didn't know that Dangerfield lived here, I'd guess that this was a holiday home. We used to have a caravan in Wicklow for the summer and it was a bit like this room, nothing that gives an indication of who inhabits the space other than his love for books and his taste in theatre and films. The bureau is a bust. No personal papers whatever. There's a nail in the wall over there where something must have hung.'

Fiona followed Tracy's finger. There was a stain on the wall beneath the naked nail.

'And I found this behind the couch.' Tracy held up a broken frame that might have housed a painting.

'Interesting.' The naked nail and the broken frame were out of character with the rest of the cottage. Fiona wondered if the killer had removed whatever had hung on the nail and had been contained in the frame. She looked around the room, no photographs. Maybe Tracy was right. Dangerfield was renting on Inis Mór, but he could possibly live somewhere else. The way he died wasn't the only mystery surrounding the man. She looked at her phone hoping that she had missed a message from Brophy – nothing.

The door opened. Foley and O'Malley entered and joined Fiona and Tracy.

Foley looked at his watch. 'We have less than two hours to process this place, so we'd better get moving.'

O'Malley was already unpacking her gear.

'Anything new to report from the keep?' Fiona asked.

Foley laid his metal case on the floor. 'Nothing of a forensic nature. It's a hell of a location for a murder. Way out of sight. You could scream your lungs out and no one would hear you.'

'There are lots of questions that need answering. Tracy and I will get out of your way.' She walked to the door followed by Tracy.

'Where to next?' Tracy peeled off his overalls.

'Your guess is as good as mine. We have an older reclusive gentleman who died in what could be ritual fashion. He appears to have made no attempt to avoid his death which could mean that he agreed with the ritual. He knew no one and nobody knew him even though he's lived on the island for the past year. Everyone seems to be skirting around whether there's a group on the island who might not worship who the Pope considers the one true God. There's a lot to sift through.'

CHAPTER TEN

Fiona stood at the entrance to the quay watching the passengers assemble for the five o'clock sailing from Kilronan to Rossaveal. She recognised many of the faces who had arrived with her earlier that morning. They were the usual mixed bag with the largest group being the young backpackers closely followed by retired Americans, then a mixture of locals and day-trippers from the mainland. Tracy and Clarke were in the ticket office checking that the names and the identities of those about to leave were being checked. O'Flaherty had been sent to fetch Foley and O'Malley from Dangerfield's house in Kilmurvey. Fiona wondered how long they could keep this circus operating. The word from Galway was that isolating Inis Mór was out of the question. She reckoned that there might be a fifty-fifty chance that the killer had departed on the morning boat. Every day they permitted people to leave the island the chances that the killer had departed would increase and she would be left to carry the can for the failure to solve the crime. That was if a crime had been committed in the first place. She would never have said so openly but a possibility existed that Tracy might be right about the killing being a human sacrifice. It appeared outlandish. She'd never heard of a similar case but that didn't mean that there wasn't one some-where. Stranger things had happened. She remembered the case of a cannibal who had put an advertisement in the local paper looking for someone who wanted to be eaten. That was strange enough but even stranger was the fact that he had received several replies. Whoever said that it took all kinds wasn't lying. What if they were dealing with a willing victim? Could it have been suicide by ritual murder? Only someone above her pay grade could answer that kind of metaphysical question. Her job was to identify the person who had plunged the knife into Dangerfield" chest. Horgan had informed her that the autopsy would take place the following morning and that the state pathologist would carry out the procedure himself. While she had him on the line, she'd asked that Brophy be assigned to the case and he told her that her request was under consideration. There was no need to rush with such a trivial decision. She pointed out that she and Tracy would handle the investigation on the island, but they would need someone at base to man the telephones and do the computer research. Horgan conceded the point and would add it to salient points such as the effect on the budget before giving her an answer. Horgan had managed to rustle up six uniformed officers who would arrive on the first boat in the morning. They would carry out a search of the area around the crime scene and depart in the evening. She also learned that although the ferry hadn't yet arrived, she could expect a television crew to be on board and possibly one or two reporters. There would be an interview in Gaelic on the quayside, and she should keep it simple and short. No details of the crime were to be discussed. Rumours were already flooding Galway about the nature of the crime and had sparked a level of interest beyond a simple stabbing. Murder was front-page news, but ritual murder was sex and drugs and rock and roll. She contemplated a drink at Tigh Watty before the boat sailed. It had been a strange day and there was the potential for a lot of stranger days in the future. She had made up her mind that a pint of Guinness might be an antidote to her feeling of disquiet when she saw the ferry on the horizon. The pint of Guinness would have to wait.

'What's the plan?' Clarke had joined her at the edge of the quay.

If Fiona were honest, she would have said that there was no plan. 'We'll be back tomorrow. Or at least one of us will be back tomorrow.'

Clarke looked at the clouds massing on the western horizon. 'The weather is expected to turn. You'd best bring your rain gear. Met Eireann is predicting the arrival of a storm.'

Fiona wasn't worried. The national weather authority seldom managed to get it right.

'Do you need anything more from me?' Clarke took out his notebook and pen.

'Ask around, see if anyone saw activity at the cottage in Kilmurvey. Maybe someone saw Dangerfield leave and head up the path to the fort. It's a long shot but someone has to have seen something. This has got to be a once in a generation event. People are going to talk. Don't push them. Just listen and make a note of anything that might be useful.'

He put away his notebook. 'I'll follow your instructions but don't expect too much. The islanders don't talk much about each other and there's a healthy disrespect for the law hereabouts.'

I wonder why, Fiona thought. 'I'm from a small village in Connemara myself. Leave the interviewing to Tracy and me.' She looked along the quayside to where Tracy was using his mobile phone to make a video of the waiting passengers. The ferry had reached the mooring and the passengers shuffled as one man in the direction of the gangplank.

Tracy finished videoing and ambled over to where Fiona and Clarke were standing. 'All done,' he announced as he joined them.

They watched as the ferry tied up and the passengers streamed off. There were far fewer than on the morning boat. Tracy's girlfriend, Cliona Gallagher, was carrying a large camera at the front of the queue. Fiona recognised one of the local telejournalists accompanying her.

'I didn't expect that,' Tracy said.

Fiona wiped her eye with her finger. 'The hell you didn't. You're the bloody source of the rumours in Galway about the nature of the crime.' Fiona walked to the edge of the quayside and stood waiting for the two-man TV crew.

'DS Madden,' the telejournalist extended his hand. 'Simon Toner, ready for the interview? We need to catch the ferry back to Rossaveal.'

Fiona ignored the extended hand. 'I don't know if it crossed your mind, but we could have done this at Rossaveal and saved you the trip.'

'We need to get Kilronan as the background shot.'

Fiona turned to Tracy who stood beside his girlfriend. 'Where's O'Flaherty? He's supposed to have Foley and O'Malley here.'

Cliona pointed the camera at Fiona and Toner. 'Ready when you are.'

'What can you tell us about the murder on Inis Mór?' Toner said in Gaelic.

Fiona went on autopilot, speaking for the mandatory two minutes that would appear on TV and giving away absolutely nothing.

'Great.' Toner turned to his camera operator. 'Get a shot of Kilronan and the passengers boarding the ferry.'

O'Flaherty's van pulled up on the end of the quayside. Foley and O'Malley exited and took their gear from the rear.

Cliona took a shot of the two techs carrying their metal cases.

Foley came past Fiona. 'That's cutting it fine,' she said.

'We just finished processing the cottage. We don't want to

come back and I'm praying there's some alcohol on that boat. It's been a tough day.'

'For us all. And we'll be back tomorrow. Find anything useful?'

'We bagged what we found, and we dusted the whole place. We have three good sets of prints. I guess one belongs to Dangerfield. The other two belong to a man and a woman but until we have exclusion prints, I don't know how useful they're going to be. The knife will be at the lab tomorrow and that might be your best chance of a lead. You'll have the report ASAP.'

All the passengers were on board, and Foley and O'Malley picked up their cases and made a beeline for the gangplank accompanied by the TV crew.

'Are we leaving?' Tracy asked.

Fiona strolled towards the gangplank. 'We're fucked,' she mumbled under her breath.

CHAPTER ELEVEN

Fiona had found a table in the small bar area of the ferry and the four police officers sat cradling their cups of tea as the boat left the quay. She had rejected an invitation to join the captain on the bridge and she regretted that decision as soon as she tasted the weak liquid that passed for the tea supplied to passengers. 'No leads from the forensic examination then?'

'Bad day at the office,' Foley said. 'I would have liked to have found his clothes. There would be some DNA transfer from the killer. The site was a nightmare. It's a popular tourist attraction so there's DNA all over the place. Is the killer's DNA there? I have no idea. We've collected a lot of trace but nothing that's of immediate value to you. We took hair from a brush at the cottage so we'll have a DNA profile on the victim but that could have been done at the morgue. We've taken his fingerprints as well.'

'Any ideas?' Fiona asked

Foley sipped his tea. 'Either it is what it looks like, a ritual killing, or someone thought long and hard about it. Looks like the crime scene has some significance and possibly the weapon as well. There are no ligature marks on the victim, so he wasn't carted up that hill. He went up willingly. Did he know he would die when he reached the keep? Your guess is as good as mine. Dozens of people had trampled the area around the platform. Either a group of cloaked crazies dancing or a couple of hundred tourists walking back and forth could have been the culprits. I hate processing an outdoor crime scene. There's an abundance of trace and very little of it turns out to be relevant.'

Fiona noticed Tracy's girlfriend videoing them from the door of the saloon. She nodded at Tracy. 'Tell Cliona it's not cool.'

Tracy stood and went to join his girlfriend.

'Bloody journalists,' Foley said.

'She's actually a nice girl,' Fiona said. 'Just doing her job like the rest of us.'

Foley finished his tea. 'Did Horgan manage to enlist any troops for a search of the surrounding area?'

'They'll be on the morning ferry,' Fiona said.

'If they find the clothes, get them to me immediately.'

'What about the cottage?'

'Strange place.'

'What do you mean?'

'Lack of personality. I don't think I've ever processed a location where someone lived that I didn't get a feeling for the person. The cottage might have been a rental where the guests changed every week. Aside from the books, there was nothing that pertained to the victim's life. No photos, no letters, nothing about the victim's life.'

'I noticed that too.'

'What's the next step for you guys?'

'Looks like we might be on the island until we either find the culprit or we declare the killing unsolved.' Or Horgan runs out of budget for the daily allowance she might have added.

'From what I hear you wouldn't like that at all.'

Fiona's phone rang. She took the call and moved away from the table.

'You've got Brophy but only pro tem,' Horgan said. 'And I don't want him swanning off to Inis Mór like you and Tracy.'

She hated it when the hierarchy thought that solving a murder was a holiday. After she and Tracy paid for their digs, they'd be lucky to have enough in the kitty for an evening meal of burger and chips. 'Thanks, boss, Brophy will handle the Internet stuff and whatever needs doing in Galway.'

'Any lines of enquiry?'

'It looks like a ritual killing.'

'I hope to God you didn't say that on camera.'

'Perish the thought, boss. I was the soul of discretion.'

'Doesn't sound like you. What do you think?'

'I think that whoever killed Dangerfield could be in Timbuktu by tomorrow.'

'That doesn't sound good.'

'There were more than a hundred people on the morning ferry. We have their names, and the majority provided their IDs.'

'We couldn't cordon off the island. The Americans would have lost their heads completely. They'll be on a schedule. Inis Mór today and the Giant's Causeway tomorrow. I told the superintendent I have my best team on the case.'

Fiona didn't know whether Horgan meant it or was bull-shitting. She decided on the latter. Through the window, she could see that they were approaching the harbour at Rossaveal. 'I want Brophy at the autopsy, but I'll call him in the morning with instructions.'

'This is going to get a lot of press. The tabloids have already been on the phone. I have a feeling that you'll have more than a few journalists on the ferry tomorrow.'

'We're arriving, boss. Have a nice evening.'

'Get a result on this one, Madden.' The line went dead.

'Horgan?' Tracy asked as Fiona rejoined her colleagues.

She nodded. 'He wants a result.'

Foley laughed. 'Don't they always. I'm afraid you're up

against it on this one. There's a TV drama about a murder that takes place on a nuclear submarine. The suspects are the crew. You've got the opposite problem. There are the nine hundred islanders and God knows how many tourists.'

Fiona stood. 'We're coming in. I'm going up on deck.'

She leaned on the rail and watched the land approaching. It was all going to be uphill on this one. A victim who kept himself to himself. No apparent friends and more importantly no apparent enemies. The murder method was certainly unique but not so unique that no one had ever used it before. No murder is unique. If it was murder, the killer thought himself very clever. It was early days and all she could see ahead were problems. But wasn't that the way every case started. Tomorrow, she and Tracy would start peeling away the outer layers of the crime to expose the core. The locals might have thought Dangerfield a singular man, but every human has a backstory, and they were going to scour Dangerfield's life. He didn't end up naked and dead on a black stone platform in Dun Aengus because he was an angel.

CHAPTER TWELVE

F iona had been prepared to have Tracy drop her home,
but her mood brightened when she saw Aisling's smiling
face at the end of the quay at Rossaveal. She watched as
Cliona tossed her camera into a TG4 van before jumping into
the police car with Tracy. There was a possibility that if she
tried hard enough, she could find the administrative notice
outlining the regulations against the use of police cars to transport one's girlfriend. But at the end of the day who cared about
police regulation XXX.

Aisling linked her arm and led her to the car park. Fiona
flopped into the passenger seat. 'Drink,' she said simply.

'A tough day on the Aran Islands in the sunshine. Am I
supposed to feel sorry for you?'

'Drink.'

'Where will we have this drink?'

'Tigh Wally on the way home.'

'Not the most salubrious spot, it's a pub in a house.'

'It suits my mood.'

'Oh dear, one of those days. You have fifteen minutes to
spill it all.'

Fiona told her about the body at Dun Aengus.

'You live a very exciting life. A naked man with a very particular dagger in his chest, a pentagram painted on the ground. How very mysterious. I suppose you've already considered the obvious.'

'What obvious?"

Pagan ritual.'

'The thought crossed my mind. It's so damn obvious that it's already crossed Tracy's mind. The techs even mentioned it as a possibility. Maybe it's a little too obvious.'

'The pentangle or pentagram is interesting. For some, it is said to have illustrious origins. The great biblical King Solomon supposedly designed the shape. Each point of the pentangle stands for a list of virtues or wits, including the five joys of Mary and the five wounds of Christ. For others, it has its origin in the legends of King Arthur. It's the emblem of truth, known as the "endless knot". It's particularly suitable for the knight Sir Gawain because the five points of the star represent the five different ways in which Gawain, like purified gold, embodies faultless virtue.'

'Thanks for the lecture. There was I thinking it had something to do with devil worship.'

'You're not wrong. The pentagram as a symbol has been adopted by many world religions and cultures, including the Freemasons, the Babylonians and the Baha'i and Christian faiths. What you're thinking of is the notion that neopagans, generally referred to as Wiccans, and satanists employ the pentagram in their symbolism.'

'So, our victim might have been murdered by any manner of group. The chief tech, Foley, has Inis Mór full of pagans. Apparently, he read a book that had an island full of pagans.'

'I wouldn't dismiss the pagan angle so easily. Pagan and Satanic ritual is still practised in many parts of the world. It's not inconceivable that there's a group of Wiccans on Inis Mór.'

They had arrived at Tigh Wally, and Aisling parked

outside. 'I don't know what the attraction of this pub is for you.'

'We'll be the only patrons and the barman never listens.'

They sat on a bench at the rear of the former front room of the house that now constituted the pub. Fiona knew her pubs, they were the only patrons.

She had downed the first half of her pint of Guinness before Aisling had started on her orange juice. 'That was one tough day and it's not over yet. The bad aspect of this job is that you can't shut down your brain at five o'clock in the evening.'

'Are you back on the island tomorrow?'

'Tracy and myself for the duration. I suppose Horgan would have insisted that I stay there except he'd be afraid that I'd submit a chit for fresh knickers and laundry.'

'You're awful hard on that man.'

'You think. I've been in this job for twelve years and the only bosses that have treated me like a human being have been the men who wanted to get into my pants. Women have been university professors for hundreds of years. The first women joined the Garda Síochána in nineteen fifty-nine. I live in a man's world, and I know it. I didn't tell you, but Horgan boought drink for Tracy and me after the business in Clifden. As we left the pub, someone in the group said "fucking dyke" loud enough for me to hear. Tracy was the only one who reacted. Horgan probably saw who made the remark but did nothing about it. Even the boss must be seen as one of the boys. Although I didn't see the misogynist in question, I have my suspicions and if I ever get a chance to skewer the bastard, I'll take it.'

Aisling sipped her orange juice. 'We can't change the world.'

'As long as we believe that, nothing will change.'

'What about an evening out. There's live music in Kitt's.'

'It'll end late and I'll be like a wet rag tomorrow.'

'You don't have to drink.'

Fiona finished her pint and called for another. 'Fat chance. I want a shower and a nice meal. Then I want to put my feet up.'

The barman deposited the drinks and went outside.

Aisling waited until the publican had disappeared before kissing Fiona. 'I don't like to see you this way. Maybe you should give up the police.'

'You really are a clever clogs. Why didn't I think of that?'

'Cynicism doesn't become you. Finish up your drink and let's find the makings of the dinner you were talking about.'

'Yeah, tomorrow is another day and hopefully, it'll prove better than today.'

DAY TWO

CHAPTER THIRTEEN

Fiona sat in the cramped saloon of the ferry. She wondered whether Garda Clarke might be a Wiccan because he was certainly right about the weather. Rain beat a tattoo on the roof of the saloon and sluiced down the windows; only the hardiest of souls had ventured onto the deck. Outside the window, Fiona could see what looked like stair rods falling from the heavens. The boat ploughed through the choppy water with more motion than the previous day and there were a lot of pale faces in the packed saloon. Unfortunately, one of them belonged to Tracy. Yesterday's shower and dinner had done much to dispel the despondency she had felt after her first day on the case. However, there was a long way to go before she was ready to toss her towel into the ring on the Dangerfield murder. She had called Brophy before she left home that morning. He'd drawn a blank on Dangerfield but there were still a few avenues he hadn't explored. She'd convinced herself that the genesis of the murder resided in Dangerfield's past. It was a trite conclusion. The genesis of almost every murder is in the victim's past. The exceptions are those victims who happen upon a psychopath on a murder spree. The random murder is the most difficult to solve. Someone you meet in a pub and take home, or you're out for a walk and the guy walking behind you has a baseball bat under his coat and he's looking for someone to kill. Brophy would eventually find something; like a snail, everybody leaves a trace of their slime on the planet. The autopsy was scheduled for eleven o'clock and Brophy would attend. She didn't think that it would add significantly to their store of knowledge. As far as she could see there were no defensive wounds on the body. There might be something interesting under the fingernails. It would be nice to have the DNA of the killer, but she doubted they were going to be that lucky. She'd told Brophy to put a rush on the tox screen. She also told him that his duties included the maintenance of the murder book, an important document that consisted of a compendium of all the reports, statements and photos that would be collected during the investigation. Every now and then she glanced across to the other side of the saloon where four glum Garda officers sat dressed in their best foul weather apparel that, although well designed and fabricated, would have zero chance of keeping them dry on a day like this. If they looked glum now, it would be nothing to how they'd look on the return trip. Horgan had promised her six officers but at Rossaveal she learned that two of the intended search party had conveniently fallen ill overnight. She didn't blame the *sick* men nor the unhappy quartet. Searching a rocky hillside in a downpour was no way to spend a day especially if the chances of success were minuscule. If Dangerfield's murder were planned, the murderer would have had a plan for the victim's clothes. If she were a betting woman, she would lay her next month's salary that the clothes were incinerated immediately after the killing.

'Not got your sea legs yet?' she asked Tracy who sat in a huddle beside her. 'You won't have to suffer for long, we're already making our approach to the harbour.'

Tracy looked up exposing his pallid face. 'I never much

liked the sea and I'm usually smart enough to stay on dry land on days like this. As usual, it doesn't appear to affect you.'

'We're made of stern stuff out here in the wilds.' She looked out of the window and saw that they were manoeuvring into Kilronan harbour.

'If you can hold it for another ten minutes we'll be on dry land.'

Clarke stood at the end of the quay and the now ever-present O'Flaherty stood beside him wearing a black slicker and a brown leather cowboy hat from which rain ran in front of his face like a mini waterfall. Fiona had insisted on maintaining the list of passengers and associated IDs for at least another day. The passengers streamed off the ferry and made for the shelter of the four pubs in Kilronan. From experience, Fiona could tell them that the rain wasn't about to let up and they were lucky to miss out on Dun Aengus because a visit there would have left them looking like drowned rats. The bags under Clarke's eyes had bags under their eyes and she assumed that he'd had a big night. She could imagine him holding court in the pub regaling the patrons with his story of Dangerfield's murder while the pints and whiskeys arrived in front of him as though they were on a conveyor belt. That meant that everyone on the island was up to speed on the state of the investigation.

'We need to drop our bags off,' Fiona said. 'And let's get the hell out of this damn rain.'

'Absolutely, sergeant,' Clarke said. 'The local parish priest, Father Flanery is most anxious to speak with you. I told him you'd be available as soon as you arrived.'

'If I wanted a secretary, I would have brought one along. Don't make arrangements for either me or Tracy. We make our own plans.'

'Sorry, sergeant, it's just that he seemed a bit upset.'

'We're not here at the clergy's beck and call.' She turned and pointed at the four Garda officers who had accompanied her. 'Those stalwart lads are going to search the area around the fort and you, Garda Clarke, are going to supervise them. Right now, I want you to explain the terrain to them while they have a cup of tea in a pub. Tracy and I will drop our traps at the B and B and then O'Flaherty here will drive you all to Dun Aengus.' She noted that the glumness had spread to Clarke. 'I'll keep in touch with the search during the day.'

'That's Thomas, sergeant.' O'Flaherty had his hand out. 'My sister is waiting for the two of you. She has tea and scones ready.'

Fiona handed him her bag. 'Detective Garda Tracy has a dicky stomach and I think tea and scones might be just what he needs.'

Two hundred metres outside Kilronan on the road to Kilmurvey, O'Flaherty pulled into the driveway of a house. The island was famed for its Man of Aran thatched cottage accommodation, but O'Flaherty's sister's house consisted of a modern two-storey construction with a porch supported by two pillars at the end of a tarmac drive and a well-developed front garden.

'My sister's husband owned a construction company in Boston,' O'Flaherty said by way of explanation for the substantial property.

'Why the hell did he come back here?' Fiona asked.

'He didn't. He fell off a roof and killed himself.'

Fiona reminded herself to stop asking stupid questions. They entered a hallway with a tiled floor and O'Flaherty led them into a comfortable sitting room where tea and scones were laid out on a coffee table. She decided it would be no penance to spend a few days on the island after all. Then she remembered she hadn't discussed money with O'Flaherty.

'Take off your coats and sit down.' O'Flaherty had already disposed of the slicker and hat. 'Maureen will be around the place somewhere.' He slipped from the room.

'Nice digs,' Tracy said as soon as they were alone. 'That's a sixty-five-inch TV in the corner. I think I'm going to like it here.'

'Don't get too used to it. I think Horgan will start mentioning the budget sooner or later.'

A woman with dark flowing hair, resembling her brother entered the room cleaning her hands on her apron. She looked to be in early middle age and had curves in all the right places. Fiona thought her Rubenesque. She had beautiful blue eyes and a classic Celtic face with skin that was unblemished. 'I'm in the middle of making a spotted dog for dessert this evening. Would you like to see your rooms before you have tea?'

'Thank you but we'll skip the viewing,' Fiona said. 'The trip over was a bit rough and Detective Garda Tracy needs to put something in his stomach. I'm Detective Sergeant Madden, but you can call me Fiona.'

Maureen poured their tea. 'Of course, you are, doesn't the whole island know your name. You can call me Maureen. Shocking business up at the fort.'

'Murder is always a shocking business,' Fiona said taking a scone from the plate that her landlady offered.

'Things like that don't happen around here. In fact, I don't think we've ever had a murder on the island.'

'Did you know Mr Dangerfield?' Fiona added milk to her tea.

Tracy started on his scone. The colour was returning to his face.

'No, but I often saw him walking from Kilronan on the road to Kilmurvey. He was a fine, strapping man, good-looking in a rugged way. People said he wasn't married but he would have made a good husband for some woman.'

'You sound like you might have been interested,' Fiona said.

'I lost my man when I was young. Some advised me to put myself up for marriage again, but I didn't have the heart for it at the time and sure with four children there wasn't a queue forming to take me to the altar. Now that my children are grown up and I'm in need of company I'm sorry I didn't heed the advice.'

'So, you never spoke to him?' Fiona buttered her scone.

'No, what would an educated man like him want with someone like me?'

Fiona wondered if Dangerfield knew what he was missing. She had eaten half her scone and Tracy had finished his. 'Thanks, Maureen. Tracy and I have a lot of work to do today so we probably won't be back until late this evening.'

'I'll have the dinner on the table for you at seven and I'll have your bags in your rooms.'

The two detectives looked at each other and smiled.

CHAPTER FOURTEEN

Fiona folded the umbrella that Maureen had kindly provided, shook the rain off, and pushed in the door of Dangerfield's cottage. Foley and O'Malley hadn't had time to clean up and a fine dusting of fingerprint powder sat on the furniture. The two detectives stood inside the door and looked around the room.

'Where do we begin?' Tracy asked.

'Take your pick. Foley and O'Malley are trained forensic detectives and they found little or nothing according to Foley. But we were both struck by the absence of personal objects. We need to find something that tells us what kind of man Dangerfield was aside from being interested in books and reclusive.'

Tracy walked to the small library. 'The books are personal. I think what people read says a lot about who they are.'

Fiona joined him and picked up a book. 'What do these tell us?'

Tracy chose a book titled *Magic in Celtic Mythology*. He opened it and saw it had been read from cover to cover. Many paragraphs had been highlighted in yellow. He took from the shelf a second entitled the *Religious Practices in Neolithic*

Tribes in Ireland. It had also been well-read and passages were highlighted. 'First off, I'd say that he was a university graduate, a very educated man and erudite. He had a deep interest in ancient cultures and religions to the extent that he didn't just read about them, he studied them.'

'We have a saying in Gaelic *athnion ciarog eile.*'

'And what does that mean?'

'One beetle can recognise another.'

Tracy had a bemused look.

'One university graduate can recognise another,' Fiona said. 'Go on with what his reading habits tell you.'

Tracy looked along the shelf and pulled a book out. 'He likes good food.' He held up a copy of *Larousse Gastronomique* in French. A few of the pages had been marked. 'And he knows enough French to read the recipes.'

'Since you're so keen on books. I want you to go through every one of them and see if he left any papers in the middle. For such an erudite man, there must be a pen and paper around somewhere.' She moved to the bureau. 'There's no sign of a landline or a modem. So, it's odds on he didn't have a phone, so he must have had a mobile. There's a TV but no sign of a box of any sort, so TV wasn't his thing. We'll have to check it, but I bet the landlord has the electricity in his name. I don't think we're going to find a single bill in this cottage that relates to our victim. I wonder why that is.'

'If he took a mobile phone up the hill, it could be anywhere. Most people use apps these days. He could have a bank account that he operated online.'

'We need to find that phone.'

Tracy looked at the window. The rain smashed against it, and he shivered. 'I'm glad I'm not out in this weather. It won't be pleasant searching for evidence on the hill. Maybe one of the lads will find the phone.' He continued flicking through the books.

'Yeah.' Fiona pulled out the top drawer of the bureau.

Nothing. Why didn't the Wiccans have a membership card? She supposed that they might not like to announce themselves to the world. The local parish priest might not be happy to count among his flock a dozen Wiccans who might get off on dancing naked around a pentagram and sticking knives into each other. The Garda Síochána had gone to the enormous expense of sending her on a short management course when she'd been promoted to sergeant. She realised that she risked falling into a trap pointed out on the course. She was suffering from groupthink. Tracy had started it off in the keep yesterday. Foley had continued it and Clarke had joined the group. She bet that a proportion of the islanders believed that Dangerfield was murdered in a satanic ritual that ended with a knife in the chest. But did they also believe that their neighbours might count themselves among the Satan worshipers? Aside from the pentagram and the knife, there was no proof for the satanic ritual theory. She would have to try to keep her mind open despite the constant reiteration of the speculation. Dangerfield was flying below the radar. There were a million and one reasons why that might be the case. They could range from hiding from a spouse to avoid paying maintenance to being in a police protection programme. She left the living room and went into the bedroom. The cottage was an example of Dangerfield's minimalist life. She noted that Tracy didn't use the word aesthetic. The man had a right to live any way he pleased. He even had the right to worship Satan if he so wished. She didn't bother to go through the clothes again and went back to the living room. Tracy wasn't flicking through the books; he was engrossed in reading one.

'Look at this.' He held out the small book to Fiona.

Fiona looked at the drawing. The image could have been of the scene in the keep at Dun Aengus. A man lay on the stone platform just as Dangerfield had. Surrounding him were a dozen cloaked figures and one of them held a knife aloft. She looked at the first page and saw that the book was written in the first decade of the twentieth century. It wasn't a real representation but an artist's impression and only went to substantiate the pagan theory. It was in the same vein as Frankenstein, werewolves, witches and warlocks; a fantasy but an intelligent man like Tracy was buying it. The investigation was heading onto a single track, and she needed to force it off. Dangerfield might have been the victim of a ritual murder, but she would have to find proof to substantiate that theory. She took out her phone and called Clarke. 'Have you found anything?'

'You mean aside from empty cider bottles and condoms.'

'I'll ignore that remark because I understand it's a crap job on a day like this.'

'Sorry, sergeant, nothing so far. You could say that the level of enthusiasm for the job is at an all-time low.'

'I understand. Keep at it. We need to show Galway and the Park that we did our best to find evidence.'

She cut the call and rang O'Flaherty. 'Get over to the cottage at Kilmurvey.'

CHAPTER FIFTEEN

F iona sat in the rear of O'Flaherty's van and listened to the rain hammer against the roof. She took her phone from her pocket and checked her messages for the tenth time. Nothing from Brophy or Clarke. She imagined the group up on the hill looking for evidence and thanked God that neither she nor Tracy were among them. She wondered whether she had been wise to leave the autopsy to Brophy. They were drawing a blank in Kilronan, and she could have remained in Galway and seen whether the autopsy tossed up the lead they so desperately needed. Dangerfield was an enigma. If she hadn't seen his corpse, she might have thought that he didn't exist. People had seen him but didn't interact with him. It appeared that he eschewed social contact with the islanders. His cottage bore no trace of personality aside from his love of books and literature and his interest in myths and magic and possibly the occult. He lived an aesthetic life, much like the monks that had set up the many churches on the island. It was the strange dichotomy of Inis Mór between the Neolithic pagans that built Dun Aengus and the monks who built many more churches than the small population warranted. Despite his desire to stay aloof, Dangerfield had made an enemy who felt strongly enough about him to want to kill him. Maureen Leavy had called Dangerfield *a fine man*. There was a chance, despite the evidence to the contrary, that Dangerfield had had a liaison with a local married woman. It was a possibility that had to be examined.

'Where to?' O'Flaherty asked.

Fiona had been asking herself the same question. Murder on a sparsely populated island didn't fit neatly into the normal process of crime investigation. There were no neighbours to interview. No witnesses to obtain statements from and no damn leads from the murder itself. 'Take us to the parish house.'

Tracy turned and stared at her. 'I thought you gave Clarke a mouthful about making appointments with the clergy for you.'

'You know that an investigation in France begins with a search for the woman.'

'Cherchez la femme.'

'Whatever, well in Ireland we begin with a visit to the local parish priest who knows all and hears all every Saturday evening in the confessional.'

'I thought that he couldn't repeat what he hears in confession.'

'Don't believe that old bollocks. That's only for the movies.'

O'Flaherty pulled up before the parish house in Kilronan which turned out to be a modest stone structure located close to the Church of St Bridget and St Oliver Plunket several streets back from the quay. Fiona and Tracy raised their umbrellas and dashed for the cover of the small porch that held the front door. A small wooden plaque on the wall beside the door bore the legend *Fr Liam Flanery*. Tracy did the honours by knocking.

A bent elderly woman wearing an apron opened the door.

Tracy smiled involuntarily because the woman was the living image of the priests' housekeeper in the television series *Father Ted*. He finally composed himself enough to say, 'Is Father Flanery at home?'

'And who would you be?' she asked.

Tracy stood aside. Fiona already had her warrant card in her hand. 'This is Detective Sergeant Madden and I'm Detective Garda Tracy.'

The housekeeper stood aside. 'Father wants to speak with you. You'll wait in the parlour.'

Fiona and Tracy entered a short corridor before turning right into a small but cosy room. There were three armchairs and a small coffee table. Two of the armchairs were on one side of the coffee table and faced the third. The two police officers continued to stand, and they were joined two minutes later by a middle-aged priest dressed in standard black suit, black shirt and white clerical collar. He was an imposing man standing over six feet with a head of steely grey hair and a stomach that indicated he didn't take a great deal of exercise. He had a ruddy face, and his nose was a testament to a lifetime attachment to whiskey. Fiona could see that Father Flanery was probably a traditionalist. Many of the young priests in Galway looked more like schoolteachers than priests. She noticed there was no welcoming smile, so she introduced herself and Tracy, and didn't bother to shake hands.

'Please sit.' Flanery didn't introduce himself. He was an important man in the community. The two simple coppers should know that. 'Can I ask Mrs O'Donnell to get you tea?'

'No thanks, we've just had tea with our landlady.' Fiona sat in one of the two chairs on the far side of the table, Tracy sat beside her and Flanery took the chair facing them.

Flanery stared at Fiona. 'You're Madden. I've heard about you from Father Flanagan. He wasn't very complimentary.'

'I don't think your colleague is an independent observer. I understand from Garda Clarke that you wished to speak to us, and we certainly wish to speak to you.'

'I'll be writing to the bishop concerning the events of yesterday. I went to Dun Aengus in order to give the poor dead man the last rites and you prevented me from entering the fort.'

If Flanery was as good as his word, the super would be adding the letter to her file. Beside her, Tracy was busy taking notes. She would make sure this exchange was removed from the note of the meeting. 'The fort was a crime scene, and we had a number of technicians there collecting evidence. You would have contaminated the site.'

'You prevented me from doing my duty as a priest.'

'The body had been exposed for at least ten hours and we needed to get it to Galway as quickly as possible to preserve any evidence it might contain.' She thought about Brophy and decided to give him a rocket up his arse if he didn't call soon. 'I have it on good authority that the victim received the last rites at the Regional.'

'Nonetheless, I'll be writing to the bishop. What did you want with me?'

'We're having a certain amount of difficulty getting a handle on Mr Dangerfield. We know he arrived here last year, but nobody appears to know too much about him.'

'The word around is that Dangerfield was the victim of a satanic ritual.'

'That hasn't been established.'

'There was a pentagram on the ground and a distinctive dagger was in his chest. Doesn't that confirm the hypothesis?'

'You're well informed.'

Flanery laughed. 'The dogs in the street have the story.'

'Did you know Dangerfield?'

'No, not really, I only met him once.'

'Where?'

'I call on all new arrivals, so two weeks after he settled, I called to inform him of Mass times and to establish whether he would become a member of the parish.'

'You called at the cottage at Kilmurvey'

'I did. He invited me in, and we had tea together.'

'And did he become a member of your congregation?' She already knew that he didn't.

'He did not. I had the impression his faith had lapsed. However, there was no doubt that he had a deep knowledge of Catholic liturgy and he had studied the Bible. You examined his library?'

'We did,' Fiona said.

'Then you know that his reading concentrated on the unusual aspects of ancient religion, the more exotic and erotic the better.'

'Were you surprised that he died the way he did?'

'Not really.'

'So, you think he was killed in the course of a satanic ritual?'

'It would not surprise me. He showed me a few pieces he had collected.'

'Such as?'

'He had a druid's dagger in a presentation case above the fireplace and a mask with horns coming out of the side hung on the wall.'

Fiona and Tracy looked at each other.

Fiona pushed ahead. 'If you believe the ritual theory, it will suppose that there is a group of satanists on the island. Have you ever come across satanists before?'

'There is evil everywhere, Detective Sergeant. But no, I haven't come across satanists before. However, I don't think they would advertise themselves to me.'

'But have there been any other instances of satanic activity? Since you are the opposition, have there been any attacks on the church or on you?'

'No.'

'Then it's possible that the theory about the satanists might be farfetched?'

'It might.'

'So where should we look?'

Flanery opened his hands wide. 'Why are you asking me?'

'Do you know anyone who would like to see Dangerfield dead?'

'Offhand, no. The man was a bit of a hermit. I never heard he had a falling out with any of the locals.'

Another nail in the cuckolded husband theory, she thought. If Dangerfield was playing around with a local, Flanery would have heard about it. 'Then why do you think he was murdered in a way that would suggest a quasi-religious ceremony?'

The colour rose in Flanery's face. 'Satanism isn't a religion.'

'What about Wiccans? Are there any pagans on the island?'

'The islanders are good God-fearing people.'

'No Wiccans?'

'That I know of. You appear to be discounting the ceremonial aspect of the killing.'

'That couldn't be farther from the truth. It's the early days of the investigation and we don't discount any theory, do we Garda Tracy?'

Tracy looked up from his notebook. 'We certainly do not, sergeant.'

Fiona locked eyes with Flanery. 'No, if there are Wiccans or satanists in this parish, Tracy and I will find them and if they're responsible for the death of Mr Dangerfield then they will all go down. I assume that you've heard of conspiracy to murder.'

'I have heard of it.'

Fiona stood. 'Thanks for your time.'

Flanery stood and faced her. 'I understand that you're something of a pagan yourself"

Fiona went to the door and Tracy followed. She stopped and turned. 'You shouldn't believe everything you hear.'

CHAPTER SIXTEEN

The umbrellas went up again as soon as they left Flanery's house. They sprinted to the end of the driveway where O'Flaherty held the side door of the van open, and jumped in. They settled themselves in the rear seats while their driver took his place behind the wheel. Traditional Irish music blasted from the speakers and Fiona motioned O'Flaherty to turn it down. She called Brophy. The message on her phone said he was unavailable. She thought she would give him unavailable when she got hold of him. She called Clarke and he answered after half a dozen rings.

'You're still in the land of the living,' Fiona said. 'I've called you twice without reply.'

'I think I might have picked up a dose of pneumonia,' Clarke said. 'We're all wet through to the skin.'

'My heart bleeds for you. Have you found anything?'

'We've done a sweep of the keep and there's nothing hidden around the place. We're now on the patch between the two walls and so far, we've drawn a blank. After that, we'll move to the path from the car park to the outer wall.'

'Pay particular attention to the standing stones. Something might be lodged in there.'

'Yes, sergeant.' The phone went dead.

Fiona looked at the phone. 'Did that clown cut me off?'

'The line must be crap given the rain and wind and all,' Tracy said.

'I've a good mind to call him back and read the riot act.'

'Probably wasn't his fault.'

'Nothing from Clarke and I can't get Brophy. I've been kicking myself all morning for not keeping you in Galway and bringing Brophy with me, but the autopsy will be finished this morning, and he can spend the afternoon following up on Dangerfield's background.' She looked at O'Flaherty and saw that he was listening attentively. 'Why don't you drive us to the police station. Tracy and I need to have a few confidential words.'

O'Flaherty turned around. 'All the locals have heard that Dangerfield died in a ritual manner.'

'So?' Fiona said.

'It doesn't fit. I'm a tour guide and I've researched the island. There's no history of satanism and the pagans were here more than a thousand years ago.'

'Maybe the people who killed Dangerfield weren't listening to your spiel.'

'They weren't reading any books about the island either.'

'So, you don't subscribe to the theory that there's a group of pagans organising moonlight rituals that end up with a human sacrifice?'

'No, I don't. I'm not saying that there aren't pagans around or even people who practise the occult and worship Satan. But nobody ever tried to enlist me in any pagan or satanic group. We've had all sorts here over the years. The monks came here for the remoteness and there's no history of the Vikings having any interest in a rock in the Atlantic. In the 1970s, we had an invasion of hippies and at one time it was rumoured that John Lennon had plans to set up a commune. Most of the islanders would have appreciated a commune set-up based on love.'

Fiona wasn't sure but the rain appeared to be getting heavier. Who in heaven's name would set up a commune here? 'Did any of the communes survive?'

'Not the hippy communes. We have a so-called House of Devotion run by an extreme Catholic group led by a man who claims that she can speak to Jesus, his mother and assorted saints. And there's a guy who runs a drug rehab centre.'

'You're a strange fish, Thomas,' Fiona said. 'You don't speak like a local tourist guide.'

'I did law at Galway University. I was born in the States, so I had US citizenship, and after college, I went to work for a corporate law firm in Chicago. I stuck at it for five years and I decided that life wasn't worth living if you had to spend eighty hours a week working. The official story is that I had a breakdown and came back here to have a quiet life. The truth is I came back to *have* a life. I understand that you and Tracy have to have confidential conversations, but my knowledge of this island is an asset and I think that you should use me.'

'No insult intended,' Fiona said.

'And none is taken. I'd like to help as much as I can, and I don't need to know all the details.'

'Thanks for the offer and we'll be happy to take you up on it. But we still need to pass by the station.'

'Yes, sergeant.' O'Flaherty started the van and drove them the few hundred yards that separated the priest's house from the Garda station.

The building housing the station turned out to be a two-storey, white-washed house with a small entrance porch in the front. The local budget hadn't stretched to having a *Garda Síochána* sign anywhere in sight. The rain had eased off a little but there were still plenty of black clouds approaching from the west. Fiona had procured a set of keys to the station from Clarke. She opened the front door, used a second key to enter the office at the rear, and flopped into Clarke's office chair.

'This is probably where I'll end up, running my own little station in the middle of nowhere.'

'Maybe you'll end up as the commissioner. The glass ceiling has already been broken.'

'So young and so naive.'

Tracy poked around and found the kitchen. 'He has tea and instant coffee and the icing on the cake is a packet of chocolate biscuits.'

'No thanks.' The wall clock facing her showed eleven thirty. She realised that Brophy would only be halfway through the autopsy. She'd been mad at him for nothing. The case was already getting to her. 'I think your right, I am being a bit hard on Brophy.'

'I looked at the text he sent last night and the background check on Dangerfield doesn't seem to be going particularly well.'

'For a young man, you have a fine sense of understatement. We have nothing on the electoral roll, no social media presence, no police record. I suppose he checked if Dangerfield might be in a police protection programme.'

'He might have to get approval from higher up for that. Whatever he is doing, I guess it's his best. So maybe you shouldn't hound him.'

'It's just so damn aggravating. You were at the cottage. We should have found a passport, a bank card, a bank statement, photos, letters, postcards, some bloody thing. What the hell is going on here?'

'Maybe the killer beat us to the cottage and cleaned the place. Just like the business in Clifden, this could be an attempt to muddy the waters and keep us messing around.'

'Meanwhile, our killer or killers might already be off the island.'

'What do we do next?'

'I'm convinced that whoever murdered Dangerfield had a personal motive.'

'What about the dagger and the missing mask?'

'I'm willing to bet that the dagger is the one we found in Dangerfield's chest. We'll get a picture of it and a confirmation from Flanery. The mask is another matter. It would be nice to find it along with Dangerfield's clothes, but I fear both are long gone.'

'Then why leave the dagger in Dangerfield's chest?'

'To support the ritual killing hypothesis and to send us off like chickens with their heads chopped off looking for pagans and satanists. I think what we're looking at is plain old murder. The killer wanted Dangerfield dead and he had a motive for that desire. We just need to find it. I've changed my mind, make us a cup of tea and bring the chocolate biscuits along.'

CHAPTER SEVENTEEN

B rophy threw off his scrubs, left the autopsy room in the basement of the Regional Hospital and made straight for the gents' toilet. He barely made it to a cubicle when he dumped his breakfast into the toilet bowl. He'd never attended an autopsy and it would be some time before he attended another. He flushed, dropped the lid, sat on it and waited while his stomach gave another lurch. He tasted bile and decided that he needed a drink as soon as he pulled himself together. The autopsy had been a nauseating experience. He ran his hand over his brow and felt the cold sweat. During the procedure, he had made a phenomenal effort in keeping his bowels in check and not fainting. The state pathologist turned out to be an arrogant bastard which stiffened his desire not to let the side down despite his aversion to the scene of blood and guts that he had just witnessed. He'd done his best to cry off, but Sergeant Madden had pointed out that it was deemed necessary for a detective to witness the autopsy and that it was obligatory to attend at least one postmortem during one's career. He removed his phone from his pocket and turned it on. The sergeant had tried to reach him multiple times, but he had been required to turn off his phone while the pathologist worked. The overriding question was whether he should have the drink first or call the boss. He decided to call.

'I thought you'd gone AWOL on me,' Fiona said.

'The pathologist has just finished, and his assistant is what they call closing up.'

'And how are you?'

'Fine.'

'I hate that word. You don't sound fine. I hope you didn't faint or puke all over the place.'

'No, boss, I managed to hold it all together.'

'Until it was over. I can hear from the acoustics that you're speaking from the toilet. There's no shame in feeling a bit queasy. I understand that quite a few medical students faint or toss their lunch at their first autopsy. Anything interesting to report?'

Brophy took out his notebook. 'The cause of death was the knife through the heart. There were no defensive wounds and there was only dirt under the fingernails. It's been bagged and sent to the Technical Bureau. There was evidence in the lungs that Dangerfield was a heavy smoker and there was liver damage consistent with alcohol consumption. A load of samples were taken, and they'll all be sent off for testing. There was a whole load of medical mumbo jumbo that I didn't understand, and I got the impression that I would have been stomped on if I'd asked questions. The bottom line is that everything will be revealed in the autopsy report which will be delivered to you at the pathologist's earliest convenience.'

'Then you might as well go to the station and get me background on the victim.'

'You read my text from yesterday?'

'Tracy did.'

Brophy closed his notebook and returned it to his pocket. 'I know I'm not the greatest detective in the world, but I should have turned up something by now. I've searched the Internet, but Dangerfield is an unknown quantity. This guy is so far off the grid that it's ridiculous.'

'We've tossed his cottage and we've come up with nothing. There are no personal items whatsoever. I would be thinking that we're dealing with a ghost if we didn't have the body.'

'I'll give the property register a second look. Maybe he has a house somewhere else.'

'Good thinking. Before you get back to the office drop into a bar and have a coffee or a stiff drink. Celebrate your first autopsy.'

'Thanks, boss.' Brophy killed the call, stood, lifted the lid of the toilet, and vomited into the bowl wondering all the while where it had come from.

CHAPTER EIGHTEEN

Fiona withdrew a chocolate biscuit from the packet and bit into it. The news from the autopsy was disappointing but not altogether unexpected. She sat back in the office chair and stared at the ceiling. Her partner Aisling had acquainted her with the Pareto principle which stated that you get eighty per cent of the result from twenty per cent of the effort. In other words, eighty per cent of the effort produces nothing. She thought that the principle was appropriate when applied to crime detection. They were constantly improving their procedures and employing new technology, but an enormous amount of time and energy went into finding the criminals and getting the cuffs onto them. Where did that leave them with their current case? Dangerfield wasn't on any database. He had no family or work connections with Inis Mór, and he had been living quietly there for a year. Was there a place in Ireland more off-grid than the Aran Islands? She doubted it. That meant that Dangerfield must have wished to be off-grid. People who have a wish to be off-grid generally have a reason to be below the radar. She would need to find that reason but before that, she would have to delve into Dangerfield's life. But that was her current problem. The dead man didn't appear to have a life. That might have been possible before the advent of the computer and the insidious Internet. Brophy had demonstrated that he was an adept researcher and he had drawn a blank. It was possible that the dead man had compounded his desire to be anonymous by using an alias. In which case, they might be up shit creek. But how did that resonate with his ending up with a dagger in his chest? Lots of questions but very few answers. She sat up straight, picked up her cup and drained the remaining tea.

Across Clarke's battered desk, Tracy stared at her. 'Anything to share?' he asked.

'Not really. I'm waiting for either a piece of actual evidence or a bolt from the blue.'

Tracy stood up and went to the window. 'The rain has eased off.'

Fiona joined him. 'Maybe it's an opportune moment to show our faces to the lads on the hill. We wouldn't want them to think we were sitting snug in the station drinking tea and guzzling Clarke's chocolate biscuits. Be a good lad and rinse the cups out and while you're at it put the biscuits back where you found them.'

Tracy stared hard at her for a moment then picked up the cups and biscuits and headed to the kitchen.

Fiona smiled. It was a lesson in rank and hotshots like Tracy needed such lessons.

As they were leaving the station, Tracy's phone rang, and he took the call. 'Doctor Noelle Burke,' he put his hand over the speaker. 'She'd like to have a word.'

'Now that's a bolt from the blue,' Fiona said. 'Tell her we're busy now and we'll drop by the surgery when we have time.' She locked the station door and headed for the van.

THE RAIN HAD EASED but the wind howled and shook the van as they pulled up beside the ticket booth.

'I wouldn't put a beast out in weather like this,' O'Flaherty said.

They exited and saw that a handwritten sign had been affixed to the entrance gate indicating that access to Dun Aengus was restricted until further notice. The ticket office was unmanned and there didn't appear to be any local personnel in evidence. Who could blame them? The rain had made conditions on the hill even more treacherous than the previous day. Fiona pushed the gate open, and they climbed towards the chevaux de frise. After they'd gone a hundred yards, she could see orange-clad figures moving among the standing stones. Away to the right, Clarke had already exited from the stones and sat on a large rock enjoying a cigarette. Fiona made her way towards him.

As she approached, Clarke stubbed out his cigarette and stood.

'Find anything?' Fiona asked. She knew the answer already from the look on his face. It had probably been a useless exercise from the beginning but if she hadn't done it, some smart bastard would have pointed it out later. It was part of the investigation protocol.

'Divil a bit. We've searched the area from the keep to here. Bloody waste of time, if you ask me.'

'Thankfully nobody *is* asking you.'

Clarke looked at his watch. 'We'll be done in less than half an hour. I suppose you have no objection to us having a spot of lunch in Kilronan.'

'None. I'm sure the lads will appreciate a chance to dry off. But I'm afraid that it's not the end of their day. The boat for the mainland leaves at five o'clock and until then they're mine. After lunch, I want you to organise a door-to-door in Kilronan and Kilmurvey. I want to know if anyone saw or heard anything strange two nights ago. I'd also like to know if anyone had any dealings with the dead man.'

Clarke slumped.

'You have a problem with that?'

'It's another waste of time. You don't know the islanders like I do. They don't like the police or authority. If they know something, they'll likely keep it to themselves.'

Fiona knew he had a point. However, the search of the surroundings of the crime scene might have produced a result and the door-to-door might do the same. She would have to follow the protocol and hope that it produced a lead. Although, like Clarke, she would be surprised if the door-to-door produced a viable line of enquiry. Investigating a murder was like painting by numbers; the entire picture had to be filled in before it became clear. She glanced to her left and saw that all the team had emerged from the standing stones and were poking the ground and the heather with their sticks as they made their way back to the entrance. Tracy moved among them and chatted them up. The boys at the Park were probably right; he had the personal touch and he would go far. 'After lunch, carry out the door-to-door. Despite your misgivings, we might get a shred of evidence. We'll meet up later to review the day.'

As she walked back towards the entrance, her phone rang. She looked at the caller ID and sighed before hitting the green button. 'Yes, boss.'

'Any news?''Horgan said. 'What's that infernal noise in the background?'

'It's a thing called wind. I'm standing on a hillside on Inis Mór and it's blowing a gale. We've just completed the search of the surroundings of the crime scene, and we'll use the lads for a door-to-door this afternoon. The search was a bust. The killer or killers took everything with them.'

'The press have got wind of the special circumstances surrounding the death. And that means Superintendent O'Reilly has developed an interest. Whatever you do keep your bloody mouth shut about ritual murder.'

Tracy came and stood beside her.

'Didn't hear that, boss. The wind is howling. Maybe we should talk later.'

'Don't talk to the press,' Horgan shouted.

'Didn't catch that. Sorry, boss.' She held the phone up to amplify the sound of the wind and then cut the call.

'You're incorrigible,' Tracy said. 'What didn't you want to hear?'

'The part about not speaking with the press.' She continued down the hill with Tracy at her side. 'I don't like Brophy drawing a blank on Dangerfield. The consensus is that despite his bulk, Dangerfield didn't have an enemy in the world. That might be true but there was someone who wanted him dead. At some point, we may need the press to help us kickstart a look into the victim's backstory. The meek may not inherit the earth but they rarely end up being murdered in ritual fashion.'

'I read up a bit last night on the ritual murder stuff.'

'Bedtime reading. Cliona will be disappointed.'

Tracy ignored her and took out his notebook. 'I know you've discounted the ritual murder theory, but I think you may have been hasty. Human sacrifice was part of many occult belief systems. The word occult is important here because many of the adherents keep a low profile. For most believers, violence perpetrated in the name of religion is not a crime although in the eyes of the law it certainly is. Research into the motivation for ritual killings has shown that the practice is thought to lead to transformation, self-deification and healing. It could be that the killing was used to awaken dark forces. Our colleagues in the police generally assume that ritual killers are mentally disturbed and hiding behind a belief system that justifies their actions. The bottom line is that ritual killing is difficult to investigate and solve.'

'So, all we have to do is find who's been treating himself like a god these past few days.' Maybe the killer had read the same research that Tracy had. Perhaps the ritual aspect of the murder was intentional and aimed at making the murder difficult to solve. If that was the case, the killer had probably called it right.

Tracy put his notebook away. 'Maybe if we try to understand the beliefs behind the person who killed Dangerfield, we might be able to work out who he is.'

'Bullshit. Murder is murder whether it's dressed up as something else or not. Maybe you're right with all this ritual crap and I'll eventually have to eat humble pie. I agree that we need to trace the reasons that led to this crime. And the answer to that problem might lie with the perpetrator but I'm sure it lies with the victim.'

They reached the road and O'Flaherty pulled back the door of the van. 'Where to?'

'Lunch.'

CHAPTER NINETEEN

Although the place was jammed, O'Flaherty used his influence to find them a table in Joe Watty's pub. The building was a two-storey traditional house with an extensive outdoor area that was empty due, no doubt, to the inclement weather. Steam rose from wet clothes hanging on any protruding knob that might support their weight. For most of the tourists crammed into the pub, the trip to the Aran Islands would not rank among the fondest memories of their visit to Ireland. Fiona and Tracy had barely installed themselves at their table when O'Flaherty pulled up a stool and sat across from them. Fiona toyed with informing him that she and Tracy might like to dine alone but she could see from the look on his face that he considered himself a member of the team. The pub was doing a roaring trade and waitresses were busy distributing plates and alcoholic drinks to the patrons.

'The owner wants to take a photo,' O'Flaherty said.

Fiona gave him her best scowl.

'If that's all right with you guys,' O'Flaherty continued.

'I suppose you used our current notorious status to get us the table,' she said.

O'Flaherty smiled. 'You might find your picture on the celebrity wall one of these days.'

A waiter arrived, took out a mobile phone and took a picture of Fiona, Tracy and a smiling O'Flaherty. Luckily, the waiter didn't ask the detectives to smile.

Fiona ordered a burger and water, and Tracy chose the fish and chips. O'Flaherty settled for a club sandwich.

'How long do you think you'll be here?' O'Flaherty asked.

'It depends,' Tracy answered.

O'Flaherty looked at Fiona. 'You should come back here tonight. The Irish music will be massive.'

Fiona leaned forward. 'I've noticed that returned Yanks like to use words like big, great, beautiful, massive.'

'A former president noticed that as well,' O'Flaherty said, smiling.

Fiona pushed Tracy aside. 'I need the ladies' room.'

O'Flaherty watched her as she made her way past the tables. 'She's a bit feisty.'

'You could say that,' Tracy said.

'For coppers, you're both easy on the eye. Most of the cops we've had here could audition for the part of Quasimodo. The two of you seem to get on.'

'We've been working together for a while.'

'Are you sure that there's nothing going on with the two of you?'

Tracy burst out laughing. 'My girlfriend works for TG4.' He could barely get the words out.

'That's the second time my interest in your boss elicited laughter. What's so bloody funny?'

Tracy pulled himself together. 'Nothing, I just got a fit of the giggles.' He looked up and saw Fiona threading her way towards them.

She sat. 'You boys seem to be getting on well.'

'Just yapping,' Tracy said.

The arrival of their food coincided with the door opening and Clarke entering with four Guards in tow. Conversation in the room stopped as the patrons saw such a show of force from the constabulary. Clarke and his troops were ushered into a rear room and the pub gradually refilled with animated conversation.

Fiona tried her burger and declared it to be good. Tracy tucked into his fish and chips and O'Flaherty started on his sandwich. Fiona looked around the room and wondered whether the killer might be present. It was useless speculation. She had no leads so it could be anyone. She didn't even know whether she was dealing with a man or a woman. She decided to give her brain a rest and concentrate on her food. The next time she looked up she saw a woman standing in front of her holding a stool.

'Mind if I join?' she said placing the stool on the floor and elbowing O'Flaherty sideways. 'Ginny Hinds.'

'Fuck off, Ginny.' Fiona took a bite of her burger.

'Detective Sergeant Fiona Madden, you're exactly as I imagined you,' Hinds said. 'I watched the video on YouTube a dozen times.'

Fiona looked up. Ginny's blonde hair must have been perfectly coiffed before the wind got at it. She estimated Hinds as early thirties; she was pretty with regular features and beautiful blue eyes. She wore a short suede coat which led Fiona to believe that her clothes had been chosen before she knew she was to visit the island and that she hadn't checked the weather forecast. Her skirt finished just above the knee and displayed well-formed legs. There was no wedding ring on her finger. 'What paper do you work for?'

'You *are* a detective,' Hinds said. 'The Irish Daily Post.'

Fiona frowned. It was a tabloid, and the story would feature naked women dancing around a pentagram while the warlock drove the dagger into the chest of the sacrificial victim before everyone had wild abandoned sex. And it would certainly appear on the front page. So, Ginny was from the Irish Post.

'How did you get here, Ginny?' Fiona asked. 'You weren't on the ferry this morning and there hasn't been a boat since.'

'My editor splurged for a flight.'

'Aer Arann?'

Hinds smiled. 'Twin engine job from Dublin.'

'Sounds like more money than sense.'

Not if the story we heard is true.'

'And what story did you hear?' Fiona asked.

Tracy and O'Flaherty had stopped eating.

Hinds leaned closer to Fiona. 'The man whose death was announced yesterday was found naked on a stone platform in Dun Aengus. There was a pentagram on the ground indicating that there had been a satanic ritual underway. From a newspaper point of view, it's box office.'

'It's also bullshit. Who fed you this line of rubbish?'

Hinds picked up a chip from Tracy's plate and ate it. 'I'm a member of the National Union of Journalists and I never reveal my sources. If it's bullshit, then what's the truth?'

'You're in luck. There's going to be a press release from the Park. You've wasted your time and your editor has probably blown his travel budget for the month. So far, a man has been found dead, the circumstances are suspicious, and we are currently investigating the death.'

Hinds leaned forward revealing cleavage to Tracy and O'Flaherty. 'That won't sell papers. Do the suspicious circumstances include a sacrificial dagger in the chest and the pentagram on the ground?'

'No comment"

'I'm only the vanguard. When our rag hits the streets tomorrow, every journo worth his salt will be on his way here.'

'Bye, Ginny.' Fiona continued eating her burger.

'You had your chance.' Hinds stood and left.

'You handled that well.' Tracy resumed eating

'She'll concentrate on the salacious end of the murder.' Fiona finished her burger. 'That will make our murderer very happy indeed and our lives will be made miserable. Whoever killed Dangerfield wants the world to think that the murder involved the occult. That would be fodder for the press and the TV but it's not the truth.'

'But it is plausible.' Tracy pushed his empty plate aside. 'Shouldn't we at least consider it?'

'It's only plausible if you believe that there are people wandering around trying to raise the Devil by sacrificing humans. We've come a long way from societies that believed that human sacrifice could change weather patterns. Personally, I don't have the time to follow up on oddball lines of enquiry. We're going to follow correct police procedure and if we trip over a few pagans or Wiccans or whatever, then so be it. The arrival of Hinds has set the clock ticking. Stories in the papers will only stimulate the hierarchy to put pressure on us. Our leisurely investigation is out the window.' She took out her phone and called Brophy.

CHAPTER TWENTY

B rophy looked at the caller ID then at Horgan across the desk from him. His finger hovered over the green button on his phone.

'Madden?' Horgan said.

Brophy nodded.

'Don't take it.'

Brophy reluctantly dumped the call. He had been called upstairs to Horgan's office for a briefing on the Dangerfield murder. The boss's office was located on the same floor as the troops in the TV dramas he watched but since the station had once been a house and the architect who designed the refurbishment didn't watch crime programmes, Horgan's office was placed one flight of stairs above the worker level and was rarefied air for grunts like Brophy. He didn't like to have people leaning over his shoulder while he worked so he preferred to have the boss out of sight.

Horgan pointed at the chair in front of his desk. 'You've failed to locate this Dangerfield character. It shouldn't be that difficult after all it's an unusual name and not very Irish. I haven't run across a Dangerfield in my fifty-five years on the planet.'

Brophy sat on the edge of the proffered chair. 'I've tried all the databases – the electoral roll and the property register and there's no sign of a Sebastian Dangerfield anywhere. The man's a ghost.'

'What does that mean?'

''Probably that Dangerfield isn't his real name. Foley sent over his fingerprints, and I put them through the system. Nothing. To all intents and purposes, this man doesn't exist.'

'I don't like it,' Horgan said. 'I hope to God it has nothing to do with terrorism or spies. Used to be in this country we had the very rare murder case. Since the advent of drugs and social media, people are going around murdering each other daily.'

Brophy didn't see the link between social media and murder, but he knew better than to question his superior's deductions.

Horgan stroked his chin. 'I don't like Madden overseeing this investigation. She's a bull in a china shop. God only knows whose back she's going to put up.'

Brophy liked and respected Madden. She was the best detective he'd worked with. However, he kept that opinion to himself.

Horgan took a vial of pills out of the desk drawer, shook two into his palm and swallowed them. The facial grimace that followed indicated that the pills didn't taste nice. 'I want you to be my eyes and ears on this investigation. Madden will only tell me what she wants me to know.'

Brophy shifted uneasily in his chair.

'I'm only asking you to do your duty and keep your superiors informed. This is no run-of-the-mill murder. If the victim was a local who got himself mixed up with the local branch of Satans Anonymous, I wouldn't bother my arse looking over Madden's shoulder. My first thought was to have Tracy report independently to me, but it looks like he's drunk the Kool-Aid.'

'Coolaid? 'Brophy sometimes wondered about Horgan's sanity.

'Before your time. Jim Jones and the business in Guyana. He made a suicide pact with his followers and had poison mixed in with a soft drink called Kool-Aid. Then he told them all to drink it. They did as he asked thereby committing suicide. For God's sake, man, it means Tracy has bought into Madden.'

'Okay, I get it. Tracy won't inform on Madden, but I will.' Brophy noticed the tic in Horgan's eye. The word *inform* was one of the most emotionally reactive words to an Irishman.

'Brophy, a career in the Garda Síochána is a long hard road. It's important to have friends to help negotiate the bumps on that road. Do I make myself clear?'

'Crystal.'

'Keep me informed especially if there's a sensitive issue that I should be made aware of. Now get out and figure out why this victim doesn't exist.'

Brophy left the room vowing to ignore everything Horgan had said, except the bit about the Coolaid. He would look that up.

CHAPTER TWENTY-ONE

The secretary in the reception room of Noelle Burke's surgery asked them to kindly wait as the doctor was currently with a patient. She indicated a couple of metal chairs that faced a television in the corner showing a series of slides that had been produced by the Health Service Executive informing patients about different ailments they might be suffering from. In effect, it should have been called the *Hypochondriac Channel*.

Fiona had finally got through to Brophy who had sounded nervous on the call. She put it down to the aftermath of his first autopsy and his apparent failure to locate Dangerfield. The butterflies in her stomach indicated that she was a little nervous herself. They should already be generating lines of enquiry that would lead them to the killer or killers. The crime scene search had produced nothing, and she would be surprised if the door-to-door didn't prove to have the same result. She had been running over possible solutions to her problems. Dangerfield wasn't a ghost as Brophy had intimated. He was a flesh and blood man who had a reason for using an alias. One sure way to find out would be to release his photo to the press. Except the only photos of him they had were those taken by Foley at Dun Aengus and the autopsy. He didn't look too fresh in either and she thought that even his mother might have difficulty recognising him. Ginny Hinds was right. The *Post* would print a salacious story in tomorrow's paper and consequently, the island would be crawling with journalists. She needed to get a good likeness of Dangerfield and get it out to the media. The Kilmurvey cottage didn't contain a single photo and Dangerfield didn't conveniently leave his passport behind, if he had one. As she considered the options the consulting room door opened and a woman leading a young boy with a bandaged right hand exited. Burke appeared behind them and motioned Fiona and Tracy to enter.

Fiona shook Burke's hand. 'Another bicycle victim?'

'Par for the course.' Burke extended her hand to Tracy.

'You wanted to see us,' Fiona said. Burke wore loose-fitting black trousers and flat shoes. She was not what Fiona's mother would call an oil painting. She wore the obligatory white blouse and was rather flat-chested. She wondered why Burke hid away on a remote rock in the Atlantic.

'Please sit.' Burke indicated the two chairs facing her desk.

Fiona and Tracy took the chairs that still held the heat of the woman's and her son's bottoms. Tracy took out his notebook and pen.

'I'm afraid I was a little discombobulated yesterday. Seeing Sebastian like that made me wobble a bit. Most unprofessional of me.'

Fiona noted the use of the forename. 'You appear to have known him better than you indicated yesterday.'

Burke scratched her right cheek. 'As I said, I was taken by surprise.'

'You said he was a patient and you treated him for eczema.'

Burke tried a smile. 'He was as healthy as a horse. He had a bad case of eczema in his ears which caused a build-up of wax. He needed to have his ears cleaned every three months.'

'Can we see his patient file?'

Burke hit several keys on the computer and printed off three pages then passed them to Fiona.

Fiona scanned the pages. 'The field for his social welfare number is empty and you didn't get his birthdate.'

'He couldn't remember it on his first visit, and I must have forgotten to ask him on his subsequent visits. I don't know how I missed the birthdate. And he always paid cash.'

'That's a pity,' Fiona said.

'Why?'

Fiona ignored the question. 'I notice that you never performed any tests, no bloods, et cetera.'

'Every visit was simply a matter of helping him hear properly again.'

'What did you think of him?'

'He was a very charming and erudite man.' She looked wistful.

'You liked him.' Fiona thought it might be more than that. Gentlemen callers would be few and far between on the island.

Burke reddened. 'Yes, he was easy to like.'

'Did you meet him outside the surgery?'

'I had tea with him several times at the cottage.'

Tracy looked up from his notebook.

'It wasn't a sexual attraction,' Burke continued quickly. 'He was charming and knew how to behave around women. We had tea, played a game of chess and discussed books.'

'I don't suppose there's a chess club in Kilronan,' Fiona said.

'Not that I know of.'

'We've looked around his cottage. There's a distinct absence of personal items.'

'I noticed that too. I got the impression that Inis Mór wasn't a permanent home, more like a stop along the way. I had the feeling he had a more permanent residence somewhere, but he never said where.'

'His library contained a lot of interesting books.'

'His taste was eclectic.'

'Did you discuss his interest in the occult?'

Burke frowned. 'Not one of my interests.'

'You weren't really upset by the sight of a dead body. What was it that caused you to wobble as you called it?'

Burke paused before answering. 'I was sad. In the medical profession, we're trained to keep our emotions in check. I was surprised that his death hit me so hard.'

'I noticed you shivered when you saw the pentagram on the ground. Did the presence of the occult symbol cause your wobble?'

Burke's head dropped. 'Yes, Sebastian talked a lot about what I would term spiritual issues.'

'He wasn't a Christian?'

'Rather an agnostic, he had several run-ins with the House of Devotion people. He thought they were a bunch of charlatans.'

'What kind of run-ins?'

'Not really run-ins, more heated discussions.'

'Were you surprised he died the way he died?'

Burke's brow furrowed as she thought. 'I suppose not. He came across as a man who would accept an adventure.'

'Anything you'd like to add?'

'Not really, do you have any idea who killed him?'

'The investigation is in its early days. Our net is cast wide at the moment. Would it surprise you if |I told you that we can find no evidence that a Sebastian Dangerfield exists?'

Burke laughed. 'You're not serious.'

'I'm always serious.'

'When he told me his name, I was a little taken aback. Sebastian Dangerfield is the main character in a 1950s novel called *The Ginger Man* by JP Dunleavy. It was obligatory reading when I was at college.'

Tracy slapped his forehead with his right palm. 'I told you

I'd heard that name somewhere before, I just couldn't remember where. I dated a girl who studied English, and she was obsessed with that book. It's a cult classic.'

'You've been very helpful.' Fiona stood.

Burke stood, walked to the door and opened it. 'I hope you find who killed him. He was a nice man.'

'We'll do our best,' Fiona said. 'And you really have been very helpful.'

CHAPTER TWENTY-TWO

Rain blew in sheets across the front lawn as the two detectives exited the surgery. It was the wispy kind of rain that could drench you without you really knowing it.

Tracy put up the umbrella. 'She fancied him.'

'I think so. The pool of eligible bachelors is probably very limited, and he was a man at the same educational level as her.' She took out her phone, called Brophy and told him to drop the search for Dangerfield. They had established he used an alias. She would be in touch when she had something for him to do.

'Nice lady,' Tracy said.

'So, she's not in the frame.' Fiona didn't want to leave the porch just yet.

'Was she in the frame?'

She watched the rain being blown across the lawn. 'Everybody is in the frame until we find the killer.'

'What's her motive?'

'You came up with it. Hell hath no fury like a woman scorned.'

'How could she get him up to the fort?' Tracy asked.

'An assignation, a promise of sex. She has access to drugs.'

She stared up at the sky. There were black clouds as far as the eye could see. 'We need to get inside so that we can process what we've learned.'

'Back to the station for tea and chocolate biscuits,' Tracy said hopefully.

'Sounds like a plan.'

The van was waiting while O'Flaherty dozed at the wheel. He stirred when Tracy pulled back the door to the rear.

Fiona took her seat behind the driver. 'Back to the station and Tracy and I would like you to join us for tea.'

O'Flaherty smiled before putting the van in gear for the short drive to the station.

They sat together in Clarke's small office cradling their hot cups of tea. Fiona sat in Clarke's chair and O'Flaherty and Tracy sat facing her. She looked at O'Flaherty. 'Tell me about the House of Devotion.'

'It's a pity you didn't take my island tour.' O'Flaherty bit into a chocolate biscuit. 'While some people concentrate on the early Neolithic structures that have been found on the island like Dun Aengus itself, the real history is the remains of a lot of early Christian churches that are visible throughout the island. The most famous are the Seven Churches although the name is loosely applied to the remains of two small churches, *Temple Brecan* and *Teampall an Phoil*. Beside the churches is the Holy Ghost Bed and there are fragments of High Crosses all over the place. We were very big in early Christian times.'

'We'll take the tour when the case is over, get to the House of Devotion.'

'About fifteen years ago, this charismatic guy called Michael Meaghar claimed to have visions of angels and saints. He built up a following and bought a deserted convent located two kilometres outside Kilronan. He used donations to rebuild the place and install it as a church. People flocked to the island to attend Mass and listen to the description of Meaghar's visions. The flock grew and Meaghar attained celebrity status.'

'What did the Catholic Church do?' Tracy asked.

O'Flaherty poured himself a second cup of tea. 'Meaghar was on message, so they adopted a don't-rock-the-boat approach. They didn't like the vision bit, but they did like the fervour of the congregation. And he has a tame priest who says Mass and sucks up to him. But Meaghar is very much on the line of what they call televangelists in the States. It's all about the money. And the cash rolls in. What's your interest in them?'

'Apparently, our victim didn't see eye to eye with them. He called them out as a bunch of charlatans.'

O'Flaherty looked surprised. 'I didn't know that. Meaghar and the people that work for him wouldn't like that. There have been problems with journalists being invited to vacate the property.'

'The police weren't involved?' Fiona asked.

'Meagher's people insisted that they only use reasonable force in ejecting protesters. One of the national newspapers did an exposé and branded Meagher a fake. But it's a cult and the faithful still flock to hear him. I suppose you want to go up there.'

'I do.'

O'Flaherty finished his tea. 'There's no chance that you'll get to see Meagher. As far as I know, he doesn't even live here. People say he's got a mansion somewhere in England and he only comes to the House of Devotion when there's an event.'

'Or I suppose when Jesus or the Blessed Virgin want to speak to him,' Fiona said. 'Since they've been mentioned as having problems with the dead man, we'll have to investigate. Now be a good man and leave Tracy and me to have a little private conversation.'

O'Flaherty put on a theatrical peeved face before handing his cup to Tracy.

Tracy took the cup and looked at it in his hand. 'I suppose

I'm on cleaning up duty. You think this House of Devotion crowd has something to do with our victim's death.'

'I think if you'd remembered your old girlfriend and the literary illusion to this Ginger Man book, we would have wasted less time.'

Tracy stood and returned the cups to the kitchen. 'I never read the book, but the name stuck in my memory. I just couldn't remember where I'd heard it.'

'I'm not sure about the House of Devotion but they appear to be the kind of people that might go in for a theatrical end to one of their enemies. Although the altercation doesn't appear to be heavy duty. What did you think of Doctor Burke's opinion of our victim?'

Tracy didn't reply for a few minutes. 'I just ran through the interview and the only thing of note was that she fancied the man.'

'I think we learned something new. Put everything together, the library, the chess set, the use of the literary alias, the ability to stay under the radar.'

Tracy's cheeks flared. 'He was a spy,' he said in an excited tone.

'I don't think so but it's a possibility. But even a spy would have a couple of low-brow books on his shelves. Burke used the word erudite. Now why did she use that word above all others? Because she thought he had great learning. And what kind of people have great learning?'

Tracy smiled. 'University professors.'

'Or teachers in general. What if our victim was a teacher, professor whatever? How many teachers would you say there are in Ireland?'

Tracy had his phone out. 'Primary or post-primary?'

'Post-primary.'

'My trusty search engine tells me that there are nineteen thousand teachers affiliated to the Teacher's Union of Ireland.'

'Get on to Brophy, tell him that our victim is most probably a teacher and he's to find out if the union has photos of all their members. If not, then we'll have to depend on Ginny Hinds and her pals, and I really don't want to go there. The hierarchy will resist using the media because it conflicts with the concept that the family must be informed first. But our options are diminishing by the day.'

Tracy did the necessary while Fiona sat back and contemplated the ceiling.

CHAPTER TWENTY-THREE

Thankfully the rain had stopped and although Fiona didn't believe her eyes there were rays of sunlight breaking through the banks of cloud that still covered the island. On their two-kilometre drive to their destination, they encountered tourists wandering the streets finally freed from their prisons in the pubs and restaurants. The first observation Fiona made about the House of Devotion when O'Flaherty's van pulled up in front of the two-storey 1930s building was that visitors were not welcome. The ten-foot-high cast-iron entrance gates to the tarmacked area in front of the renovated building had thick chains encircling them that were terminated in a stout lock.

'Maybe we should have called ahead,' Tracy said.

'An open church in name only,' Fiona said opening the rear door of the van. She stepped outside and made her way to the gate. The building inside was large and looked institutional except for a conservatory which had been added at the side and which bore the legend *ENTRANCE*. The building appeared deserted although O'Flaherty had advised that there were always staff about. She shook the gates. The heavy metal chains jangled but the gate didn't move.

Tracy joined her. 'Looks like we'll have to abandon and move on.'

'Maybe but we'll be back.' Fiona was about to turn back to the van when she heard an angry shout.

'Get away from the gate.' A man had exited from the glass annexe and strode towards them gesticulating wildly.

Fiona took out her warrant card and held it up. 'Garda Síochána.'

The man slowed and stopped shouting. He stood on the other side of the gate, craned his head forward and read the warrant card.

'I'm Detective Sergeant Fiona Madden and this is Detective Garda Sean Tracy. Who are you?' The man on the other side of the gate was in his late thirties. He was short and stocky and what little hair he had was prematurely grey, his face pale, round and featureless except for his eyes that appeared to blaze with what Fiona took to be religious fervour.

'My name is Pearse Connelly, and you have no business here.'

'That's for us to decide. Open the gate.'

'This is holy ground. You can't enter here.'

'That makes you wrong twice. The House of Devotion is not a church, and we can enter where we please. If you don't open the gate, I'll send Garda Tracy off to find a bolt cutter and we will gain entry. I am investigating a murder and you are obstructing me in fulfilling my duty. Your actions constitute a crime.'

Connelly produced a key from his pocket, opened the lock and unwound the chain. He held the gate open. 'What's your business here?'

'We'll discuss that inside.' Fiona strode off in the direction of the glass annexe followed by Tracy.

Connelly busied himself by relocking the gate.

'Looks like the House of Devotion definitely doesn't

welcome visitors,' Tracy said when they reached the double glass doors that led into the annexe.

When they entered, they found themselves in a large room that had been set up as a shop. It resembled the other tourist shops on the island except that the items on sale all had a religious theme. At the far end of the annexe, a set of double wooden doors were open, and Fiona could see a substantial church lay beyond. She turned and viewed the items on sale. A nondescript picture of the Virgin Mary in a cheap plastic frame was on sale for two hundred and fifty euros with corresponding prices in US dollars and sterling. Beside the picture a small box contained two base metal medals for sale and she whistled when she read the price: one hundred and twenty-five euros. Nice work if you can get it, she thought.

Connelly closed the door and turned to face the detectives. 'What can I do for you?'

Fiona dragged herself away from the display cases. There had to be a Trades Description Act covering prices that high. 'We'd like to speak to Mr Meagher.'

'He's not here now. He only visits when we hold a Mass for the congregation.'

'Not too fond of the weather, is he?' Tracy said.

Connelly stood facing Fiona. 'We have other houses, and he spreads his time between them. He has a large flock. I'm in charge here so how can I help you?'

'You may have heard that we discovered the body of a man in Dun Aengus. We're investigating the death.'

'What does that have to do with the House of Devotion?'

'It's a man who called himself Sebastian Dangerfield and he lived in Kilmurvey. We have information that he had a run-in with someone, possibly yourself, at the House of Devotion. There's no police record of an altercation but we're wondering whether there was any bad blood between Dangerfield and yourselves.'

'Are you trying to intimate that someone at the House of Devotion had an involvement in this man's death?'

Fiona tried to get a handle on Connelly's accent; it mixed Dublin with Galway and added a tinge of Oxford. 'I'm not trying to intimate anything. I'm simply trying to find out if the altercation between Dangerfield and an individual at the House of Devotion had any bearing on his murder.'

'Okay, I'm the one that had the row with Dangerfield. It wasn't an altercation; no punches were thrown. In fact, there was no physical contact whatsoever. This is a house of peace and devotion to the Virgin Mary. Dangerfield sounded off about Michael being a charlatan and fleecing his flock. That is not a fact. Michael receives visions from the Virgin Mary and a collection of saints. He actually had visions while attending Mass here in Inis Mór.'

'So, you bore Dangerfield no ill will.'

'The man upset the older members of our flock. We banned him from the grounds, and we threatened to have a banning order issued in court.'

'What's your role here?'

'Is that relevant?'

Fiona stared into Connelly's face.

'I manage this facility.'

'And you believe strongly in what Meagher is doing?'

'I know that Michael is genuine in his visions. I believe strongly in the grace of God, and I have devoted my life to Michael's ministry.'

'Are you here alone?'

'No, three others are supporting the ministry. We organise the events and advertise to the flock.'

Fiona took a last saunter around the shop examining the items on sale as she went.

Connelly had already moved to the door, and she joined him there.

'Thanks for your time. We may need to talk to you again. Is there any way we can contact you to avoid unpleasantness at the gate?'

Connelly handed her a card. 'You have my phone number. I'm always here. I'm sorry about the way I reacted but there are people committed to bringing Michael down.'

'And you don't like that.'

'No, I don't. They say that Dangerfield died as a result of a satanic ritual. Here we praise God and abhor Satan.'

Fiona and Tracy sat in the van. They watched as Connelly replaced the chain and turned the key in the padlock.

'How did you get on?' O'Flaherty asked.

'Like a house on fire,' Fiona said.

'Christ and his mother spoke Aramaic,' O'Flaherty said. 'But I hear that when they converse with Meagher, they speak in a west of Ireland accent.' He burst out laughing and Tracy joined in.

Fiona yawned and leaned against the side of the van. 'If what we saw inside is anything to go by there's money to be made in religion.'

'What you saw was the tip of the iceberg,' O'Flaherty said. 'There are the bequests and the DVDs. It's a business.'

'I think it's time that Tracy and I headed back to your sister's place. It's been another long day.'

'What about Bridget Heaney?' Tracy asked.

Fiona frowned.

'The housekeeper,' Tracy said.

'She didn't get back to you?'

He shook his head.

'I wonder why that is.' Fiona tapped O'Flaherty on the shoulder. 'Kileany House, driver. If Mohammed won't come to the mountain.'

. . .

KILEANY HOUSE WAS a large two-storey house with an extensive two-storey annexe to the side. There was a substantial parking area that allowed O'Flaherty to pull up close to the entrance.

Fiona and Tracy entered a hallway where a wooden desk stood on the right side. There was no one at the reception and Tracy hit an ornate brass bell that stood on the desk with his right palm. A well-dressed middle-aged lady emerged from a door behind the desk and smiled at the two police officers. Tracy had his warrant card out and introduced himself and Fiona.

The smile disappeared from the woman's face. She introduced herself as Treasa Kenny the owner of the establishment. 'How can I help you?'

'We'd like to speak with Bridget Heaney if she's around,' Fiona said. 'We left a message for her to call us back, but we haven't heard from her.'

'I'll get her for you.' Kenny disappeared through the door at the rear of the desk and returned several minutes later with a younger woman who entered the hallway with a noticeable reluctance. She was in her mid-twenties and dressed in black shirt and trousers. She was pretty and had a full head of curly fair hair. 'This is Bridget,' Kenny said. 'I'm afraid that she's a bit apprehensive.'

'There's no reason to worry,' Fiona said. 'We only want to talk about her work for Mr Dangerfield.'

Heaney suppressed a fit of sniffles.

'Perhaps you'd be more comfortable in the library,' Kenny said. 'There's no one in there now.' She didn't wait for an answer but strode down a corridor off the hallway.

'Thank you,' Fiona said as Kenny ushered them into a room with a large bookcase lining one wall. There was a selection of antique chairs and tables spread throughout the room.

Kenny retired, and Fiona led Heaney towards one of the stuffed chairs and sat her down. 'This won't take long.' She and Tracy sat facing Heaney. 'You worked for Mr Dangerfield?'

Heaney sat on the edge of her seat and held a handkerchief in her right hand. 'Yes, one day a week on my day off. I cleaned, changed the bed linen and ironed. He did the washing himself.'

'What did you think of him?'

'He was always good with me. He paid me every week and even gave me a bonus on my birthday.' She began to cry and wiped her eyes with her handkerchief. 'It's a sin that he was murdered.'

'He doesn't appear to have had any friends.'

'He kept to himself right enough. He used to go out for a walk and let me get on with the work, but I never saw any sign that someone else had been in the house. He could have set a bed in the spare room, but he never bothered.'

'Did you ever see any photographs or personal items around?'

'Never.'

'Did he have a mobile phone or a computer?'

'Not that I saw. He was always looking after them books of his. He was one of them intellectuals, always learning new things.'

'Did he ever tell you what he did for a living?'

'Not directly. I don't know why but I thought he might be a professor with all them fancy books.'

'There was a broken frame on the floor of his cottage. Was it broken the last time you cleaned the place?'

'No, I cleaned that place within an inch of its life.'

'Did you ever have an inkling that Dangerfield wasn't his real name?'

Heaney looked confused. 'No, he was always Mr Dangerfield to me.'

Fiona stood. 'Thanks for your time. You obviously liked him.'

Heaney looked relieved. 'He had a way with him. I never heard a cross word from his mouth.'

Fiona and Tracy stood at the entrance. 'A riddle, wrapped in a mystery, inside an enigma,' Tracy said.

'It's all of that.'

CHAPTER TWENTY-FOUR

F iona wanted to call it a day after the visit to the House of Devotion and Kileany House but in a murder enquiry time had a habit of telescoping. She called Clarke and learned that the door-to-door had proved as useless as they'd both anticipated. She thought it highly unlikely that Dangerfield's trip to Dun Aengus in the dark had gone unseen, but it was likely that whoever witnessed it had no idea what they were looking at. There was a well-known psychological phenomenon in police work called change blindness which is a term used to describe a situation in which someone fails to notice that a key element of their surroundings changes, for example, a fifty-odd-year-old man traipsing up a hill in the dead of night. That was the kind explanation for the lack of evidence produced by the door-to-door. The unkind version was that someone had witnessed Dangerfield's journey to the fort but like Bridget Heaney was loath to get themselves involved in a police enquiry. The bottom line was the same. She had used up valuable police resources in a fruitless exercise. It was a quarter to five when she and Tracy made their way to the quay. Clarke stood with the four Guards amid the crowd waiting for the ferry to arrive. Fiona didn't want the men to leave before expressing her gratitude for the tough day she'd organised for them. She went among them shaking hands and apologising for the ball aching waste of their time. She was grateful that they took it as part of their job. Except for Clarke whose sullen look indicated that he didn't take kindly to his cushy life being disturbed. Fiona waited until the ferry arrived at its mooring before leaving the group. She had no doubt that the pub in Rossaveal would be the next stop on their journey home. She was at the edge of the quay when she heard her name being called and she turned to see Aisling waving from the foredeck of the ferry. She smiled and turned back down the quay.

Aisling hugged her as she stepped off the gangway. 'I thought I'd give you a surprise.'

Fiona linked her arm as they joined the stream of passengers heading into Kilronan. 'It's not really the ideal time for a visit. Don't get me wrong. I'm delighted to see you, but this is turning out to be a tough case.'

'I'm only staying overnight. I'm booked on the morning ferry back to Galway. I'm sorry if I overstepped the mark.'

Tracy arrived and hugged Aisling. 'If I'd known you were coming, I would have invited Cliona.'

'Tomorrow night is yours,' Fiona said. 'I don't know about you two, but I need a drink. Let's give The Bar a try. The last time I was in Inis Mór it was called the American Bar, but it appears the adjective has been dropped.'

The Bar is in a two-storey house that overlooks the yacht anchorage in Kilronan. The outside tables and chairs were sodded as a result of the day's rain. Fiona marched straight into the lounge. A blast of nostalgia hit her. The only thing that had changed about the pub was the name. The years fell away, and she was a twelve-year-old again. The two Galway flags that hung over the bar might very well be the same ones she remembered, and the painting of Elvis still stared at her from the back wall. She walked to the other side of the bar and saw the table that she and her parents had sat at was still there and free. She stopped for a second and got a mental image of her parents sitting there. She took the seat where her younger self had sat. The reason the memory was so vivid was because she had replayed it so many times. It was the last trip they had made as a family. Two weeks later her father went to Galway on *business* and never returned. And life changed for her and her mother.

'You look tired,' Aisling said.

'Just having a bout of nostalgia. I sat in this room twenty-two years ago and it hasn't changed. Except for the two guys playing music at the end of the room. They look to be in their twenties.'

Tracy sat facing the two women. 'This place grows on you. I've only been here two days and I feel I've been here all my life.'

'I'll have a pint of Guinness,' Fiona told Tracy. 'And Aisling will have a gin and tonic.'

Tracy held out his hand, but Fiona ignored it. 'I suppose it's my turn, again.' He slipped off his chair and headed to the bar.

'Cut the poor man some slack,' Aisling said.

'I'm mentoring him. When he starts to rub shoulders with the big boys, he'll be expected to keep their whistles wetted.'

'Is that what you did when you rubbed shoulders with the big boys?'

Fiona laughed. 'The big boys had other places they wanted me to rub.'

Aisling joined in the laughter. 'I'm just getting a mental image.'

Tracy deposited the drinks on the table. He'd chosen a pint of lager for himself. 'What's so funny?'

'I'll tell you later.' Fiona pulled the pint glass towards her.

They touched glasses before drinking.

'How's the case going?' Aisling asked.

Fiona gave her a brief rundown.

'Not your run-of-the-mill murder,' Aisling said. 'A victim using an alias, a set up ritual murder, all on an island in the Atlantic. Sounds like it might be difficult to solve.'

'I would have preferred to have found the murderer standing over the body with the knife in his hand,' Fiona said. 'But that wasn't to be. Do you have something to add to our thinking?'

'Dangerfield is an interesting character,' Aisling said. 'He appears to be a worldly individual, but he hides himself away here. He could have buried himself in Paris or Rome, why here?'

'Just another question to add to the many we've already developed. The autopsy hasn't turned up anything so far. We're still waiting on the tox screen. The techs are sifting through what they collected, and we should have a report in a few days but in the meantime, the trail is going cold, and the murderer might already have left the island.'

'Sounds pretty hopeless,' Aisling said. 'But if you'd like my professional opinion, I'd say that your best chance of finding the culprit would be to dredge through the victim's life. The murder was very personal which indicates that the perpetrator and the victim knew each other. Maybe not just knew each other but knew each other well enough for the victim to have severely injured the killer.'

'I'm already there. There's no such thing as the perfect murder. Or at least I hope not. The hardest murder to solve is the indiscriminate one.' Fiona finished her pint, took a twenty-euro note from her pocket and handed it to Tracy. 'Same again.'

'It's going to be one of those nights,' Aisling said.

'Just working up a bit of Dutch courage before introducing you to my landlady.'

'Ireland's a different place now. She probably won't bat an eyelid.'

'Tell that to the lads up at the House of Devotion.'

'I've seen Meaghar on TV. How could anyone believe that drivel?'

'It's all about the money.' Fiona saw Ginny Hinds entering the lounge. 'Speaking of drivel, here comes a purveyor of lies and half-truths.'

'Your hackles are showing,' Aisling said.

Hinds marched over to Fiona's table and took out her mobile phone. 'I thought I'd give you a look at the mock-up for tomorrow's front page.'

Fiona looked at the picture on the phone. The background had a large image of Satan with obligatory horns and bulging red eyes. The headline read *Satanic Murder on the Aran Islands*. There were just two paragraphs of text, and the rest of the front page was devoted to a small picture of two celebrities who were divorcing. The byline was Ginny Hinds. 'At least they got your name right.'

'Why don't you give me the real story. There's time to send fresh copy if you'd like to comment.'

'You'll still run the image and the headline. You only missed out the naked women. But I suppose they're on page three. Now it's been a long day and we're having a quiet drink so why don't you crawl back under whatever rock you came out from.'

Hinds laughed. 'I heard you were a ballbreaker. You better find the killer because if you don't, I'm going to skewer you.' She turned and made for the door.

Tracy put Fiona's drink in front of her. 'There's a book you should read: *How to Win Friends and Influence People*.'

Fiona held out her hand. 'Change.'

Tracy dropped coins into her empty hand.

Fiona lifted her drink. 'Slainte. I think I'm about ready to face Maureen Leavy and I need a shower to wash Ginny's stink off.'

DAY THREE

CHAPTER TWENTY-FIVE

F iona's phone rang at two minutes past eight in the morning while she, Aisling and Tracy were wolfing down an Irish fry that would feed a horse. Maureen's home-made brown bread was among the best Fiona had tasted and as Aisling had anticipated not an eyelid had been raised about the two women sharing after a financial consideration had been agreed.

'Good morning, boss,' Fiona said answering her phone. She was surprised that Horgan was up and about at the early hour.

'Have you seen the newspapers?'

'The quality newspapers or just the *Post*?'

'What did you say to that Hinds woman? The Garda Síochána do not discount the possibility that the murder had been carried out by a group of devil worshipers.'

'I never said that, and Tracy witnessed every conversation I had with Hinds. But it's true we haven't discounted the possibility nor have we discounted the possibility that the murder was carried out by the local book club members.'

'You and Tracy are as thick as thieves. I'm worried about

that boy. I suppose you and he are keen to extend your holiday on Aran.'

Fiona's first reaction was to tell her boss where he could shove his *holiday*. But she was a professional crime solver. 'I think there are a few more avenues that we need to explore.'

'Have you considered the possibility that the killer might already have left the island?'

She explained the system of collecting the names and IDs of departing passengers. 'Dangerfield is an alias but we're still in the dark as regards his real name. We need to find out who he is and what he was doing on Aran. I have a feeling that will throw some light on the killer's identity. The people we've spoken to here would put the victim up for sainthood.'

'And how long do you think that might take?'

'Anything between a day and twenty years.'

'Don't get fucking smart with me, Madden. I doubt very much that the commissioner or the super read the *Post*, but they have people who do. And when they see the front page, they'll call me and ask for an explanation which I don't have. What I'm afraid of is a tsunami of press coverage will follow.'

'It'll be a flash-in-the-pan. I'm sure the press know that there are more important things going on in the world.'

'I want a written report of each day's activity starting with yesterday.'

'Just the highlights or do we go into issues like toilet breaks?'

Horgan cut the call.

'In case you didn't catch the name of that book,' Tracy said, it's *How to Win Friends and Influence People*. You obviously don't believe in the saying that you catch more flies with honey than with vinegar.'

Fiona pushed her plate away. 'Have you heard of the phrase lions led by donkeys? Horgan typifies it. He doesn't know his arse from his elbow where murder investigation is concerned. And I'm not about to patronise his ignorance.'

Aisling looked at her watch. 'Very interesting discussion but my ferry leaves at eight fifteen so I'd better get a move on. When you get more information on Dangerfield give me a call if you want a professional opinion.'

'I'll come down to the quay to see you off.' Fiona turned to Tracy. 'We'll rendezvous at the station at eight thirty and make sure that Clarke is in attendance.'

GARDA CONSTABLE CLARKE sat in his ergonomic chair and didn't move when Fiona entered. He smiled at her. 'That journalist set the cat among the pigeons. Everyone on the island is trying to get hold of a copy of the *Post* but they're like gold dust.'

'It's bullshit,' Fiona said.

'But it's putting the island on the map. I wouldn't be surprised if the news went global.'

Fiona hoped to God that he was wrong. It was time to get the show on the road. 'Did you take a copy of the responses to the door-to-door?'

Clarke opened a desk drawer, withdrew a sheaf of papers and tossed them on the desk in front of Fiona.

'Pick them up and hand them to me,' she said.

'What!' Clarke looked surprised.

'You heard me, or I'll have you on report for a lack of discipline.'

He picked up the papers, straightened them and handed them across the desk. 'Sorry, sergeant.'

'Find something useful to do. Tracy and I need to go through these notes in peace. We'll need this office.' She watched as the red colour deepened on Clarke's face.

'What about opening up the visits to Dun Aengus?' he asked. 'They had a couple of lads up there yesterday cleaning up the blood and erasing the pentagram.'

'They can go ahead. We're finished up there.'

He stood up, put on his cap and left the office.

'What?' she said to Tracy when the office door closed. 'There's no way I'd let that prick disrespect me. I worked too hard to get where I am to allow a lazy bastard to look down on me.'

'We may need him later.'

There were about forty photocopied pages from the notebooks of the four Guards. 'We'll have to be pretty desperate.' She handed half the pages to Tracy.

She sat in Clarke's chair and began reading. The previous night she hadn't slept well despite the comforting presence of Aisling. She didn't need Horgan to tell her what she was up against. Murders came in all shapes and sizes. Their solutions, therefore, required an individual approach. The process of detection was much the same, the collection of evidence and the interviewing of witnesses leading to the development of a hypothesis of how the crime had been committed and who the murderer might be. But what happened when there was little or no evidence and no witnesses? That was where she and Tracy found themselves. There had been several cases in the state where her colleagues had failed utterly in both finding and collating the evidence and in interviewing witnesses, and those cases were still open decades later and were generally the subject of TV documentaries. She was worried that the murder in Dun Aengus might be that kind of case. She stared at the papers in her hand and hoped that the nugget that would spring the lock that was on the case lay within.

The notes made by the individual policemen were an exercise in human psychology. Many of the pages contained only one phrase denoting the fact that the interviewee, name and address supplied, knew nothing about Dangerfield. This was a rather strange statement given that the island's population could be squeezed into a space one-fifteenth the size of the 3Arena in Dublin. As a local of Connemara herself, she would suppose that the dead man, as a stranger, would have been

seen or pointed out by a local. Fifty per cent of the intervie-
wees asserted that they had no knowledge of the man and that
was accepted by the Guard in question. The other fifty per
cent knew the victim but had no dealings with him. They had
seen him about Kilronan and Kilmurvey but had never spoken
to him. She noticed that most of the latter lived in Kilmurvey.
However, no one remembered a man heading towards Dun
Aengus on the evening of his death.

'Anything?' she asked when she had finished.

Tracy put his pages aside. 'Not really. I've underlined
anything I found out of the ordinary. What about you?'

'An exercise in futility and human nature; the three wise
monkeys were very much in evidence, see no evil, hear no evil,
speak no evil.' She handed across her papers and took Tracy's.
She found a similar theme in the notes that Tracy had viewed.
She had almost finished when she came across one that Tracy
had underlined. One of the locals in Kilmurvey, a Mrs
Dirrane, didn't know much about the victim but she had a
major bee in her bonnet about the kids from the refuge who
she didn't trust. It was a typical complaint from an older
person about the activities of the younger generation. She laid
the note of the interview aside. It might be useful to interview
the younger people who might have been out and about the
evening that Dangerfield was murdered. She worked her way
through the rest of the notes and then sat back in the chair.
They'd come up dry. That was why the modern copper
preferred CCTV to witness information. Witnesses were
unreliable and could be easily manipulated by a clever
policeman into fingering the wrong miscreant. The camera
didn't lie and didn't suffer from the psychological baggage of
the human.

Tracy tossed his finished stack onto the desk. 'Another
dead end.'

'Agreed. I'd hoped for more but got exactly what I expected.' She looked at the clock on the office wall, nine twenty-five.

'What next?'

'Tea and biscuits. Put the kettle on like a good man.'

'After that feed we had this morning?'

'That was an order.'

FIONA SAW Clarke looking at the empty packet of biscuits on the desk when he entered. 'Don't worry, Tracy will replace the biscuits before the day is out. There's still a cup of tea in the pot if you're interested.'

Clarke poured himself a cup. 'Find anything in the door-to-door notes?'

'Nothing jumped out at us.'

'Bloody waste of time.' Clarke sipped his tea. 'Who made this?'

'Tracy's working on his technique,' Fiona said. She picked up the sheet she'd left aside. 'Do you know this Mairin Dirrane lady?'

'Know her? I regret the day I ever met her. The woman is a pest. She's always ringing up complaining about something or other. I wouldn't take a blind bit of notice of anything she says. Always going on about antisocial behaviour and people watching her house.'

'She seems to be a bit preoccupied with the group of young people who live close by.'

Clarke pushed his half-full teacup away. 'The refuge you mean. Yeah, that's the centre of her attention now. She thinks it's a commune.'

'O'Flaherty mentioned it earlier. What exactly is it?'

'Young fellah called Grealish set it up a couple of years ago. He brings in young people who have drug-related problems. They help around the farm and learn how to grow their own food. I suppose you could call it drug rehabilitation. The idea is that there are no drugs on Inis Mór but of course, there are drugs in every parish in Ireland.'

'We'll have a word with her anyway. I suppose O'Flaherty will know where to find her.'

'Speaking of which...' Clarke withdrew an envelope from the pocket of his tunic and handed it to Fiona. 'O'Flaherty's bill for driving you around for the past two days.'

Fiona took a single page from the envelope and started laughing. 'Our friend Thomas O'Flaherty is a comedian.' She put the note in her jeans pocket. 'I'll sort this out later.'

'Come on, Tracy, let's hit the road.' She stood up and strode to the door.

'Who's going to clean up?' Clarke said.

CHAPTER TWENTY-SIX

'Did Clarke speak with you?' O'Flaherty said as he pulled up outside Marin Diranne's house located a hundred yards from the cottage which had been specially constructed for the *Man of Aran* film.

Fiona tapped her pocket. 'He did and it will be dealt with by the accounts department of An Garda Síochána in Galway. You'll be contacted by them in due course.' She didn't tell him that he would be sorely disappointed when he received his money.

O'Flaherty laughed. 'I think I've been stitched up. There was great craic in Joe Watty's last night. The music was top drawer. Tracy put in an appearance, but I thought you'd show up.'

'It was a long day, and I needed my bed.'

'Maybe this evening.'

'Maybe.' She nodded at Tracy, and he opened the van door.

A gravel path led to the front door of Marin Diranne's thatched cottage which was set back from the road and could itself have been used in the famous film classic. Tracy rapped on the front door and had his warrant card ready for examination.

The woman who eventually opened the door was in her late seventies with a mop of curly grey hair. She was bent forward and leaned on a walking stick. Her face was thin and lined and her turkey neck narrow and sinewy. She wore a black oversized pullover and a wide full-length wool skirt. She closely examined Tracy's warrant card through a pair of wire-rimmed spectacles, then opened the door and stood aside to permit the two detectives to enter.

'*Fáilte romhibh* – you're welcome.'

'*Tá Gaeilge agam ach ní labharann Garda Tracy*. Do you mind if we continue in English?' Fiona introduced herself and Tracy before entering. She looked at Diranne's face and saw that while there was age there was a brightness in the eyes that bespoke an inner energy.

'You have fine Irish. Where are you from?' Diranne asked.

'Glenmore on the mainland.'

'I don't know too many places on the mainland. I haven't been off the island in years. Come in and sit.'

The cottage was a carbon copy of Fiona's. They were standing in the living room and Fiona noticed the two doors, one right and one left, that would lead to the bedrooms. A door at the rear would lead to the kitchen. The cottage hadn't been modernised and the open fireplace looked far too big for the small living room. A turf fire smouldered gently, and a black cast-iron kettle hung directly over it. Every available wall space and shelf was filled with religious pictures and paraphernalia, mainly plastic statues of Jesus, the Virgin Mary and Saint Anthony. One section of wall was devoted to black and white family photos, probably taken in the 1950s given the clothes the subjects were wearing.

Diranne sat in an armchair that faced the TV while the detectives selected a pair of kitchen chairs.

'So, Garda Clarke finally sent somebody to listen to me,' Diranne said.

'You've no doubt heard that one of your neighbours has been found murdered. Garda Tracy and I are investigating,' Fiona said.

'The work of the devil,' the old woman said. 'Not just what happened up in the fort. The devil has been active on Inis Mór ever since that young man set the commune up.'

Fiona had an idea that in Diranne's opinion most of the happenings on the island would be the devil's work. 'Did you know the victim?'

'Faith and I didn't expect to see him passing up and down the road. He wasn't much of a neighbour. Never called around when he moved in. Stayed to himself. But he was a stranger and a fine cut of a man. I didn't have anything to do with him. I don't get out much and I have to depend on my nephew to get me a few messages and to take me to Mass on a Sunday.'

'Garda Clarke said that you might have information for us regarding the murder.'

'I saw a group of them young drug addicts walking near his house.'

'Which drug addicts are they?'

'I don't know which particular ones. They come and go but they're all the same, bringing their filthy habits to the island. Clarke should do his duty and get rid of them. Spawn of Satan.'

'Are they the young people from the refuge?'

She sat forward in her chair and leaned her two hands on her walking stick. 'Refuge be damned. They cling to each other don't you know. The priest has read them out from the pulpit several times. He wasted his time; they never go to Mass. Bunch of heathens.'

'Did you see them talking to the dead man?'

'No, but I've seen them skulking around his cottage. What are you going to do about them?'

'There's nothing we can do about them. They don't appear to have committed any crime.'

Diranne shook her walking stick at them. 'You're no better than Clarke. I don't feel safe in my bed with the drug addicts wandering about the place.'

'Have they ever bothered you?' Tracy asked.

'They came around here asking if they could do anything for me. I saw the way they looked around. They were looking to rob what little I have.'

Fiona stood. 'Thank you, Mrs Diranne, you've been a big help.'

Tracy tried to help the old woman rise but she shook his arm off. 'I'll stand on my own. And it's Miss Diranne. I never married.'

'Forgive me.' Fiona marched out of the door and along the gravel path.

'Waste of bloody time,' Tracy said when he caught up with her.

'Looks that way. Maybe Clarke called it right this time.'

O'Flaherty had the van door open.

'How far is it to the place Clarke calls the refuge?'

'Half a mile up the road there's a small lane off to the right. It's about two hundred yards along the lane.'

'Tracy and I need a walk. You can wait here or if you prefer to pick up a group of tourists, we can make our own way back.'

'I'll hang around. The money is obviously going to be shit but I'll probably never have another chance to be part of a murder investigation.'

O'Flaherty couldn't possibly believe that he was part of the investigation. Fiona opened her mouth to burst his bubble then she held her tongue. She had had too many of her own illusions shattered in her short life.

CHAPTER TWENTY-SEVEN

They walked away from Diranne's cottage and headed west along the road. Clouds drifted across the sky, but they were of the fluffy white variety and patches of blue sky were visible. There would be no repeat of the previous day's rain. Several groups of cyclists and a couple of horse-drawn carriages passed them before they came to the small lane that led off to the right in the direction of the ocean. Tracy stopped at a bush and pulled off a couple of blackberries. 'They're out early this year.' He popped two of them into his mouth.

Fiona wasn't listening. They were floundering. Neither of them had verbalised it but she got the vibe from Tracy. Even his normal exuberance had deserted him. It would end up like the case of the baby washed up on the shore in Kerry or the murder of the French documentary maker in West Cork. They would be famous as the detectives who screwed up the case of the man found stabbed in Dun Aengus. She took out her mobile; no word from Brophy. They had almost reached the ocean when they saw two thatched cottages surrounded by well-cultivated gardens. A group of young people worked in the fields. Fiona made for the door of the larger of the two cottages and had just arrived when the door opened and a young man exited. They almost ran into each other.

'Sorry,' the young man recoiled. 'I wasn't expecting anyone to be outside.'

'My fault,' Fiona said. She fished her warrant card from her pocket. 'Detective Sergeant Madden.' She pointed at the field. 'That fellow chatting with your friends is Detective Garda Tracy.'

'Charlie Grealish.' He held his hand out. 'I'm sort of in charge here.'

Fiona took his hand. She reckoned that he was in his mid to late twenties, fair-haired and tanned. He was attractive and well-built and wore an old work shirt with blue jeans and a battered pair of work boots.

'I don't suppose you're just out for a walk,' he said.

'I'm afraid not. I'm investigating the dead body that was discovered in Dun Aengus.'

'Why don't you and your colleague come inside.' He pushed open the door to the larger cottage.

Fiona motioned for Tracy to join them before following Grealish inside.

They entered a large living room where a table surrounded by ten chairs dominated the space. The cottage had begun life as a single storey but had been converted to include an upper floor.

'Take a seat,' Grealish said indicating the chairs. 'I'll make tea. Everybody here offers tea to visitors. And there are scones that we baked ourselves.' He disappeared into the kitchen at the rear of the cottage.

'I stayed in a place like this last year in Kerry,' Tracy said when he arrived. 'A hostel in a place called Glencar.'

Fiona looked around. Tracy was right, it was set up like a hostel. They were sitting in the central meeting place. There was no sign of a TV but there was a small library in one corner. There were no easy chairs.

Grealish returned and placed a pot of tea and three cups on the table. He went back into the kitchen and returned with a plate of scones, butter, a jar of homemade raspberry jam and two knives. 'So, how can I help you?' He poured tea into the cups.

'You've heard about the body up in Dun Aengus.'

'News travels fast in Inis Mór,' Grealish said.

'Did you know Dangerfield?' Fiona ignored her tea and watched Tracy put butter and jam on a scone. When he finished, she took half of his scone and bit into it.

'Never had the pleasure. As you can see, we're a bit off the beaten track. Intriguing name though, Dangerfield. Any idea about his first name?'

'Sebastian,' Fiona said.

Grealish burst out laughing. 'No relation to JP Dunleavy's Ginger Man?'

'You've read the book?'

'Yes, at school. The locals believe that the death has something to do with a satanic ritual up at the fort. They think the victim was a sacrifice to the devil.'

'Is that what you think?'

'I don't know enough about the circumstances to have an opinion. But it appears a bit prosaic.'

Both Grealish's arms were heavily tattooed. It was a good job, but Fiona could still see the marks of self-harm. She absentmindedly rubbed at similar marks on her thighs. 'You're not from the island.'

'No, I'm what the locals call a *strainseir*, a stranger. None of us here are locals.'

'What exactly are you doing here?'

'My father left me a sum of money, a very small sum of money I should add. I used it to buy this place. I was a drug addict in my teens, and I always had this idea that if I could get away to an island where there were no drugs, I could get clean. It was a bit fanciful. I've learned that you have to get clean despite the availability of drugs.' He finished his tea. 'The cottages were derelict so the first group of addicts I had here helped rebuild this cottage. Subsequent groups rebuilt the second cottage and cleared the fields. We've had over ten groups down the years. The cottages are comfortable, and the garden provides most of our food. Our approach to getting clean involves eating well and having the support of like-minded individuals.'

'It's a rehab facility.' Tracy buttered a second scone. 'These scones are good.'

'That's praise indeed,' Fiona said. 'Since his arrival in Galway, Garda Tracy has become a connoisseur of scones.'

'This is not a rehab facility, neither is it a commune. People come here to help each other get clean. They stay as long as they like. We take on ten people max and if one leaves, we accept the next person on the list. We don't advertise. People apply because they've heard of us by word of mouth. There are no lectures, we just meditate, cook and eat together.' He looked at his watch. 'The group will be here soon for their morning break.'

'Are you successful?' Fiona asked.

'It depends how you measure success. When most people leave, they've been clean for six months. We're not so stupid to think that everybody leaves here cured of their addiction. This is one step on a very long journey. I've been clean for six years but I'm still an addict.'

The door opened and a group of muddy young people entered the room. They ignored Fiona and Tracy and made their way into the kitchen where water immediately started running. Eight of the new arrivals, five men and three women, joined Grealish, Fiona and Tracy at the table.

'Our guests are police officers,' Grealish said.

'That old biddy at the top of the road has been complaining about us again,' a young man with a heavy Dublin accent said.

'They're investigating the death of the man found in Dun Aengus several days ago.' Grealish looked at Fiona. 'Sergeant Madden.'

Fiona took the invitation to speak. 'Did any of you meet or talk to a man called Dangerfield? He was in his fifties, big and distinguished-looking.'

There was a general shaking of heads around the table and muttered nos.

'We rarely move out of here,' Grealish said. 'The workday is long, and we're tired in the evenings.'

A young man and woman entered with tea and a plate of scones.

'You're right about the lady at the top of the road,' Fiona said. 'She has made complaints against you, but we're satisfied that there's nothing in them. If anyone remembers seeing Mr Dangerfield, I'd appreciate a call.' She took out one of her cards and placed it on the table, stood and turned to Grealish. 'Thanks for the tea and scones.'

'I'll see you out.' He followed the two detectives to the door. Grealish held Fiona's arm gently and restrained her from moving forward. 'How are you doing?'

'What are you talking about?' Fiona looked sharply at Grealish, her heart pounding.

'I'm an expert, sergeant. And you were once one of us. It leaves an indelible mark.'

Fiona held out her hand. 'Good luck.' She had to make a mental effort to keep her hand steady. She'd been clean for more than sixteen years. How the hell had Grealish spotted it? Probably the same way she had spotted the marks on his arms.

Grealish took it and shook. 'I hope you catch whoever did it.'

'So do I.'

They walked back towards the main road.

'Are you feeling alright?' Tracy asked.

'Yeah, why do you ask?'

'You lost the colour in your face back there. You looked like you were about to get sick.'

'I probably stood up too quickly. I'm fine, so forget about it.' But she wouldn't forget about it so easily. She would wonder long and hard about what telltale signs she still bore from her misspent youth.

'They could all be Satan worshipers,' Tracy said as they reached the T-junction.

Fiona stared at him. 'You think. How far is it back to Kilronan?'

'Five kilometres give or take.'

'You go back with O'Flaherty. I need to walk, and I need to walk alone. We'll meet at the police station.'

'Shit, I forgot to get Clarke a packet of chocolate biscuits.'

'Pick them up on the way back.'

CHAPTER TWENTY-EIGHT

F iona and Tracy walked together as far as Diranne's cottage where Tracy climbed in with O'Flaherty while Fiona tramped off alone in the direction of Kilronan. There is generally a stiff breeze blowing across the island but fortunately, it was at Fiona's back. She stopped for a few minutes and took in large gulps of the ozone-laden fresh air that swirled around her. She passed Kilmurvey Beach at a moment when the sun broke through and the white sand of the beach glistened invitingly. She was still brooding about Grealish's ability to recognise her past addiction when she came to the first T-junction and the choice of her route back to Kilronan. The road to the left would straddle the coast and pass the Seal Colony while the one on the right would cut across country on the more direct route to her destination. She allowed her legs to make the decision and she took the longer route. She needed to think whether she had missed an obvious lead. Dangerfield was the key. But he was an unknown quantity. Brophy's silence could be because he had failed to identify Dangerfield as a teacher. The teacher's union was one of the strongest in the nation and it would have a detailed register of all qualified members. But did that register include a photo ID? Or perhaps her hunch was wrong. Not every erudite person in the country was a teacher. If she reviewed every fact that she had learned about Dangerfield, it pointed to the conclusion that he was or had been in the teaching profession but at what level. Nobody had mentioned that he had a feeling for small children and both people closest to him, Bridget Heaney and Noelle Burke, were agreed that he had the manner of a teacher of older children or even university students. She passed the beach at Stigutha when a thought struck her. Was it possible for a man to live in a cottage without any form of identification? If for example, he needed to go to hospital he would be required to produce his social welfare card, or a bank card or some form of identification. She could imagine that if Dangerfield were a criminal, he would have had contacts that could provide him with false papers, but she doubted he was a criminal. The dead man could play an intellectual game by claiming to be Sebastian Dangerfield the protagonist of a famous novel that she had never read. He and the few people on Inis Mór who had read JP Dunlevy's work could smirk at his intelligence. She had assumed that the murderer, or murderers depending on how Dangerfield had been ferried up the incline to the fort, had removed his various types of identification. But what if that assumption had been erroneous? Perhaps she had been influenced by the recent case in Clifden where the murderer had muddied the water by removing all the victim's identification. But suppose that the person who had hidden the real identification was the man himself. Foley and O'Malley had searched the cottage as had she and Tracy on two occasions, but all three searches had proved fruitless. However, the searches had been perfunctory. At least hers and Tracy's were. There was something hidden in the cottage or the surrounding area. She supposed that there would be no chance of getting the uniforms back to carry out a detailed search of the area around the cottage. The overtime budget would preclude that. So, it would be her, Tracy and Clarke and they would tear the place apart if they had to. It might be the last throw of the dice, but they had to get over the bump that the victim had placed in their road. She noticed that her step had got lighter as the road ahead became clearer. She literally flew over the ground, and she was past the Seal Colony Viewpoint before she realised it. When she saw the sign on the right for the Aran Islands Goat's Cheese factory she was almost home.

Fiona opened the station door and went straight to Clarke's office which was empty. She took out her mobile and called Tracy. 'Where are you?'

'Joe Watty's, I have the biscuits, but Clarke locked up the tea.'

'I'll be there in five minutes. Order me an Americano, I'm tired of drinking tea.'

Five minutes later, she flopped into the vacant seat with an Americano in front of it.

'The walk has certainly brought the colour back into your cheeks,' Tracy said.

'Did you come around by the coast road?' O'Flaherty asked.

Fiona sipped her coffee and nodded.

'It's a much finer walk than the Kilmurvey loop that everybody does.' O'Flaherty stood and headed for the toilet.

'I've been thinking,' Fiona said. 'I'm afraid that we screwed up at the cottage in Kilmurvey.'

'How so?' Tracy pulled his chair closer to the table.

Fiona leaned forward and dropped her voice. 'There's got to be something there that we missed. We've led ourselves astray by thinking that the murderer was the one who removed Dangerfield's real ID. I think the murderer didn't give a damn about Dangerfield and his little nod to one of his favourite authors. I think he just wanted him dead. He knew exactly who he was. It was Dangerfield that didn't want people to know his real identity. I'm positive that Heaney was the height of discretion but I'm more positive that she's a nosy islander who would have the occasional root among the victim's papers. That means Dangerfield would have made sure that they were well hidden. We need to get back to the cottage with Clarke and O'Flaherty's brother-in-law. It's all hands to the pumps. Dangerfield was a clever man, and he will have made it difficult to just come across something that he'd hidden. That's why Foley and O'Malley drew a blank and you and I screwed up. I pity poor Brophy. We've tied his hands behind his back and given him a series of impossible tasks.'

'You two definitely look like there's something going on between you.' O'Flaherty sat.

'You didn't tell him,' Fiona said.

'It's not my business.' Tracy sat back.

'Tell me what?' O'Flaherty looked from Tracy to Fiona.

'Nothing,' Fiona said. 'We need to lay hands on your brother-in-law and tell him to meet us at the rented cottage.' She took out her phone and called Clarke. 'Where are you?' She heard pub noises in the background.

'Having a break. I've been on the go all morning. I've been on to Galway about the way you've been treating me like a slave.'

Fiona laughed. 'And I bet that they believed you. There's the look of a slave on you. Get back to the station and we'll meet you there.' She looked at Tracy. 'Garda Clarke is going to be lucky to make it out of this case in one piece.'

CHAPTER TWENTY-NINE

I t was approaching midday when O'Flaherty's van pulled up in front of the cottage Dangerfield rented in Kilmurvey. O'Flaherty's brother-in-law was running late and hadn't yet arrived. Strings of yellow crime scene tape crisscrossed the door.

'When did you put the crime scene tape up?' Fiona asked Clarke whose face was more florid than usual.

'This morning, I was afraid that some of the locals might use the occasion to collect personal items they could later sell.'

Tracy ripped the tape off and used a key to open the door. He stood aside to permit his boss to enter.

Fiona's nose began to twitch as soon as she entered the room. She turned around quickly and stared at Clarke. His colour rose to a light purple. 'I knew you were an idiot, but I had no idea that you were this big of an idiot.'

'What's up?' Tracy asked.

'Ginny Hinds is what's up.' She marched over to Clarke until their faces were almost touching. 'She's been here, and this idiot is the one who let her in. Because the doors and windows have been closed the remnants of her perfume are still in the air. Isn't that right, Garda Clarke?'

'I d-d-didn't think it was any harm.' Clarke forced the words out.

'Come off it,' Fiona said. 'Permitting a civilian to enter what could have been a crime scene. How much did she pay you?'

Clarke was rooted to the spot.

'You're already on report for dereliction of duty. If you've taken money, and I know you have, I'll add a charge of corruption. If you come clean, I'll stay with the former charge, otherwise, I'll throw the book at you.'

'She gave me five hundred quid. She said what was the harm of five minutes to look around.'

'Did she take photographs?'

'Yes, on her mobile.'

'Did she take anything away with her?'

'No, she had a root around and then we left.'

'Get out of my sight, you gobshite, and that five hundred quid is going to charity.'

Clarke left the cottage.

Fiona noticed that the landlord had joined them. She walked over to him. 'We're looking for a place where your tenant might have hidden something, something small. You know this place well.'

The landlord scratched his head. 'It's not the largest there couldn't be too many places, but he's been here a year which would have given him the chance to create a hiding place.'

'What about loose stones or floor coverings?'

'I had the cottage fully renovated two years ago. If there were any loose stones or floor coverings, they would have been dealt with.'

'Then I'm sorry for you because we're going to have to take this place apart.'

'Good God, no, this is my livelihood.'

'Any damage we do will be fixed by workmen from the

Office of Public Works in Galway. The sooner you think of a place that could be used for hiding documents the better.' She turned to Tracy. 'Let's get at it partner.'

Tracy went to the bookshelves. 'I'll start here.' He took a pile of books from the shelves and began searching behind them.

Fiona headed for the door on the right. 'I'll take the main bedroom.' She was angry with herself for not thinking of carrying out a finger search of the cottage. But she would have needed resources and she wouldn't have got them. She was furious with Clarke for letting the side down. She didn't blame Hinds; she was only doing her job. She took the duvet off the bed and felt the length and breadth of it. There were no unusual bumps. She threw it aside and removed the sheet. She looked under the mattress before examining it for signs of a cut and repair but found nothing. She moved on to the drawers. It was an old police adage that people hide their valuables in their sock drawer because no burglar would rummage among the socks. Given time, burglars will turn a house upside down including the sock drawer. Dangerfield's drawers contained only his clothes. She turned the drawers over and looked underneath. She searched the panels of the wardrobe for a secret hiding place but there was none. The stone floor of the room appeared solid, but she tested each flagstone with her foot for movement. She took a quick look in the cistern of the toilet and the cabinet beneath the handbasin before returning to the living room and going directly to the second bedroom where she checked the lining of the suitcases and overnight bag. She checked the floor and walls before leaving.

'Anything?' she asked as she re-entered the living room.

'Only this.' Tracy held up a couple of sheets of paper. 'Stuck behind some books. It's an auction receipt and a provenance statement. Dangerfield bought the dagger that ended up in his chest and a goat-head mask from an auction house in London. The provenance states that they were once the property of a guy called Aleister Crowley. I've looked him up on Wiki. He was an English occultist who founded his own religion called Thelema of which he was the chief prophet.'

'The goat-head mask is missing,' she said. 'Interesting but not what we're looking for.'

'I've finished the bookcases,' Tracy said. 'I'm about to start on the soft furnishings.'

Fiona looked at the landlord. 'It might be time to send for a couple of pinch bars. It's looking like the floor is going to come up.'

Michael O'Flaherty's face went pale. 'You're joking, right,' he said.

'I know what I'm looking for is here. We just must find it. My first guess would have been the book collection.' She looked at Tracy. 'None of them has been hollowed out?'

He shook his head. 'I've checked every one.'

'Before we start wrecking the cottage let's try to think this through. I don't think Dangerfield was a spy so he would have chosen somewhere an ordinary civilian would have hidden their precious items. It would be somewhere innocuous, somewhere he could reach easily if he had to make a trip to Galway and he had to have an ID, and possibly somewhere in plain sight, somewhere nice and dry. She walked around the living room. The couch was a possibility, so was the base of the reading lamp. She kept circling and taking in every item in the room, no matter how trivial. She kept thinking where she would hide personal papers she didn't want found. Then her eyes fell on the large plant that stood in the corner of the room. She walked over and felt the leaves. They were plastic. It was a fake plant. She pulled it out and there was no root. She bent, rummaged in the earth in the pot and came up with a small package wrapped in plastic and kept together by rubber bands. She held up the package. 'What did that Greek guy in the bath shout?'

'Eureka,' Tracy said.

She looked at the landlord. 'Looks like your cottage just dodged a bullet. You can leave now.'

'Thanks be to God,' O'Flaherty muttered as he left.

Fiona unwound the rubber band and pulled aside the plastic wrapping. She held the contents aloft. 'Double Eureka.'

CHAPTER THIRTY

Fiona leaned back in Clarke's chair and looked at James
Mangan's passport. The photo was of a younger man, but
the ten-year passport was about to expire so Mangan was in his
forties when the photo was taken. Under profession, Mangan
had opted for *educator*, not teacher or lecturer or even professor. She had already decided that he was a pretentious prick;
the passport only proved the point. There was no time to dwell
on Mangan's psychology. They needed to know everything
about the life and times of James Mangan from birth to death.
She had already called Brophy and set him on the trail which
meant that there would be news soon on what they were
dealing with. It had taken two days to breach Mangan's hidden
identity. She now turned her attention to the investigation of
the reason behind Mangan's need for anonymity. She was sure
that it was the reason someone had murdered him.

'What about Clarke?' Tracy said, fingering the packet of
chocolate biscuits he had bought to replace the ones he and
Fiona had eaten.

'What about him? He sold us out for a measly five hundred
quid. You remember your passing out day at Templemore?
You remember the oath you took?'

Tracy nodded.

She closed her eyes and recited. *I hereby solemnly and sincerely declare before God that I will faithfully discharge the duties of a member of the Garda Síochána with fairness, integrity, regard for human rights, diligence and impartiality, upholding the constitution and the law and according equal respect to all people. While I continue to be a member, I will to the best of my skill and knowledge discharge all my duties according to law, and I do not belong to, and will not while I remain a member, belong to or subscribe to any political party or secret society whatsoever.'*

Tracy gave her a silent clap. 'You know the bloody oath off by heart.'

'Don't you?'

'You don't believe that every officer holds to that crap.'

'No, not while all the top jobs are handed out by the party in government. Professional Services are there to catch the boys who are in the pockets of the organised crime groups and the drug lords. Clarke screwed you and me. That makes it personal. Ginny Hinds would have great pleasure in skewering us if she got information that we weren't doing our jobs and on the other side of the scale she's suborning a Garda officer to break the law. She wasn't in that cottage as an investigative journalist but as a muckraker.'

'What law is that?'

She leaned across the desk. 'You're such a bleeding heart. Don't cry any crocodile tears over the likes of Clarke. This thing of ours only works when we're all in it together.'

'Where do Horgan and O'Reilly fit in?'

'They don't. We'd be better off without them. They contribute nothing to fighting crime. Neither of them is capable of independent thought. They need to call the Park before deciding to take a piss.'

'The gospel according to Fiona Madden. My God you are

so far up yourself it's unreal. You should learn to be a little less judgemental.'

'Tell that to the people who have been judging me all my life. Tell it to the shithouse poet who thinks my sex and my sexual preference should be the subject of his sick mind.'

'Did Clarke's little trip to the dark side anger you that much or are you always angry?'

The telephone rang. She put Brophy on speakerphone and laid the phone on Clarke's desk. 'Go ahead.'

'I've only just started but I'll give you what I have.' The pitch of his voice was higher than usual. 'James Mangan has never been involved with the Garda Síochána. He's never had so much as a speeding ticket. He is registered with the Irish National Teachers Organisation. He has a degree in English and French from the National University of Ireland in Galway. Up to last year, he was teaching at St Cormac's, a private school run by the Jesuits on grounds outside Loughrea. He has a registered address in Loughrea. I can find no evidence that he was married but he has taught at several schools prior to St Cormac's. I'm digging into other databases, but I think that you'll get most of what you need from interviewing people who knew him. He's kept a low profile during his life and paid his taxes. That's it for the moment.'

'Any next of kin?'

'Not so far. I'm looking into that.'

'Move that along. If there's someone we need to inform, let's do it and then we can release his name to the papers.'

'I'm on it, boss.'

'Good man,' Fiona said. 'Keep up the good work.' She killed the call.

'We have momentum.' Tracy was rubbing his hands.

'Do you want the good news or the bad news first?'

He immediately stopped the hand rubbing. 'I wasn't aware that there was good news and bad news.'

'Well, there is.'

'What's the bad news?'

'You're staying here.'

'And the good news?'

'I'm not.'

Tracy's frown said it all. 'Don't you think I could be more use back in Galway helping to follow up on Mangan's background?'

'No, I think you'd be more use here holding the fort.' Fiona sent a text to Aisling asking her to meet the five o'clock boat. 'Let's have a bite to eat before I pick up my things and catch the ferry.'

'What about Clarke?'

'Fuck Clarke, he's only a diversion. I'll deal with him when we have someone behind bars for killing Mangan.'

CHAPTER THIRTY-ONE

Fiona's meal arrived at the same time as Horgan's phone call. She took the call and asked the waitress at Joe Watty's to put her meal in the oven.

Horgan started speaking as soon as the line opened. 'Brophy has established that Mangan's parents are dead and his only living relative resides in a place called Rockhampton in Australia. Our communications people are preparing a press release. You know the usual palaver *The man found dead on Inis Mór two days ago has been identified as.* There's no need to go into the rigmarole of the alias. We'll also be asking the public if they have any information relevant to the death. This case has all the characteristics of that Sophie Toscan du Plantier case in West Cork, and we all know what a monumental fuck-up that was.'

Fiona raised her eyes and sighed. 'You may not wish to go into the rigmarole, but you can bet this month's salary that Ginny Hinds will. The *Post* will be all over why this man was hiding on the Aran Islands.'

'Where do we go from here?'

'I still believe that the answer to Mangan's death is here on the island. We need to find out everything we can about the victim's past. I'm coming back to Galway this evening on the ferry. Tracy will stay here and continue the investigation locally. I've already phoned St Cormac's and I have a meeting with the headmaster, sorry I mean the president, tomorrow morning.'

'I don't know why but my waters are telling me that we might have trouble ahead on this one.'

'We might indeed.' Fiona's conclusion had nothing to do with her waters which were in perfect condition, thank you.

'Check in with me when you finish with St Cormac's. And don't conveniently forget.'

'Of course.' She killed the call and waved at the waitress.

Across the table from her, Tracy moved a goat's cheese salad around his plate but ate little.

'What's up with you? You usually have the appetite of a hungry horse. Cliona give you the push?' The waitress arrived and put a plate in front of her. It didn't look as appetising as it had done on its previous visit.

'No, she's coming over tonight and I don't know how to approach the landlady about the two of us in the same room. Inis Mór isn't like the mainland. They didn't get electricity until sometime in the seventies. The government is trying to keep it as a heritage park.'

Fiona started on her meal. 'Wake up and smell the coffee. Maureen doesn't give a damn who you bring home if you pay the additional costs. It's a lot more traditional to have a hetero-sexual couple in a room than having a lesbian couple. Just try and keep the noise down. You're pissed that you're going to be here on your own tomorrow.'

'What will I do? I'll be bored out of my tree.'

Her roast beef was dry and had the consistency of an old boot. She cursed Horgan for spoiling her meal. 'No, you won't. Go through the photos and the IDs of the people who left on the ferry the morning the body was discovered. See if there's anything strange. I've been working on the assumption that the killer is still on the island. We must always challenge our assumptions in case they lead us down the wrong path. If the investigation moves to Galway, you'll be back tomorrow evening.'

'I still think that I'll be bored out of my tree.' Tracy picked at his salad.

Fiona ate as much of her meal as she could manage and ignored the roast potatoes. All this eating in pubs would pile the weight on.

As she dropped her knife and fork on her plate, Ginny Hinds entered the pub and pulled up a chair beside Tracy.

'Hiya handsome.' She smiled at Tracy and then turned to Fiona. 'I thought I'd find you here.'

The two detectives looked at each other.

'Celebrating, are we?' Hinds continued. 'Now that you've got the real name of the victim.'

Fiona tried to hide her surprise, but she knew that the hierarchy leaked like a sieve especially to the short-skirt brigade at the *Post*.

'Bit of a breakthrough for you. I've just sent my copy for tomorrow's paper.'

'Does it include a picture of the inside of the dead man's cottage?'

Hinds' eyebrows rose.

'You'll have to change your perfume or at least wear less of it. I'm going to make sure that Clarke pays for taking your filthy lucre and letting you in. By the way, you'll be contributing five hundred euros to the homeless in Galway.'

Hinds screwed up her face in anger. 'I bet you're a vindictive little bitch. You'd be surprised how many of your colleagues are on the payroll. I wonder how you'd react if I waved a wad of notes in front of your face.'

'You can stop wondering,' Tracy said. 'She would shove them up your arse.'

Hinds looked at him. 'It speaks.' She turned back to Fiona.

'I thought you had him around as eye candy. Most people think that you're having it off with him, but we know your little secret.'

Fiona laughed. 'Everybody knows my little secret, but I wonder how many people know yours. I'd advise you to get out of my face. Otherwise, I might make you a project and that wouldn't be so good for you.'

'I'm quaking in my shoes.'

Fiona pushed her plate away. 'You've overstayed your welcome.'

'You're an interesting character, Madden. I think my editor might be interested in you.'

Tracy leaned over and put his hand on Hinds' arm. 'I think Detective Sergeant Madden would like you to quit our company. Do you think you might be able to do that unaided.?'

Hinds looked at his hand. 'I thought you were good cop to your boss's bad cop. But I can see that I was wrong. You're both arseholes.' She removed his hand, stood, and walked to the door.

'I hate this fucking job,' Fiona said when Hinds was out of hearing. 'Clarke isn't the only one who let the team down. It must have been someone in the Park that leaked. The job is hard enough without our colleagues rushing to stab us in the back.'

'It's the way of the world.' Tracy had given up on his salad. 'I think we've made an enemy there.'

'You're a sound man and I appreciate your help with Hinds.' She stood. 'I'll get the bill. Enjoy your evening and tell Cliona I'm asking after her.'

CHAPTER THIRTY-TWO

F iona smiled broadly when she saw Aisling at the end of the quay. They hugged and walked arm in arm to where Aisling had parked her car.

'You look rejuvenated,' Aisling said as she took her place behind the wheel.

Fiona sat next to her. 'We have the victim's real name and now can search for the motive. It's the first case I've had where the victim had managed to screw us up by living under an alias.'

'I don" usually read the *Post,* but I don't think I've ever seen such a scandalous front page.'

'Ginny Hinds, the *Post* journalist on the island, knows what sells papers and I'm afraid she's not one of my fans.'

'Which means?'

'She'll skewer me if anything goes wrong with the investigation.'

'That doesn't sound pleasant.' Aisling drove out of the car park and turned left, heading for the junction of the Rossaveal Road and the Coast Road. At the junction, she turned left.

'Where are we going? In case your memory is failing you should have turned right.'

Aisling smiled and kept driving. 'The publisher accepted my book and we're going to dinner at a fancy restaurant to celebrate.'

'That's great, congratulations, but I'm not exactly dressed for a fancy restaurant. Couldn't we just make dinner at home and chill out?'

'Don't be such a spoilsport. It isn't every day that I get a book accepted.'

'I'm not meaning to pour cold water on your achievement. The acceptance of your book was never in doubt. After all, aren't you the smartest psychologist in Ireland?'

'That's probably a bit of an exaggeration. But it's nice of you to have so much confidence in me.'

'What's the name of the restaurant?'

'Screebe House.'

Fiona looked at her watch. It was five minutes past six. 'But we're not going there now.'

'No, the reservation is for seven thirty.'

'We're heading in the direction of Glenmore. This is the second time that you've kidnapped me for a trip to my mother.'

'She called me yesterday. She's worried about your father's impending arrival. He sent her a message that he's arriving in a few days.'

Fiona could feel her heartbeat quicken. The man who had abandoned them, had abandoned her, was coming back after walking out on them. Only yesterday she'd had a flash of him sitting drinking and singing in the American Bar in Kilronan. She couldn't walk down a street in Galway without feeling her hands in his and her mother's. Tracy had a point about her being angry and she was convinced that she had plenty to be angry about. Twenty-two long years. Where was he when she was raped? Where was he when she'd been obliged to give birth? Where was he for all those events where she needed a father? Never a phone call or postcard, no Christmas card, nothing. And now he was coming back a stranger and expecting to walk into the bosom of his family and be greeted with open arms. She was having none of it.

'I don't like it when you're silent.'

'You wouldn't like to hear what I'm thinking.'

'You can't spend your life being bitter. It's a negative emotion. People make mistakes and we shouldn't judge them too harshly. There may be many reasons why your father left your mother and you, just as there are many reasons why your mother did what she did. Nobody is perfect and we must remember that. Your parents hurt you but right now you're hurting yourself.'

'This is the second lecture I've had today. Have you and Tracy spoken lately?'

'Not without you present.'

They had passed Screebe House and were on their way to Glenmore. Fiona was thinking of Jesus and the Garden of Gethsemane, and she sympathised. She had only recently had a reconciliation with her mother and now she was getting embroiled in a family that she had long ago rejected. She wondered whether she was happier with no family than with a new relationship with two parents who had abandoned her. The father she'd loved had simply walked away and left her. Her mother had chosen religion over her wellbeing. Aisling stood firmly on the side of creating a new family dynamic that would replace the old broken model. Fiona wasn't so sure. Aisling was attempting to dispel some of the demons that governed Fiona's actions. Fiona wasn't at all certain that the world was ready for the new kinder Fiona Madden. 'What do you have in mind?'

'Tell your mother how you feel about your father's return and listen to what she has to say. It's the way families work.'

'Do you ever think that you may be interfering?'

'Am I?'

'I think so. Maybe I would have been better left alone.'

'We all have issues that need resolving. I think you

resolving your issues will lead to us having a better relationship.' They had reached Glenmore and Aisling stopped in front of Fiona's mother's house. She turned and looked at Fiona. 'Ready?'

'No.' Fiona opened the door and exited. She walked up the short drive and knocked on the door.

'Hello.' Fiona's mother opened the door. There was an awkward moment when a hug hung in the air, but it passed when Fiona entered and made straight for the living room.

'He has some balls,' Fiona said as she flopped on the couch.

Aisling and her mother had followed her into the room.

'He's booked a ticket,' Maire said.

'Without so much as a by your leave.' Fiona crossed her arms. 'Who the hell does he think he is?'

'My husband and your father.' Maire sat beside her daughter.

Aisling sat on an easy chair facing the couch.

Fiona sat forward. 'That was a long time ago and he gave up those roles willingly. Not a letter, not a Christmas or birthday card in twenty-two years; the message was loud and clear. I got it and I'd hoped that you got it too.'

'He's arriving next Friday in Shannon.'

'So what? I won't be ordering a *Welcome Home, Dad* banner.'

Maire stared into her daughter's eyes. 'I've known him since we were in primary school. We started going out together when I was fifteen and we were married when he was twenty-one and I was nineteen. I don't think either of us realised at the time that we were much too young to marry. I think the responsibility of being a husband overwhelmed him. And then three years later you came along. We held it together as best we could. There were always money problems, but we managed to scrape by except we grew further and further apart. I suppose I wasn't that surprised when he disappeared one day.'

'Sounds like you're going to take him in,' Fiona said.

'It's the Christian thing to do.'

'You turn your cheek and he's going to slap it.'

'He's dying.'

'And you believe his shit?' Fiona stood and nodded at Aisling. 'Satisfied? Let's go or we'll miss your reservation.'

'You'll come with me to Shannon?' Maire said.

'I don't think so. What I feel for my father isn't particularly Christian.' Fiona left the room.

Maire grasped and squeezed Aisling's hand before she left. 'Thank you.'

Fiona was already sitting in the passenger seat of the car when Aisling took her place behind the wheel.

'Cancel the restaurant,' Fiona said. 'I've lost my appetite. Let's go home.'

Aisling took out her mobile phone and called the restaurant.

Fiona felt that since she had come back to Galway her past was putting out its bony hands to grab her. She didn't like her past. Too many bad things happened back there. Her stomach heaved and she prayed to an unnamed God that the past wouldn't catch up with her.

DAY FOUR

CHAPTER THIRTY-THREE

F iona practised her katas in the dojo for an hour before
heading for the station. She and Aisling had spent the
evening curled up on the sofa watching their favourite
romcoms. Her mind wasn't on the films but on Mangan's
weird death and her father's return. The job didn't stop at six
and neither did familial dramas. She smiled when she saw the
Kawasaki parked where she had left it. She looked forward to
the ride to Loughrea. At nine o'clock on the dot, she entered
the CID office, went to Brophy's desk and sat beside him.
'Tell me.'

'Good morning, sarge. I'm making progress. Mangan is an
open book as far as the early years are concerned.' He pointed
to the whiteboard at the end of the room. 'I've already written
in the essentials. During his career, he's worked at five schools,
gradually working his way up to the height of a prestigious
school like St Cormac's which means he must be pretty good
at the job. I rang two of the schools and neither one was keen
on answering my questions. They both mentioned the fact that
he was an excellent teacher but weren't happy to go into his
personality. It appeared it was a red flag for them. I think if we
want to learn about the man we're going to have to speak with

his peers. The school principals are just giving us the party line. Other than that, I've asked for his tax returns and his bank accounts which might take a day or two even with a rush on them.'

'Sound man, you'll make a fine detective. I want you to drop what you're doing and apply for a search warrant for Mangan's house in Loughrea. Let me know as soon as you have it and inform Loughrea that I might need the assistance of a few uniforms this afternoon.' She stood and went to her desk, sat down and turned on her computer. A flood of emails filled the screen. She took a quick look to see if anything needed her attention. The sun was shining and there was a light wind and she wanted to get on the road as soon as possible. There was nothing that wouldn't wait. She closed her computer and was on her way out when the door opened, and Horgan entered.

'I thought I told you to pass by my office as soon as you arrived.'

Fiona slipped on her jacket. 'Sorry, boss. I was on the way up to see you. I had to check with Brophy first.'

'I phoned you yesterday evening. Did you get my missed call?'

'My phone was out of charge and by the time I took it off the charger it was too late to call.'

'It's never too late to call a senior officer. I'm on this job twenty-four seven.' He handed her a copy of the *Post*. 'I don't suppose you've seen this.'

'I don't read trash.' She looked at the front page, the headline said it all. *INCOMPETENT GARDA INVESTIGATION OF RITUAL MURDER.*

She tossed the paper back to him. 'The murder wasn't a ritual; it was just made to look like that.'

'So you say. These kinds of headlines don't help, and this paper is selling out. We need to get control of the situation. Have you talked to this reporter Hinds?'

'Once or twice.'

Horgan blocked her exit from the squad room. 'Why do I get the impression that you managed to piss her off?'

Fiona inched closer to the door. 'She works for a newspaper that needs a sensational headline every day. That means the ritual theory. She wants satanism, murder, naked dancing and sex. That's a potent mixture for the guys in Dublin on their way to work on the Dart.'

'Speaking of you pissing off people, a guy called Michael Meagher has been on to the commissioner complaining about you harassing his people at the House of Devotion. Luckily the commissioner thinks the guy is a fraud so you can hassle away.'

Fiona looked at her watch. 'Sorry, boss, I'd love to stay but I have an appointment I have to keep.'

Horgan moved aside. 'I want a briefing this evening before closing. What's Tracy up to in Inis Mór.'

'Going through the photos and the IDs of the people who left on the ferry the morning the body was discovered.' She reached the door. 'Got to go.'

THE TOWN of Loughrea lies forty kilometres east of Galway. Fiona didn't push her bike and arrived on the outskirts of the town thirty minutes after leaving the station. St Cormac's private college lay just under the Slieve Aughty mountains and on the shores of the lake that gave the town its name. She entered the large gates that opened onto the sixty-five-acre campus. The estate had at one time been owned by a member of the Burke family who had made a fortune in India. The Burke's had somehow managed to squander their money and the estate changed hands several times before becoming a college. She drove along the road noting the well-tended gardens interspersed with small groups of trees until she came to a wide expanse of grasslands that had been turned into sports grounds. The mansion in which the school was located sat on a small hill overlooking the gardens and football pitches, and two large modern extensions had been added on either side of the main historic building. She pulled into a car park to the left of the house, parked her bike, and left her helmet on the seat. A sign at the exit of the car park indicated that the administration offices were to be found in the main house. She looked up at the roof of the main building and saw that the Irish flag was at half-mast. News travels fast in Ireland; bad news travels faster. She walked up the set of steps that led to the grand entrance. Inside was a marble-floored reception hall with offices along corridors on either side. A sign pointed to the president's office which was located on the first floor at the front of the house. She climbed the stairs, knocked on the door that bore the legend *President's Office Secretariat* and entered.

'Yes.' The woman who stared at Fiona over her spectacles was ancient and could possibly have been with the Burke's when they owned the house a hundred years previously.

Fiona took out her warrant card from her leather jacket. 'Detective Sergeant Madden' I have an appointment with the president.'

The secretary looked her up and down and didn't look impressed at what she saw. She lifted the phone and pressed a button. 'Sergeant Madden from the Garda Síochána.'

She replaced the handset. 'You can go in.'

'Detective Sergeant Madden,' Fiona said as she passed the secretary's desk.

When Fiona entered the president's office and saw that he wore a Roman collar, she realised that she should have spent the previous evening researching St Cormac's.

The president rose from his chair and held out his hand. 'Sergeant Madden, Father Joseph Locke. We meet under sad circumstances. Please take a seat.'

Fiona sat and stared at an ornamental piece of wood with a brass plaque bearing the name *Fr. Joseph Francis-Xavier Locke SJ*. The Society of Jesus, or the Jesuits as they were more commonly called, were the proprietors of St Cormac's. Locke was of medium height and cadaverously thin. Because of the thinness of his face, his nose was his most prominent feature, and his eyes were distorted by his bottle-top lenses. She assumed that his physical appearance was the result of an ascetic life of prayer, fasting and overwork. 'Indeed,' she said. 'I notice that you already have your flag at half-mast. When did you get the news that James Mangan was deceased?'

'Last night, one of our past pupils called and gave me the sad news. James was a valued member of staff here.'

'You are probably aware that his body was discovered in rather peculiar circumstances.'

Locke fiddled with an expensive-looking black fountain pen on his desk. 'One of my staff brought the article that appeared in yesterday's *Irish Post* to my attention. I thought it more salacious than informative.'

'The murder method was rather unique. He was stabbed with the dagger of a known occultist's property that he purchased from an auction. Was he known for an interest in the occult?' Fiona noticed that Locke had paled.

'James was an outstanding teacher and a rather exotic individual. I have no idea about his interest in the occult, but it does not surprise me.'

'If Mangan is still on the teaching staff, why was he living on Inis Mór for the past year?'

'James was on a sabbatical.'

'He was living under the name Sebastian Dangerfield; do you have any idea why he was using an alias?' She noticed a small smile flit across Locke's lips when she mentioned the name.

''As I said, he was somewhat exotic.'

'Right now, he's somewhat dead and I am investigating his death. Why should he have to use an alias? He has no family in Ireland that we're aware of. No wife to escape from.' She thought of her father. 'He was never married, had no children, was never in trouble with the law and yet he felt the need to hide his identity.'

'I can only tell you that James arrived here with excellent references and was a first-class teacher.'

She thought of Brophy and the red flags. 'You know of no reason why someone would want to kill him?'

'In our world of learning deaths like James' are rare. I would have said never occur, but one has. Now if you'll forgive me, I have matters to attend to.'

'Of course, I've taken up far too much of your time.' She held out her hand and Locke shook it.

'Who will be responsible for the funeral arrangements?' he asked.

'I'll let you know, and I may be back with supplementary questions.'

She walked past the secretary without comment, feeling the woman's eyes boring into her back. She had just been snowed but at least she recognised it. Locke had said nothing except that Mangan did his job. The guy who currently resided in a freezer in Galway Regional Hospital didn't have a personality. She descended the stairs and walked to the car park. As she picked up her helmet a piece of paper fluttered to the ground. She bent and picked it up. The writing was copperplate. *Meet me 11:30 Maggie May's Bar*. She looked around but saw no one. She felt uneasy and when she looked up at the mansion, Locke was in the window staring down at her.

CHAPTER THIRTY-FOUR

Maggie May's bar and restaurant on Bride Street wasn't difficult to find. Loughrea was what used to be called a one-horse town on the main road from Dublin to Galway. But that was back in the day before the government built a spanking new motorway. The local merchants screamed but the motorists cheered since Loughrea was the biggest bottleneck on the old road. Fiona parked the Kawasaki in the pub car park and padlocked it. She entered the lounge section of the two-storey building and dumped her helmet on a padded bench just inside the front door. The lounge was empty, and she ordered a coffee at the bar and returned to the bench. The clock above the bar showed eleven twenty-five. At exactly eleven thirty a middle-aged man entered the bar and looked around giving more than a passing glance at Fiona. He ordered a coffee from the bar and when it arrived, he turned and carried it back in Fiona's direction.

'Are you the cop?' he asked.

Fiona flashed her warrant card. 'Detective Sergeant Madden.'

The man set his coffee down on the table and sat across from her. 'You don't look like a cop.' He extended his hand.

'Steven Byrne, I teach maths to the Leaving Cert classes at St Cormac's.'

She took his hand and shook. Byrne looked like his job right down to the leather patches on the elbows of his jacket. He was small and slight with thinning fair curly hair over a pale kindly face that seldom saw the sun and a pair of glasses sat precariously on his small nose. She could imagine him standing at a whiteboard fiddling with equations.

'The man in the article in the *Post* was James Mangan?'

'It was. I'm investigating the death.'

'And you were talking to Locke about Mangan. I bet I know what he said. Mangan was a great teacher and popular with the staff and pupils. He couldn't imagine why anybody would want to murder him.'

'You've got the gist of it.' She sipped her coffee.

Byrne screwed up his face. 'What a load of bullshit. Mangan was a monster, a brute and a bully both to the staff and the pupils. He was the terror of the staff room intimidating and humiliating anyone he took a dislike to.'

'You don't paint a pleasant picture.' Fiona could see from the vehemence that Byrne had been the victim of Mangan's bullying and intimidation. It was a sad fact that those who had been born with a large physique sometimes used it to oppress others. Mangan would have towered over Byrne. 'I take it then that he wasn't exactly liked.'

'He was despised, hated, reviled. People who knew him will be cracking bottles of champagne this evening celebrating his death.'

That wasn't good news for Fiona. She'd hoped that the research into Mangan's background might produce a single viable suspect, not a plethora of them. 'Enough for someone to murder him?'

'Are you kidding? The line of potential candidates would run the length of this street. I've even harboured murderous thoughts myself. And I wasn't the only one, several staff members admitted to similar thoughts.'

'But I don't suppose you or the other members of staff visited Inis Mór in the past three days.'

'I can't speak for the others, but I haven't, I hated Mangan, but I couldn't take the life of another human being. But you have no idea of the relief I felt when I heard that he was dead. It was like a giant weight was taken off my shoulders.'

'Why did Locke feed me bullshit?'

'Because of the fallout for St Cormac's. He's afraid that you'll dig deep into Mangan and what you find might be explosive for the college. The fees for boarders at St Cormac's are five thousand euros a term. If there's a scandal concerning a member of the staff, the reputation of the college will suffer, and pupils might be pulled. Locke would be removed, and it would take years to recover. The Jesuits don't like failure. That's why you were told that there's nothing to see here.'

'What about the year-long sabbatical?'

'Last year the staff made representations to Locke to get rid of Mangan. But Locke was as afraid of him as the rest of us. A smart bastard thought up the idea of giving Mangan a year off on full pay. Anything except rock the boat. Nobody wanted to see him back.'

Fiona finished her coffee and contemplated having something stronger. The investigation was taking an unexpected turn. 'Did Mangan have any friends?'

'None that I know of. And there were other rumours.'

'What kind of other rumours?'

'The kind that could cause big trouble for the college.'

'Would you like to clarify?'

'No, I wouldn't. I'm only interested in speaking about what I've seen with my own eyes and what I know for a fact. You're a detective and I'm sure you know how to go about digging for the truth.'

'I know you took a risk talking to me and I appreciate it. Can I contact you again?'

'I don't think I can add anything further. St Cormac's is a good college, and we produce good results. I love my job and I want to keep it.'

Fiona thought about Locke looking down on her as she read the note. 'I hope it stays that way.' She took out a card from her jacket and handed it to him. 'Call me if there are any repercussions about you talking to me.'

'I know it sounds callous but when you find who killed Mangan tell him I said thanks.'

Byrne hadn't touched his coffee. He stood and left.

Fiona would have to write this one up herself. The question was how far she could speculate. The picture Byrne painted was at odds with the evidence of the people who had encountered Mangan on Inis Mór except for the incident at the House of Devotion. She had put her phone on silent when Byrne had entered. When she examined it, she'd had a missed call and a message from Brophy. She checked the message first. The search warrant had been signed, Brophy had sent a map with a pin dropped on the location of Mangan's house and the local station had been informed that she might need the assistance of a couple of uniforms. The last line of the message was the kicker. Foley had contacted the station to confirm that there were no fingerprints or DNA anywhere on the knife.

CHAPTER THIRTY-FIVE

L oughrea Garda station is in a three-storey building on Barrack Street facing the lake. It was a short distance from Maggie May's and Fiona pulled her bike into the small parking area in front of the station two minutes after leaving the pub. She announced herself at the reception and was led into the duty sergeant's office where she arranged for a locksmith and two uniformed officers to accompany her to Mangan's house which was no more than ten minutes from the station.

Fiona sat on her bike and looked out across the extent of Lough Rea while the uniformed officers loitered outside the well-designed bungalow in Cross Street that was listed as the official residence of James Mangan. The locksmith was late and the delay gave her the opportunity to mull over what she had learned during the morning. It was either a *house angel street devil* story or as Byrne had intimated Father Francis-Xavier Locke had snowed her. She tended to take Byrne's side in that argument. What intrigued her most was the reference to possible rumours. She didn't like rumours, she preferred facts, but that didn't mean that she wouldn't listen if somebody was prepared to whisper in her ear. The contents of the house might throw a little light on what Byrne had intimated if the bloody locksmith ever decided to turn up. Just as Fiona was cursing, a white panel van pulled up in front of the house with the word *Locksmith* prominent on the side.

'At last,' she said as a man wearing a blue boiler suit stepped out of the van.

'You the boss?' he asked Fiona.

She nodded.

'Woman locked her kiddie in the car with the keys inside.' He looked around at the house. 'I'll have this place open in a jiffy.'

The accent was English and so was the name on the van – *Fowler*. Fiona wasn't sure whether the accent was Liverpool or Manchester or maybe it was neither. It didn't much matter as long as he opened the door.

Fowler was as good as his word and had the door open in less than a minute. Fiona asked him to fit a new lock and to send the bill to the local station. It would eventually make its way to Galway for payment. She hoped Mr Fowler wasn't in a hurry for his money.

As soon as the door was open, the uniforms donned their latex gloves and headed inside. Fiona had already briefed them and supplied them with a handful of clear plastic evidence bags. She followed them into the well-maintained bungalow. The first thing she noted was a musty smell mingled with what she thought might have been cannabis. She had found no sign of drug use in Inis Mór but she, along with many others in the crime business, didn't consider cannabis as a dangerous drug. She entered the living room in which two walls were covered with floor to ceiling bookshelves. There was a desk facing the bay window with what looked like an antique captain's chair pushed underneath. On the desk had been a laptop computer that was now being stuffed into an evidence bag by one of the uniforms. Beside it had been a horned goat statue that was also being bagged. There was an easy chair set in one corner where the bookshelves met and along the back wall was a well-used two-seater couch. A thirty-two-inch TV sat in another corner. There were a series of what might be very expensive paintings on one of the walls. As in Inis Mór, there were no personal items on view and no photos. There was a bag on the floor under the desk and Fiona pointed it out to one of the uniforms. He lifted the small bag, opened it and took out what looked like a very expensive SLR camera and a set of lenses. 'Bag it,' she said.

She opened the desk drawers. There were a series of files, most pertaining to the house and containing bills and certificates. 'Collect every piece of paper and I mean every piece, bag the lot,' she instructed the uniforms. She looked around the room; there was no sign of a feminine touch. It was very much a man cave.

'Check the inside of every book and replace them exactly as they were.' She moved to the kitchen which was at the rear of the house and looked as though it had recently been refurbished; there was a selection of cookery books on a shelf. She took each one down and flicked through the pages. There was nothing inside. There was a small breakfast table in the kitchen with one chair. She opened each drawer and sifted the contents before closing them. The room had a haunted look, it was as lonely as its owner. Mangan's house confirmed what she had already thought about its owner following those first interviews in Inis Mór. He was a loner and introvert. She would never learn what tortured him but there was a reason that he found no pleasure in friendship and concentrated on humiliating those weaker than him. She could almost feel the anger reverberating from the walls. She moved on to the bedroom and recoiled when she saw a large red wall hanging that covered one wall. It depicted a pentagram with a goat's head drawn in the centre and surrounded with what looked like occult symbols. She got an immediate feeling of restlessness and wondered how someone could sleep in a room with such a dreadful image staring down on them. She took out her mobile phone and took a picture. There was a single bed that had been made up and one bedside table on the left-hand side of the bed. A built-in wardrobe covered an entire wall and inside she found only clothes. She felt all the garments and found nothing in the pockets, and nothing hidden. She removed the drawers and looked underneath – nothing. On the bedside table, there was a book entitled *The Book of Law* by Aleister Crowley. She picked it up and flicked through the pages. Mangan had highlighted one phrase *Do what thou wilt shall be the whole of the law*. She shivered despite the warm weather. She wanted to be out of that room and out of the house as quickly as possible. A feeling of nausea swept through her and bile rise into her mouth. She felt she was in the presence of evil and was afraid that she would be sick if she didn't get some air. She put down the book and left the bedroom, retracing her steps to the living room. The uniforms were working their way through the books, so she took the opportunity to go outside. She walked down the driveway and stood on the edge of the lake taking in great gulps of the water-laden air. She needed desperately to speak to someone. She took out her phone and called Tracy.

'How is it going on Inis Mór?' She tried to keep her tone normal.

'What's up,' Tracy said. 'Your voice sounds funny. Is everything okay?'

She took a deep breath. 'Yeah, I'm at Mangan's house with a couple of uniforms. Anything new your side?'

'The faces have turned into a blur but there are a couple of shifty-looking people on the quay. It wasn't a bad idea to go through the photos and the IDs.'

It was a shit idea, she thought. She'd prefer to have him here. 'Catch the ferry back this evening and sort the landlady out if I left a bill behind.'

'Missing me already?'

Yes, but she didn't say it. 'We're bagging a lot of stuff from Mangan's house. I need you back here. We need to go through his stuff together.'

'I'll see you tomorrow.'

'Yeah, don't get seasick.'

'You didn't have to mention that.'

'I know.'

She re-entered the house and saw the two uniforms were the equivalent of twiddling their thumbs. She spoke to the elder of the two. 'Check the bathroom.'

He opened the door of the bathroom and went inside.

She turned to the younger man. 'When your colleague gets back, I want both of you to sign the evidence bags and put them in the panniers attached to my bike outside.' She took a last walk around the living room taking photos with her mobile phone as she went. She didn't want to come back to this house although she would probably need to. It was something she would avoid like the plague.

The uniforms loaded up her bike with the evidence bags while she locked the front door with the new keys. She called the desk sergeant at the local station and thanked him for his help, then thanked the uniforms. Then she hit the road for Galway.

CHAPTER THIRTY-SIX

Fiona sat in an interview room at the station and sorted the evidence collected at Mangan's Loughrea house. Brophy had taken away the laptop to see if he could crack the password and her mobile to print the photos she had taken of the interior of Mangan's house. They had examined the pictures on Mangan's camera together and she was disappointed to find that they consisted entirely of landscapes. She was left with the files she had removed from Mangan's desk. They had the usual titles found in every small filing cabinet – tax, insurance, car, bank, etc. A thought struck her; where was Mangan's car? She would have to check with the car park at Rossaveal. It was difficult to believe that he would leave a car in an expensive car park for an extended period. She continued through the files but found nothing that would be pertinent to her investigation. She was thinking of calling it a day when Brophy entered the room with Horgan hot on his heels.

'I suppose you were on your way up to see me,' Horgan said.

'I was anxious to get a start on the stuff from Mangan's house.'

Brophy winked at her. 'I can't crack the laptop's password

so I've sent it up to Foley in Dublin and if he can't crack it, he knows someone who can.' He tossed the prints of the pictures from Mangan's house on the table.

Horgan picked up the pictures and flicked through them. 'What in the name of God is that?' He showed the picture from Mangan's bedroom to Fiona.

'A piece of satanic paraphernalia is my guess.' Fiona placed the statue of the goat-head man on the table. 'Just like this little fella.'

Horgan picked up the statue and stared at the enlarged penis. 'I hope the *Post* didn't get it right and we got it wrong.' He replaced the statue on the table. 'I wonder if any of this crap is cursed. Are you still sure it wasn't something to do with Satan worship?'

'I am.' She briefed him on the interviews with Locke and Byrne.

'What do make of it?' Horgan asked.

'I'm still processing it. I'm inclined to believe Byrne. Locke will try to protect the college at all costs. You know the fees are five thousand euros a term. They must be raking it in.'

'Aren't you glad you've no children?'

Fiona gave him a dark look.

'I've made copies of a couple of the photos and added them to the whiteboard,' Brophy said. 'Along with a copy of Mangan's birth certificate. I tried to get details from the school he attended and the schools he taught at but they're screaming about the EU's General Data Protection Regulation, so it looks like we're going to be seeking more warrants.'

'What a fuckin' mess,' Horgan said. 'There's not a suspect in sight and Hinds is waiting, proctoscope in hand, to probe us.'

'You paint quite a vivid picture, boss,' Fiona said. She didn't bother to mention that the problem wasn't not having a suspect in sight, it was having too many suspects.

'The commissioner won't blame *you* if this case goes pear-shaped.' He glanced at his watch. 'Where's Tracy?'

'On his way back from Inis Mór.'

'I don't like the direction the case is taking. I won't mention the involvement of the Jesuits to O'Reilly. We don't want to open that particular can of worms. I want to be briefed twice a day from now on and I don't want to have to look for you again.' He turned and went out of the door.

'Have a good evening, boss,' Fiona called after him.

'Why don't you two get on?' Brophy asked.

'Probably because he's an incompetent misogynistic arsehole.'

'He doesn't trust you. He asked me to spy on you and report back if you were taking any shortcuts.'

'You're not much of a spy, are you? But you're a nice person.' She took up the pictures from the table and put them into her messenger bag. 'Tomorrow is another day.'

'Good evening, sarge.' Brophy left her alone in the room.

What she had learned already led her to conclude that the motive for the murder probably lay in Mangan's past, but she hadn't expected the kind of past that she'd found. She picked up her phone and called Aisling. 'Where are you?'

'I'm still in my office.'

'Taaffes in fifteen minutes. I'm going to get sloshed.'

'That bad, eh!'

'Worse.'

THE SUMMER SEASON was ending and Taaffes was returning to normal which meant that you could move and, more importantly, find a seat. Fiona sat in the front snug and already had a pint of Guinness in front of her when Aisling arrived. They kissed and Aisling ordered an orange juice.

'Tell me all about it.' Aisling toasted and sipped her juice.

Fiona gave a detailed account of her interview with Locke

and her subsequent conversation with Byrne. 'What do you make of it?'

'It's a pity I didn't get a chance to meet Mangan. He sounds like an interesting character. There are several red flags. His behaviour with the staff was antisocial, at a minimum. That would make him a sociopath and before you ask that's a term we use to describe someone who has antisocial personality disorder what we call ASPD. People with ASPD can't understand the feelings of others. They'll often break rules or make impulsive decisions without feeling guilty for the harm they cause. They're also prone to use mind games to control friends, family, co-workers, and even strangers. Some people may perceive them as charismatic or charming. They tick a lot of the boxes that correspond to psychopaths.'

'Are sociopaths secretive?'

'Sociopaths are extremely secretive about their lives. They don't reveal anything about themselves to others.'

A burst of traditional music came from the bar area. Fiona and Aisling clapped along until the tunes ended. 'Given what I've learned in Inis Mór and Loughrea that ties in perfectly with Mangan. He's the kind of man who made enemies which is a major problem when someone murders him and leaves very little evidence behind. Instead of the investigation throwing up leads, it's creating roadblocks. He had this book on his bedside table and he'd underlined a phrase *Do what thou wilt shall be the whole of the law.*'

'You searched his house?'

'He had a small place on the edge of the lake in Loughrea.' She shivered.

'What upset you?'

Fiona took out her phone and brought up the photos of the interior of the house. She passed the phone to Aisling. 'They're only photos so you can't get the feeling that creeps along your spine when you walk around the place. I've only had that feeling once before when we searched the house of a murderer who liked to torture his victims for days before killing them.'

Aisling had stopped at the photo of the wall hanging in Mangan's bedroom. 'This is a very disturbing photo. Mangan was seriously into the occult.'

'Can you imagine sleeping with that thing looking down on you?'

'I can't.' She moved on to the photo of the goat-head statue. 'And having this fellow around wouldn't do much for me either.' She flicked through the rest of the photos before handing the phone back. 'I can see your predicament. You're probably right that men like Mangan attract enemies like a magnet attracts iron filings.'

Fiona ordered a second round.

'Drinking won't help.'

'I'm getting a bad feeling about our victim. The school he went to and the schools he worked at are playing the GDPR card. Giving us information on Mangan would be a breach of the data protection laws. I think it has more to do with what Mangan might have been up to at those schools. And since a leopard doesn't change his spots, he must have been up to no good at St Cormac's.'

'Go back to Locke and ask him. If he won't speak, drag him in.'

'The man has SJ after his name. If I haul him in, the commissioner's phone will be ringing five minutes later, and I'll be the new Guard in the station in Ballygobackwards.'

'Times have changed in Ireland.'

'They haven't changed that much since our Minister for Foreign Affairs asked permission of the archbishop to attend a memorial in a Lutheran Church for a deceased Swedish Queen. I'm scared shitless that Mangan's connection with the Jesuits will make him Teflon. On Inis Mór the case seemed simpler.'

There was an inch of Guinness left in Fiona's pint and

when she rose to order Aisling held her arm. 'I know you want to escape but this isn't the way. Let's pick up something nice for dinner and have a relaxing bath when we get home.'

Fiona sat and finished her drink. 'Will there be white wine involved?'

'You can be sure of it.'

'Then what are we waiting for?'

DAY FIVE

CHAPTER THIRTY-SEVEN

Fiona arrived at the station at ten to nine. She hadn't slept well and had woken early. The wall hanging at Mangan's house featured prominently in her dreams. She had slipped out of the bedroom, gone to the kitchen, made herself a cup of coffee and laid the Mangan file on the kitchen table. She'd gone slowly through the file starting with Larkin's statement about finding the body. Two hours later she had viewed the entire file except for the photos from Mangan's house. There had been no bolt of illumination during the reading. She had collected the photos and added them to the file. She realised that they hadn't received the forensic report on the crime site and the only news she had came from Brophy who had learned that there were no fingerprints or DNA on the knife. She had expected that. She needed to talk to Foley.

Tracy threaded gingerly between the desks balancing a tray holding two coffees in one hand and a large file in the other. He put the coffees on his desk and handed the file to Fiona. 'The photographs and IDs from Inis Mór.' He put a coffee on her desk. 'I've circled the characters I think look dicey in red ink.' He glanced at the whiteboard. 'Brophy has been busy.'

'Both Brophy and I have been busy.' Fiona took the lid off her coffee. 'I'm writing up notes on my interview with the president of St Cormac's. The bottom line there was that Mangan was a valued member of the teaching staff and all-round good fellow. One of his colleagues, Steven Byrne, sang a different song. Mangan was a monster. I'll have the notes of the interviews and the search of Mangan's house ready in an hour. Then we sit down and assess where we are. Tracy took his coffee and wandered up to the whiteboard where several photos from Mangan's house had been added.

An hour later, Fiona and her small team stood around the whiteboard at the end of the squad room. Fiona ran quickly through the events of the previous day and passed along Aisling's contribution. 'We've got a sociopath who thinks he's above the law, who is secretive about himself, and who some people find charming, and others think is a monster.' She turned to Brophy. 'The floor is yours.'

'James Aloysius Mangan, born eleventh April 1967 in Dublin, parents Douglas and Marie both deceased, only relative Emma currently living in Rockhampton, Australia. He graduated with a degree in English and French from NUIG in 1989 and spent a year at the Sorbonne. Looks like he took a year out at that point. At least I can find no information on him, and he wasn't registered for tax in Ireland. He took a master's degree in English in 1993 at NUIG. I'll work back on his employment record.' He pointed at the details on the whiteboard. 'He's done twelve years at St Cormac's, thirteen if we count the sabbatical, ten years at Tuam High School and five years at St Finbar's in Mullingar. That's a total of twenty-eight years but it's probably safe to drop St Finbar's since that would mean someone would have carried a grudge for a very long time. We have nothing in our records on him and he doesn't appear to have ever been to court.'

'Good work,' Fiona said. 'We'll need a warrant for the school records at St Cormac's and Tuam High.'

Brophy scribbled a note.

'You think someone at the schools had it in for him?' Tracy said.

She thought about Byrne. 'I think a lot of people at those schools might have wanted to kill him. The question is, who followed through and why?'

'The suspects in this case are multiplying like rabbits,' Tracy said. 'Every time we turn around there are a dozen more.'

'Any word from Foley?'

Both male detectives shook their heads.

FIONA WENT BACK to her desk and called Foley's number at the Technical Bureau in Phoenix Park.

'I bet it's Madden,' Foley said when he answered the phone.

'You're a clairvoyant. Either that or my case is the only one you're working on now.'

'You really are a detective. You got the bad news on the fingerprints and DNA.'

'Yeah, I suppose it was to be expected. That was the bad news, now tell me that you have good news.'

'Where would I get it. The litter we collected at Dun Aengus gave us next to nothing. Ninety per cent of it is already in the trash. We've got a lot of hair and fibres but it's a site that was visited by hundreds of people every day. The laptop arrived this morning and I've passed it on to the computer technicians. We might have something for you later today or tomorrow depending on the workload The DNA guys have come up with something that might interest you. Because the knife has grooves on the handle, there's a possibility that they might be able to lift microscopic amounts of skin cells from the grooves. That might lead to microscopic amounts of DNA, it's called mitochondrial DNA.'

'I thought there had to be a certain amount of DNA to get a match.'

'That's what I thought too but I haven't been on a refresher course yet this year so I'm not up to date with the latest in DNA technology. It's not sure but we might get the DNA profile and all you have to do is give us a suspect that we can match it to.'

'Thanks for telling me my job. Keep me informed.'

'Count on it.'

Fiona's phone had just hit the cradle when it started to ring. She grabbed the receiver.

'O'Reilly's office, now.'

She let out a deep sigh, stood up slowly and made for the exit.

O'Reilly and Horgan were seated when Fiona entered the superintendent's large office. She half smiled at O'Reilly and realised that he had put on weight and looked more like a sloth than she remembered. He stared back at her with a certain amount of distaste. O'Reilly's conservative views were well known, and they didn't include women living together in a sexual relationship.

'Sit down, Madden.' O'Reilly's double chin wobbled when he spoke.

'Sir.' The only chair available was beside Horgan and she moved it aside when she sat.

O'Reilly opened a buff-coloured folder, removed what turned out to be the front pages of the *Irish Post* for the past three days and laid them in front of her on the desk. She'd already seen two of them but hadn't bothered to check the latest; the headline said it all *GARDA BAFFLED BY SATANIC MURDER*. 'Are you baffled, Madden?'

She looked at Horgan. 'I don't think so, sir. That headline is more about selling newspapers than telling the truth.'

'Tell that to the commissioner.'

I'd love to, Fiona thought. It was obvious that once the salacious aspects of the murder had lost their appeal, Hinds would turn her attention to the investigation and an attempt to skewer her. 'I've kept DI Horgan informed of the latest developments in the investigation. Our victim didn't help by living on Inis Mór under an alias, but we now know his real name and we've begun to investigate his background. We believe that the murder was personal and that the victim and the murderer were known to each other. The investigation is proceeding along the correct procedural lines.'

'DI Horgan tells me that you don't believe in the satanic ritual theory.'

'No, sir, I don't.'

O'Reilly leaned forward. 'You don't believe that Satan and his minions are among us continuing the fight against God-fearing Christians.'

The word *no* almost slipped out before she caught it. 'I'm sure Satan is busy at work.' Unlike you and Horgan, she thought.

He slapped his hand on the front pages. 'How long is this shit going to continue?'

'We're making progress.'

'I received a call from the bishop yesterday. I understand that you're looking into St Cormac's College in Loughrea.'

This was the point on which Fiona would have to proceed cautiously. 'The victim, James Mangan, worked there for an extended period. Based on our theory that Mangan and his murderer had crossed paths we need to look deeply into his life.'

O'Reilly replaced the front pages in the file. 'St Cormac's is run by the Jesuits, a fine group of men. I don't want to receive any more calls from the bishop. Do I make myself clear?'

'Yes, sir. I'm going to need additional information from Mangan's previous employers.'

O'Reilly's brow furrowed.

'Just the college rolls,' Fiona continued. 'Detective Garda Brophy is preparing the warrants and I'd be grateful if you'd sign them. It's a question of data protection.'

'Don't bother the Jesuits. Tread carefully, Madden. This investigation is taking a turn I don't like.'

Fiona nodded and stood. She waited until she was back in the squad room before punching the wall.

CHAPTER THIRTY-EIGHT

Fiona spent the remainder of the morning looking over the work that Tracy had done the previous day. She covered her desk with the photographs that had been taken of the passengers waiting for the ferry the morning the corpse had been discovered. Tracy had circled several of the faces in red, but it appeared that he'd concentrated on those who looked like they might just have committed a murder. The problem was people who have just committed a murder rarely try to look like people who have just committed a murder. She didn't dismiss Tracy's work completely but instead of just looking at what he had done she replicated the exercise which led to candidates being removed while others were added. At midday, Brophy returned with the signed warrants and Fiona decided to present them at the two most recent schools that afternoon.

Tracy looked over her shoulder and saw that she had duplicated the work he had done the previous day. 'My work wasn't good enough.' There was a tinge of pique in his voice.

'On the contrary, we should always use the four-eyes principle in our work. You have your opinion on what constitutes a shady character and I have mine. Take this character for instance.' She pointed at a man who was unshaven and a bit grubby and whose face had been circled in red. 'Take away the context of the murder and you'd assume that he was possibly suffering from a surfeit of Guinness or a very late night in Watty's or The Bar. The look is backpacker and given the high cost of accommodation on Inis Mór, I guess he might have spent his few days on the island at a campsite. My opinion against yours and both of us might be wrong.' She picked up the warrant for Tuam High School and handed it to him. 'I'll take St Cormac's.'

Tracy took the warrant from her hand. 'And I'm off to Tuam. You actually trust me after my abject failure in picking out potential murderers.'

'My, but we are testy today. Of course, I trust you. You have a brilliant mentor and teacher but you're still learning. The purpose of your trip is not only to fulfil the warrant. I want to know what they thought of Mangan. We need corroboration of Byrne's information. Just as one swallow doesn't make a spring, one man's opinion of our victim isn't to be taken at face value. We need corroboration that Mangan was a monster. If possible, talk to a woman. You have a way about you, and we might as well use it.'

Tracy smiled. 'I can't stay mad at you for long.'

'Good, because I think we should have lunch together and you can bring me up to date on your love life.'

'That is not going to happen, but lunch sounds good.'

It was Tracy's first time in Tuam. He'd been posted to Galway a year previously and he was still scratching the surface of the county. Tuam is the second-largest settlement in County Galway but because it boasts less than nine thousand inhabitants. He took a car and drove the thirty-four kilometres north of Galway in slightly over thirty minutes. Tuam High School was situated a further four kilometres from the centre of the town and was in what had previously been a convent of the Little Sisters of Mercy. The school had been established in the 1950s and was considered a second rung college. Tracy found it easily enough and the drive from the road to the buildings that constituted the college ran through ten acres of pristine parkland. The college consisted of the original convent building which dated from the 1860s, additions from the twentieth century and modular buildings of more recent vintage. He pulled into the car park and presented himself at the reception. He had phoned ahead so that what might be unpleasant business for the school could be carried out quickly. The headmaster wasn't available to meet him, but the head of administration would deal with his queries. The young woman sitting behind the desk in the office smiled as he entered.

'Detective Garda Tracy.' He held his warrant card aloft before replacing it in his jacket pocket. 'I'm looking for Mrs Hession, the head of administration.'

'She's expecting you. If you go back outside and turn to your left, you'll find her in the first office in the next building.'

'Thanks.'

She gave him a dazzling smile. 'You're welcome.'

He followed the instructions and knocked on the first door in the next building.

'Yes.' The voice was brisk and businesslike.

Tracy had his warrant card ready as he entered the office.

'You're Tracy.' There was no smile on Hession's face. The small office was filled to the brim with furniture. Hession was a woman of indeterminate age whose steel-grey hair was pulled back and terminated in a bun. Her pinched hawklike face made her look older than she was. She sat at an L-shaped desk on which stood a computer and a printer. Behind her, there was a bookcase on which a series of six-inch files were displayed while to her right there were two metal filing cabinets. 'This whole business is a bloody nuisance. The dean told me to put the papers together. Show me the warrant.' Her accent was pure Galway and Tracy deduced she was a local and was most likely employed at the school when Mangan taught there.

He handed her the warrant and stood back. He hadn't been invited to sit.

She read through the single-page document. 'What's all this in aid of?'

'A former teacher, James Mangan, was found murdered on Inis Mór four days ago.'

She looked up sharply from reading the warrant. '*The* James Mangan, the one that worked here?'

'You knew him?'

'We don't talk about him.'

'I'm afraid you're going to have to. We're looking into his death and his background is an integral part of our investigation.'

'Did you explain that to the dean?'

'Not explicitly. I asked to see him, and I was told that you could deal with me.'

'I knew he'd come back to haunt us,' she said, more to herself than Tracy.

Hession looked down at her desk. 'Was he the man who was ritually murdered?'

'He was murdered, the ritual part is not certain. From now on I'll ask the questions and you give the answers.'

'I've been here fifteen years. He was already teaching when I arrived, and he left a few years later.'

'You're avoiding the question.'

'Yes, I knew him. He wasn't popular.'

'Why?'

'You'll have to talk to the dean.'

'I tried that, and I got you. Why wasn't Mangan popular?'

'He was aloof. When you spoke to him you felt he was looking down on you. On the other hand, he could be charming when he wanted to be, but you got the feeling that he didn't really mean it. I thought him shallow, but he certainly had a high opinion of himself, and he ruled the staff room with a rod of iron. But I don't think that anyone on the staff knew him particularly well. He had no real friends.'

'Would you call him a monster?'

She laughed. 'I don't think so. He was intelligent and manipulative. There were rumours of sexual liaisons and although I was younger he never came across sexually to me, but I can't speak for the other women.'

'Sounds like a complex character.'

She carefully measured her words. 'He made an impression.' She stared at Tracy. 'I've probably said too much. You want the rolls for the period he was with us.'

'Please.' Tracy kept a mental note of what she'd said.

She handed him a large sheaf of papers. 'There were six secondary classes that makes forty-eight sheets in total. Of course, Mangan didn't teach all the classes.'

'You've been most helpful.'

'Do you have any idea who killed him?' she asked.

'Our enquiries are ongoing. I don't suppose you have any ideas in that direction.'

'No,' she said emphatically.

CHAPTER THIRTY-NINE

F iona fared worse than Tracy. She had been required to remain in a small room just off the vestibule of the main building at St Cormac's. It might have been a broom closet in a past life but had been turned into a waiting room complete with a stack of recent copies of *The Irish Times*. She had been met at the front door by a well-dressed young lady who presented herself as an administrative assistant and who took the warrant away for perusal by someone further up the food chain. A half-hour later, she was halfway through *The Times* report on the body found on Inis Mór, which did not include details of the ritual murder, when the administrative assistant returned and handed her a brown envelope and asked her to please vacate the college grounds. She handed Fiona a business card for the college's solicitor. Any more enquiries concerning James Mangan and the college would have to be directed to him. Fiona made a show of reading the card before putting it in her pocket, thanked the administrative assistant, and said that if any further enquiries were necessary, she would contact the solicitor. If it went there, she would enjoy hauling Joseph Francis-Xavier Locke SJ across the coals. She'd parked her bike directly below Locke's window and after she stowed the envelope away, she looked up and saw the man himself staring down at her. She smiled up at him and he stepped back out of view. She gunned the motor a little louder than usual before roaring off down the driveway towards Loughrea. She loved riding her motorcycle, the joy of becoming one with the machine; having the total unification of mind, body and situational awareness that riding requires can have a meditative and spiritual effect. She felt her mind at its clearest when she was riding her bike. It had been made apparent that Fiona was now *persona non grata* on the campus of St Cormac's. That didn't matter. There was nothing Locke could do to impede the investigation and if he did try, she would have the great pleasure of charging him with interfering with a murder enquiry. If she had been looking for corroboration of Byrne's information, the treatment she had just received was sufficient. People who have nothing to hide don't treat the police like pariahs. *There were rumours.* Byrne's phrase kept running around in her mind. What were those rumours and who would spill the beans? Perhaps only someone who sat across from her in a station interview facing a charge if they didn't speak. Right now, the prime candidate was Locke, but she would reserve her opinion until she had spoken to Tracy.

The Mangan murder investigation team, such as it was, stood before the whiteboard and debriefed each other. There were pages of names that had to be examined and Brophy had been handed that task. They were still waiting on the forensic report although Foley had already signalled that it would be less than inspiring. The autopsy report hadn't been filed and Brophy learned that it was imminent as soon as the results of the tox screen were available. Brophy had almost completed a clean sweep of what was available on Mangan's life. The absence of a friend or confidante who could point the way had complicated affairs. Brophy was waiting for a response from the banks and the Revenue Commissioners. The momentum created by the investigation into Mangan's work history was waning and as Fiona wound down the briefing she was wondering where they went next.

'THE SUPER IS WORRIED.' Horgan sat in the chair beside Fiona's desk.

'What's worrying him?' She nodded at Tracy, and he moved his chair closer.

'He doesn't like the way the investigation is going. He's thinking that he would have preferred to have pursued the satanic ritual theory. He's been having warrant signer's remorse all day.'

'And why is that"

'What do you think? The involvement of the Jesuits. O'Reilly would much prefer to deal with Satan himself than the Jesuit provincial. I understand that they've played golf together recently and I notice that O'Reilly has been colluding with the Park behind my back. Years ago, I turned down an invitation to join Opus Dei and I think that might have cut me out of the loop.'

'Office politics is way above my pay grade,' Fiona said. 'And thankfully no one has ever asked me to join Opus Dei.'

Horgan laughed. 'They wouldn't have you, Madden, you're a woman.'

'What does all this mean?'

'Stay away from St Cormac's and for God's sake keep the Jesuits out of the investigation.'

'No can do, boss. We follow the investigation wherever it goes and right now St Cormac's and Locke are at the heart of it. We're developing a picture of Mangan that's more complex than we originally thought. He's not your ordinary murder victim. I've talked to Professor McGurk about him and she's of the opinion that he was a sociopath. Tracy was at Tuam High this afternoon serving the warrant and what he learned there seems to confirm her opinion.'

'You shouldn't be discussing the case with outsiders.'

'I consulted her in her professional capacity.'

Horgan stood. 'Watch your step.'

They watched him leave the room and Fiona thought his shoulders were drooping more than usual.

Tracy leaned closer to her. 'Did I tell you that O'Reilly hit me up about joining Opus Dei?'

'No, you didn't. Did you follow up?'

'I've no time for that kind of thing. You know what Groucho Marx said, *I wouldn't join any club that would have me as a member.*'

'Is that the kind of thing that you learned at university?'

'No, it's the kind of thing that you learn if you have an interest in the cinema.'

'I think it's time for a drink. I'll give Aisling a call and we can meet her in Taaffes.'

'IT FITS PERFECTLY with the diagnosis I already made.' Aisling was in lecture mode. 'I don't like to make a diagnosis without meeting the client, but the weight of evidence is there. I would need to speak to him to assess his lack of empathy. There would have been evidence of it in his dealings with his colleagues, but they wouldn't necessarily have noticed. He wouldn't have worried about any hurt felt by another and he wouldn't have cared if he was the source of that pain.'

'So, we have an unsympathetic victim.' Fiona had already cadged a lift home from Aisling, so she was enjoying a pint of Guinness. 'And probably a large pool of potential murderers.' She stared at Aisling. 'What are we looking for?'

'I'm a clinical psychologist, not a profiler.'

'A professional opinion will do.'

'The literature gives several classical reasons to explain why people murder, they're labelled the four Ls, that is lust, love, loathing and loot. I doubt if the motive was lust princi- pally because Mangan's psychopathy would not lead another person to think that their lust would be returned.'

'Noelle Burke, the doctor on Inis Mór,' Tracy said. 'There's no doubt that she fancied him. Maybe he got under her skin enough to kill him.'

'I don't think so,' Fiona said. 'You saw the way she reacted when she viewed the body for the first time. She would have had to be a consummate actress to fake that reaction. Also, I'm convinced that he didn't climb up on that platform of his own volition and I don't see a slight female hefting a dead weight Mangan. Noelle Burke is not in the frame.'

'Okay,' Aisling continued. 'Lust is probably out. Love is more associated with mercy killing. The murderer is aware of the pain of a loved one and wants to end that pain. The murderer would be trying to alleviate pain and as far as the autopsy goes Mangan wasn't dying or in pain. Let's jump to the last L. You'll be checking Mangan's estate and who bene- fits. If it's his sister in Australia, then you can probably count loot out. We're left with loathing which is lethal hate directed towards one person, or a group, or even a nation. There has been a discussion around whether murderers are mad or just plain bad. In my opinion, that's the most probable motive for Mangan's murder. The killer received a deep hurt from Mangan and carried that hurt with him until he assuaged it by killing the source of his pain. Or it may be that the hurt Mangan inflicted simply drove the killer crazy.'

'So, we're dealing with a crazy,' Fiona said. 'Or maybe someone who is just plain bad.'

Ashling shook her head. 'There are a lot of crazy people who never think of killing but there are others who because of psychotic delusions or hallucinations do murder people. But defining *madness* is itself contentious and can be a default label when there's no apparent motive for murder. Correspondingly there are people who we consider bad, such as Adolf Hitler, who is responsible for millions of deaths but who were considered heroes by whole populations. Badness is a matter of opinion.'

Fiona finished her drink and called for another round. 'Sometimes I'm sorry I asked you a question.' She looked at Tracy. 'I suppose being a university graduate you got all that.'

'Sort of,' Tracy said.

'If you want the simple version. There's a guy called Pincus who published a work entitled *Basic Instincts: What Makes Killers Kill* and he links murderers with a sexually damaging childhood, but he suggests that neurological issues including drug use have to be present for the likelihood of violence; think about Jeffrey Dahmer and Ted Bundy.'

Fiona passed over the money for the round of drinks. 'We're looking for someone who had a sexually damaging childhood and who had a lethal hatred for Mangan and a possible history of drug use.'

'I told you I wasn't a profiler. It could be someone totally different. The satanic ritual thing could have something to do with a neurological disorder. Don't quote me on anything.'

'Too late.' Fiona raised her glass. 'Here's to our new profiler.'

They had just started on their drinks when Fiona's phone rang. She moved off to the end of the bar to a quiet area to take the call.

'Did someone kick your dog?' Tracy asked when she rejoined them.

'Worse than that.' Fiona took a slug of her drink. 'That was Foley on the line. He wants to do a Zoom call with us tomorrow morning at ten o'clock and he wants to add a couple of his colleagues.'

'What's on his mind?' Tracy asked.

'He didn't want to discuss it on the phone, but I get the impression that it's something important.'

'Positive or negative?' Tracy said.

'I don't know, and I suppose we'll have to wait until tomorrow to find out.'

DAY SIX

CHAPTER FORTY

Fiona woke early and was already dressed when she realised that she had no transport and would have to wait for Aisling to drive her to Galway. That realisation put paid to her plan to spend an hour in the dojo. Aisling was a notoriously late riser which was compounded by the fact that it took some time for her to come fully awake. Fiona's nerves were on edge and her usual antidote for anxiety was exercise. The sky was still dark when she put on a singlet, running shorts and trainers and slipped quietly out of the cottage. At the end of the road outside the cottage, there was a five-kilometre stretch along an old bog road that ran parallel to the coast. The sea air was bracing, and she hit her stride as she passed a group of stones that was barely recognisable as one of the dilapidated cottages that had been abandoned during the Great Famine of 1847. She made the turn in the road after twenty-five minutes and sprinted back on the return for a forty-three-minute round trip. She cooled down on the small lawn in front of the cottage by performing a series of katas. Although she meditated on both the run and while doing the katas, she hadn't managed to stop thinking of Foley and the secretive tone of his voice on the phone. The butterflies in her stomach had butterflies in their stomachs. She screwed up her katas for the first time in she couldn't remember when. She finally gave up and flopped down on the lawn and closed her eyes. She opened them when she heard the front door open.

'What the...?' Aisling stood in the doorway in her pyjamas.

Fiona sprang up. 'I was wide awake. I did a run and practised katas and after a shower, I want to get to the station.'

'You think the case is going to break.' Aisling stood back to allow Fiona to enter.

'It feels like it. There's a moment in every case when you feel that the dam is about to burst. For God's sake get your clothes on while I'm having a shower.'

'What about breakfast?'

Fiona headed to the bathroom. 'To hell with breakfast,' she shouted. 'We'll pick up a couple of breakfast rolls and a takeaway coffee on the way.'

'I've never eaten a breakfast roll in my life,' Aisling said to an empty room. 'And I'm not about to start now.' She went to the bedroom and started to dress.

FIONA PITCHED the remnants of her breakfast roll into a rubbish bin outside the station. She entered the squad room and found it empty. The wall clock said a quarter to nine. She sat before her computer. She'd brought coffees for Tracy and Brophy and deposited them on their desks. She'd drunk two herself and was so hyped that she could bounce off the walls. She opened her emails and scrolled quickly down the new arrivals – just the usual crap. She looked at the clock, the minute hand didn't seem to have moved since she last looked at it. Maybe the bloody thing was bust. She stood up and paced around the room. Where the hell were Tracy and Brophy? They should be here by now. She turned at the sound of the door opening and watched Tracy enter and walk calmly to his desk. 'I brought you a coffee, but it might be tepid.'

Tracy pulled the lid off and drank. 'You're one for the understatement alright. Tepid means that there's still a modicum of heat present. This coffee is cold. How long have you been here?'

'Ten or fifteen minutes. I picked it up on the way in with Aisling.' She walked over to Brophy's desk, picked up the cardboard cup and dumped it in the wastebasket.

Tracy put the lid back on his coffee and discarded it. 'Brophy is a lucky man. It'll take hours to get the taste out of my mouth.'

Fiona glanced at the clock; another hour to go.

'Why am I so lucky?' Brophy asked from the door.

'The sergeant bought you and me a coffee. You're lucky because she already threw yours into the wastebasket.'

'It was that bad?' Brophy said.

'Colder than a witch's tit.'

Brophy sat, switched on his computer and hit several keys. 'Sarge, the autopsy report has arrived.'

'We know" Tracy said. 'The victim was stabbed.'

'The tox report is attached.'

Fiona sat at her desk. 'Send it to me and Tracy.' The new mail arrived at the top of her screen, and she opened it immediately. She read the pathologist's report; nothing new, healthy male, years of life left, knife pierced the left ventricle, bled out, death in less than five minutes. She moved to the appendix. The contents of the stomach were appended and at the end of the document was the tox report which showed that Mangan had a high concentration of gamma-hydroxybutyrate in his system and that he had also ingested a quantity of brandy. 'What's gamma-hydroxybutyrate?'

'GHB,' Tracy said. 'Heavy stuff, people go off their heads if they take it.'

'Why the hell would he have taken that?' Fiona asked.

'Maybe he didn't know he was taking it,' Brophy said. 'It's one of the date-rape drugs. For the regular user, it can have a high that can lead to violent behaviour. For the non-user, it's a depressant for the nervous system and can cause loss of conscientious, hallucinations and even coma.'

'How come you know so much about it?' Fiona asked.

'I spent a year in the drug squad in Limerick before they shipped me up here,' Brophy said. 'Nobody in their right mind would take it in conjunction with alcohol.'

'That answers the question about why he just lay there and let himself be stabbed to death,' Fiona said. 'He had no other choice. The killer fed him the GHB mixed with brandy and then snuffed him.' She looked at Brophy. 'Put it on the whiteboard along with any other pertinent points from the autopsy.'

Brophy stood, took a marker, and started writing on the whiteboard.

Fiona and Tracy watched.

'Looks like we're getting there,' Tracy said.

'We now know that the crime was premeditated and planned. Mangan didn't just meet his killer. They knew each other. If we accept Aisling's analysis, we're looking for someone who loathed Mangan, had been grievously hurt by him and it was someone close.'

'Mangan didn't have a friend on Inis Mór.'

'Then someone went there to kill him. We need to examine those passenger photos again.' The wall clock was showing a quarter to ten. 'We'll take the call in the conference room.' She turned to Brophy. 'You're part of the team so you'd better come along for the show.'

CHAPTER FORTY-ONE

Fiona and her small team sat facing a screen in the conference room, Fiona between Tracy and Brophy. Tracy had his laptop in front of him and the desktop was projected on the screen. At ten o'clock he signed in for the call. Foley and his companions appeared on the screen, they were already seated at a table and had a laptop that looked like Mangan's in front of them. The air in the room was heavy with expectation.

'Hello,' Fiona said.

'Good to see you, Fiona,' Foley said. 'I suppose we should get the introductions out of the way. The lady on my right is Alma Griffin a computer expert in the Technical Bureau and on my left is Gerry Walters from the Sexual Crimes Unit.'

Fiona introduced Tracy and Brophy.

'We've all got lots to do,' Foley said. 'Let's get on with the purpose of the meeting. I'll let Alma start. I'm afraid that she's a bit of a nerd and I've told her to simplify things.'

Alma Griffin was an attractive woman in her mid-twenties, her blonde hair hung to her shoulders, and she wore glasses in designer frames. She appeared nervous and coughed before starting to speak. 'Detective Foley gave me what we identified as James Mangan's laptop to investigate. On the surface, it's like any other laptop and contains all the usual programs like mail, word processor, you know the kind of thing. But beneath the surface, there are a series of hidden folders. It's quite a simple process to hide folders. You simply click a box in the properties section and your folder remains hidden from someone who just looks at the computer and sees what comes up on the desktop. This laptop has a series of hidden files.'

'I didn't know that anyone can hide a folder they don't want someone to see on their desktop,' Tracy said.

'It's nothing special and you could do it in a few minutes,' Griffin said. 'But these files aren't just hidden. Mangan either knew a lot about computers or knew someone who did. The first level of protection of a computer folder or file is password protection. You have a special password, and the file can't be opened unless you supply the password. It's like putting the folder in a safe that can only be opened with a password.'

'And that's what Mangan did?' Fiona said.

Alma picked up a glass and drank some water. 'Yes, but he went further. Password protection is useful but if your password is discovered someone can open the safe and access your folder. The next level up is to encrypt your file and there Microsoft and Apple will help you. Encryption is sort of like taking the content of your document and scrambling all the letters so that it can't be read by someone who is not authorised to read it. When a file is unencrypted it's in what we call plain text, and anyone can read it. An encrypted file is in cypher text. To see the file in its original form, the user must provide a key of sorts that unscrambles the message. In the case of file and folder encryption in Windows, the key is to be logged into the correct user account. Even on the same computer, the file might be gibberish to a different user.'

'I take it Mangan's files are both password protected and encrypted,' Tracy said. 'They contain something that he didn't want people to see.'

Fiona smiled. 'My partner has a habit of stating the obvious.' She was sorry she'd spoken when she saw Tracy redden.

'And then some,' Griffin said. 'Mangan added what we call possession-based authentication. In other words, you add a *token* or key that's peculiar to you, like your fingerprint or face, it might even be a special USB. We call that inherence authentication. Mangan had the full-house.'

'Please tell me that you've been able to get over all these hurdles,' Fiona said.

'I'm working on it, but the good news is that a few of the older folders weren't as well protected as the newer ones and I've managed to crack some of them.'

'And?'

'They contain pornographic photographs of children, mainly boys, and were obviously taken by Mangan. We'll crack the newer encryption sooner or later, but we've managed to open three old folders.'

'I think we should congratulate Alma and her colleagues for working flat out on this case,' Foley said. 'They've dropped everything they were working on to produce a result.'

'We appreciate your efforts,' Fiona said. 'You've opened a door for us. Will you let us have the photos you've unscrambled?'

'I've already sent them,' Griffin said. 'I found them quite disturbing.'

'Maybe we can hear from Gerry now,' Foley said.

Waters was middle-aged and overweight. His round face was pale and topped by a mop of black greasy hair. He stared at the Galway detectives through dark hooded eyes. Fiona had met many of her colleagues from the Sexual Crimes Unit during her time in Dublin. They all wore a slightly haunted look.

'Detective Foley contacted us as soon as the photographs came to light,' Waters said. 'There's a very active community of paedophiles here in Ireland. They've been assisted by advances in encryption technology and by the existence of the dark web. We ran the photos through our database, and we got several hits. They've been doing the rounds for years. There are a series of encrypted emails on Mangan's laptop that we're very interested in. We're not dealing with the dirty-old-men-in-raincoats gang anymore. The members of the paedophile ring we're investigating are professionals and businessmen. Someone like Mangan would fit in perfectly with that crew. Being a teacher at a boy's boarding college, he would have had access to a continuous supply of vulnerable children. The photos don't include sexual acts but that could have been something that Mangan aimed towards, or we may find evidence when more of the encrypted folders are cracked.'

'Let's get this straight, Mangan was a paedophile,' Fiona said. 'And a pornographer.'

'As far as we can tell,' Walters said.

'But so far we only know that he photographed boys and distributed the photos on the Internet. Do you think he sold the photos?' Fiona asked.

'There's a ready market out there for them,' Waters said. 'The buyers are always lusting after new *material*.'

'Our murder victim was a pornographer,' Tracy said.

'And a possible paedophile,' Brophy added.

'When we catch whoever killed him,' Fiona said. 'It's going to be a toss-up between giving him twenty years or a medal.'

'That is if you do get him,' Foley said.

'It's coming together,' Fiona said. 'The pieces of the puzzle are gradually falling into place. I think you guys have driven a few nails into the killer's coffin. What about briefing the guys upstairs?'

'This is your case,' Foley said. 'We're going to keep working on the laptop and Gerry is going to follow up on the emails, but the murder is all yours.'

'By exposing Mangan to us,' Waters said. 'You've helped

us to dig deeper into the ring. There's more information on the laptop and when we get it, we'll be making arrests.'

'My super is going to piss himself,' Fiona said. 'A paedophile operating from a Catholic boys college. The murder initially looked like a satanic ritual, and I bet the super will wish it had stayed there.'

'That's why we're sitting here today with only the four walls listening,' Foley said. 'We're giving you a chance to spin it your way. We've just done our jobs.'

'And we'll do ours,' Fiona said. 'It's appreciated.'

'Fucking hell.' Tracy flopped into his chair in the squad room. 'The super will go apeshit.'

'Yes.' Fiona smiled. 'Won't he just and I know someone else who will too.' The president of St Cormac's was in for a surprise.

CHAPTER FORTY-TWO

F iona waited in the reception area and watched Tracy and
Brophy climb the stairs to the squad room, then she left
the station. She knew her colleagues would want to talk about
what they had just learned but she needed to be alone. She
turned right and crossed the Corrib at Bridge Street then
turned right until she came to Kirwin's Lane. She cut through
to Quay Street, turned right and entered Costa Coffee. She
ordered an Americano and a blueberry muffin and sat at a
table facing the door. Her first reaction on leaving the station
was to call Aisling but she realised that it was always her first
reaction when the shit was flying, so she fought it. She had
remained calm while she had been in the conference room, but
her heart was pounding, and her blood pressure was way
beyond its normal level. Whether the super wanted it or not
the case was about what happened at St Cormac's. She took a
bite of her muffin and sipped her coffee and tasted neither.
Aisling had called it right; the motive was loathing, and the
murderer probably had a good reason to hate Mangan and
want him dead. She'd left the station because she wanted to
clear her mind. She looked across the room where two young
women were deep in conversation. They were probably

talking about their boyfriends or the movie they had watched the previous evening. They weren't running away from looking at pornographic photos of young children. Her phone rang and she looked at the ID. It was Tracy and she dumped the call. All in good time, there was coffee and a muffin to finish. She tried a meditation technique to empty her mind, but it wasn't working. Years of training to meditate in any situation gone out of the window. Her phone rang again, and she was about to take the call when she saw it was her mother. For God's sake not now, she shouted inside, but she accepted the call and put the phone to her ear.

'Hello, *a stór*, I don't want to disturb you if you're busy.'

Her mother had called her sweetheart in Gaeilge, and a tear crept out of her right eye. It was what her mother had called her as a child. 'I'm not busy right now, Mom.' The last word came out naturally and surprised her.

'I wondered whether you'd decided about going to Shannon to meet your father off the plane.'

'I hadn't given it a thought and I hope you haven't either.'

'I've been talking with Father Flanagan.'

'And what does he say?'

'It's Christian to forgive and forget.'

'At least he didn't tell you to turn the other cheek.'

'The man is dying, and we survived.'

'Did we?' She thought about the loathing she felt towards the man who'd left them destitute. Did she hate him enough to murder him? Certainly there were times when the thought crossed her mind.

'I don't want to go alone,' Maire said.

'Take Father Flanagan along. I might not even have the time. I'm in the middle of a big murder case.'

'I understand. I know your father would love to have you there.'

'No, he wouldn't. We don't even know the man.' Hell, she and her mother didn't even know each other. 'He's a stranger, we have no idea what he'd love. The only thing we can be sure of is that when he left us, he certainly loved himself.'

'Don't be so harsh.'

'My boss has just called me. I have to go.'

'Let me know what you decide.'

'I will.'

She finished her muffin and coffee, but she wasn't ready to leave. Reluctantly she stood and retraced her steps back to Mill Street. There was to be no peace for the wicked.

'WHERE THE HELL did you disappear to?' Tracy asked.

'Have you been promoted in the last hour or so?'

'No.' Tracy looked bemused by the question.

She sat in her chair. 'Then you don't ask me where I've been. For your information, I needed to be alone for a while.'

Tracy moved his chair close to hers. 'I've been looking at the photographs Griffin sent. I'm getting pretty angry about Mangan.'

'Why? He didn't do anything to you.'

'Most of the kids look like they're stoned. The bastard got them high before asking them to take their clothes off. People like Mangan ruin young people's lives.'

'What age do you think the boys in the photos are?'

'I'm not an expert on children but I'd guess about twelve or thirteen.'

'Get up off your arse. We're going to see the boss.'

'I DON'T FUCKING BELIEVE IT.' Horgan thumped his fist on his desk. 'I do not fucking believe it. It's a shitstorm.'

Fiona and Tracy stood at attention before their boss's desk. They'd watched as the colour of his face had gone from red to puce as Fiona briefed him on the results of the tox screen and the meeting with Foley and his colleagues from

Dublin. 'Whether you believe it or not, that's what we've got.'

'You should have told me about the meeting with Foley. I should have been there.'

'Foley didn't tell me on the phone what was on the agenda, and I didn't want to waste your time.'

'Are the boys in the Park up to speed on this?'

'I don't think so. Foley indicated that it's our case and we'd have to pass the message upstairs.'

Horgan cast his eyes upwards and sighed. 'They'll not forget the messenger. You're a fucking menace, Madden. Everything you touch turns to shit.'

'I don't suppose I was hired to solve crimes.'

'You're good at that but there's more to the job than collars. You have to have a bit of *nous*.'

'You mean protect my superiors' ample arses.'

'Wait until O'Reilly hears this. His pal the provincial will throw a fit.'

'They've been harbouring a paedophile,' Tracy said. 'That's against the law.'

'There's no proof of that!' Horgan shouted. 'And you can keep your fucking opinions to yourself.'

Tracy leaned on the desk. 'The guy took pornographic photos of young boys in his care. You think no one was aware?'

Fiona pulled Tracy's belt until he was upright. 'Viewing the photos is an emotional experience, boss. Detective Garda Tracy apologises.'

Horgan stared at Tracy.

'I'm sorry, boss, I shouldn't have expressed an opinion.'

'She's rubbing off on you, Tracy. So much for the glittering career ahead.'

'Who the fuck cares,' Tracy mumbled.

'I didn't catch that,' Horgan said.

'I said I'll do better in future.'

'This case calls for a degree of delicacy that neither of you clowns have. I'm going to take over running it myself.'

Fiona let out a deep sigh of relief. 'That's very brave of you, boss,' she said.

Horgan's head looked like it might catch fire his frontal cortex was working so hard. 'What are you talking about?'

'You're taking on all the risk of the investigation. I'm relieved and I'm sure so is Tracy. What do you want us to do?'

'You need to find the killer double quick before any of this gets out.'

'You're going to suppress evidence?' Tracy asked.

Horgan put his head in his hands.

'If we catch the killer there'll be a court case,' Fiona said. 'Everything will come out. They'll look around for a donkey to pin the tail on.'

Horgan continued to massage his forehead. 'I've changed my mind about taking over the case. But I'll be the one to pass the message along to O'Reilly and the Park.'

'You're right about the delicacy thing, boss. Tracy and I will try to act as we think you might. Would that be okay?'

'If I thought you were winding me up, Madden, I'd do my best to put you back in uniform.'

'Perish the thought, boss. Tracy and I should get back to work.'

CHAPTER FORTY-THREE

The Mangan murder investigation team sat huddled in a corner of the squad room. The result of the autopsy and the tox screen had been added to the whiteboard but the contents of the meeting with Foley and his colleagues were too sensitive to be opened to public view.

Tracy leaned towards Fiona. 'What are you thinking?'

There was excitement in the air. 'I know this is going to cause pain, but we need to identify those boys in the photos.'

'Perhaps you should discuss this with Aisling first,' Tracy said. 'Maybe the boys don't know their photos have been circulating on the Internet for years. Knowing something they tried to forget is out there forever could cause psychological damage.'

'One of them might be the murderer,' Fiona said.

'Just as easily none of them might be the murderer. Is it worth running the risk of psychological damage? These kids have been abused already. What you're suggesting could add to the abuse.'

'Do we have another choice?'

Tracy thought for a few moments before shaking his head. 'I don't like it. Who is going to identify the boys?'

Fiona had already considered the potential candidates. There was only one. 'I think I might be able to convince Stephen Byrne, the lecturer at St Cormac's, to help us.'

Tracy looked at Brophy and then at Fiona. 'He'd be putting his career at risk if his employers found out he was your man on the inside.'

'You're being dramatic. They'll never find out.' She knew they would if it went to court.

Tracy frowned. 'Do you care what detritus you leave behind in an investigation?'

'Of course, I care. I don't want justice for James Mangan, and I don't want to cause more pain for people who have already been hurt. And I know that if we went upstairs tomorrow and suggested that we terminate the investigation, people at the schools where Mangan taught would heave a collective sigh of relief. But that's not what they pay us for. The guys upstairs think it is, but they don't. They pay us to catch people who kill other people for whatever reason, justified or not. The people with something to hide will hate us for it, but they can go fuck themselves. Has anyone got anything to add?'

She looked at Tracy and Brophy who both shook their heads. 'Make sure no one else here sees the photos and I'll make the call.'

'I'LL HAVE to think about it,' Byrne said after he'd listened to Fiona's suggestion.

She could hear fear as well as hesitation in his voice. 'Nobody will ever know you helped us and the whole matter will be kept confidential.' She knew she'd made a promise she couldn't keep, and she wasn't just thinking about Ginny Hinds' spy in the station. There would be a court case and evidence would be presented in open court and that evidence would include the photographs. If Fiona had been one of the abused boys and learned those photographs existed, she might not be too happy. It was one of the laws of unintended consequences.

'I'd like to help but it's not something I can agree to off the bat.'

'Your information may identify a murderer.'

'I understand and that's the burden I'm considering. If I identify the boys in those photos, you're going to start looking into their lives. Hasn't Mangan caused them enough distress? It seems like his claws are extending from the grave to injure them yet again.'

Fiona sighed inwardly. Byrne was a typical civilian. He didn't want to get his hands dirty. She, along with Tracy and Brophy, didn't have that privilege. There was so much dirt on her hands that no matter how many times she washed them they'd never be clean. 'I completely understand your position. How long do you need to consider my proposition? Please remember that if you decline, I'll be obliged to go direct to Locke.'

'Can you give me twenty-four hours?'

'No, I can't. Murder investigations are time-sensitive. We don't have twenty-four hours to waste. I'll give you an hour.'

'I'll ring you back.'

Fiona normally got a feeling as to how something would turn out, but Byrne was an evens call. She hadn't looked at the photos of the boys and she thought that it might be a useful exercise. She opened the computer, found Griffin's email and opened the attachment. She flicked through the photos. She'd seen pictures like these before, some many times worse than Mangan's efforts. There were sixty photos in total, and they featured twelve boys. The faces were fresh and innocent, and she agreed that they looked like they had been plied with either alcohol or drugs. She wondered whether they even remembered having their photographs taken. Then a second thought struck her. Mangan had been a paedophile. Suppose the photos were the tip of the iceberg. Suppose that under the surface lay something altogether more sinister and evil. Suppose all, or some, of these boys had been sexually abused during their sessions with Mangan. She had no proof of sexual abuse, but it couldn't be discounted. Would somebody murder Mangan for taking a lewd photo that they would hardly remember. She didn't think so. The motive had been loathing, a visceral hatred of Mangan, an injury so deep and hurtful that the murderer had to plunge a dagger into his nemesis' heart and violate his body.

'You've been quiet.' Tracy rolled his chair over towards her desk.

'Byrne didn't bite and I don't blame him. I've reviewed the photos and I've seen worse, but I had another thought. I'd hardly murder Mangan if he took a nude photograph of me. I'd be ashamed but that would be it. The hatred must run deep, and the hurt be unforgettable. Mangan raped these boys.' Fiona could have told him that she knew how the boys felt because she had had the same feelings herself. Like them, she hadn't been the guilty party in her own rape but that didn't stop her from feeling guilt. And she understood the hatred of the rapist. She could have killed hers. Her mental state had been such that she might have killed him. The memories were clouded in fog, and she had suppressed most of them. She understood these boys, their experience resonated with her. The years didn't banish the memories. There were times she could still smell her rapist's breath, times she could still feel the knife nick in her throat and the pain in her loins. She could see Tracy looking at her strangely.

'What's up?' Tracy said. 'You were away somewhere there. Care to tell me about it.'

'I just thought how horrible it must have been for them. A bully like Mangan penetrating them. That's not a memory that would fade with time.'

'Maybe that's not what happened?'

'I hope not.'

Her mobile phone rang. She didn't recognise the caller ID, but she took the call. She listened for a while then said. 'Thank you, I think you're doing the right thing.' She turned to Tracy. 'That was Byrne. He's agreed to identify the boys. He'll be here this afternoon which gives us time to get lunch if you feel like eating.'

'We need to keep our strength up. And we need to get out of this station, the atmosphere is getting a bit oppressive.'

CHAPTER FORTY-FOUR

L unch had turned into a non-event with even Tracy
playing with his food rather than eating it. Fiona had
ordered a tuna sandwich which had arrived accompanied by a
handful of potato chips. She had eaten two chips but left the
rest of the food untouched.

'The first boat trip to Inis Mór seems so long ago,' Tracy
said. 'A lot has happened since. Back then it seemed like a
straightforward case, the victim had been sacrificed during a
religious service to a Neanderthal God or even Satan himself. I
was a little naive, wasn't I? I didn't see the other possibilities.'

'Neither did I but murder investigations generally tend to
be journeys into the psyche of either the killer or the victim.
It's like a game where there is a group of players, and the
process leads to change for all the participants. The victim
leaves the game early and the police and the murderer must
play it out to the end. The main point is that we all experience
change. I think you've learned a lot.'

'Are you sorry you didn't have children?'

A moment occurs in every partnership when an opportunity arises to expose your deepest darkest secret. Fiona recognised the moment and decided to let it pass. 'Where the hell

did that come from? No, I'm not.' An image of her son floated across her mind, and she wondered where he was and what he was doing. She wondered whether he still hated her. Did he hate her enough to kill her?

'I took Cliona home to my parents last weekend and my mother has us married and expecting. I think Cliona freaked out.'

'Poor girl. And probably so did you. I didn't think you guys were that far along.'

'We're not. Don't get me wrong, I love Cliona and we get on great, but we haven't even discussed marriage. I always liked the idea of kids but so many things can go wrong.'

A waitress came and looked at the untouched plates. 'Is something wrong?'

'No, we don't have much appetite.' Fiona pushed the plate away. 'Bag it and we'll take it away. Bring two coffees and the bill.' The waitress looked at them with a sad look on her face before picking up the plates. Fiona could almost read her mind; the good-looking guy was breaking up with the slightly older woman.

'Things going wrong is called life,' Fiona said when the waitress left. 'We always seem to be trying to fix something that went wrong. Sometimes it might be better if we just accept that not everything can be perfect and not everything can be fixed.' She thought of her father and his dereliction of duty. If he hadn't flown the coop, who knows what might have happened. Maybe she wouldn't have been raped and forced to give birth to a child when she was no more than a child herself. What's done cannot be undone.

'I was thinking about those boys that Mangan abused,' Tracy said. 'Their parents had probably made sacrifices to send them to a good school never thinking that they were falling into the clutches of a paedophile. I wonder how those parents will feel when it all this comes out in court.'

'You're jumping ahead there a bit, but I love your confidence. We must find the culprit and even if we do there'll be a delay before the court case. That'll give everyone concerned time to spin events as they see fit.'

The two coffees arrived, and Fiona paid the bill.

'I'm wondering whether Byrne is going to turn up.' She stirred her coffee.

'What will we do if he doesn't?'

'We'll find another solution.' She didn't have one in mind.

'Maybe it's not one of the boys in the photos.'

'Then we'll go back to the beginning and work forward again because that's what we do.'

As they left the restaurant, she gave the waitress a sad smile and was rewarded with a wave.

THE AFTERNOON DRAGGED. There wasn't much to do except await the arrival of Stephen Byrne and it looked like he was a no-show. Fiona read every boring line of the post-mortem report. She didn't expect to discover anything new or startling and her expectation proved correct. The clock on the squad room wall was creeping towards four o'clock when Fiona's phone rang, and the duty sergeant announced the arrival of a visitor. She nodded at Tracy. 'We're on. Put the photos on a USB and bring a laptop to the conference room.'

In the reception area, Fiona extended her hand and Byrne took it. 'Thanks for coming.' Her smile wasn't returned. 'I know this isn't easy for you.' Byrne was paler than she remembered and a lot more withdrawn. He carried a satchel tight under his arm. She led him to the conference room on the ground floor where Tracy and Brophy were already seated, and the laptop's screen faced the empty chair at the top of the table.

'These are two of my colleagues, Detective Garda Tracy and Detective Garda Brophy.' Tracy and Brophy nodded as their names were said.

'Dr Stephen Byrne,' he said before taking his seat at the top of the table. He placed his satchel on the table before him. 'How many people know about the existence of these photos?'

'Only the people in this room and a few colleagues in Dublin. Why do you ask?'

'There's an amount of cleaning house going on at the college this afternoon. Locke's office has been taken over by two men I've never seen before and there's a rumour that Locke has been removed from his post and sent abroad on an extended visit to a Jesuit house.'

'You think they caught wind of the current direction of our investigation?' Fiona said.

'We've never experienced anything like this level of activity and Locke's departure has been very sudden. These kinds of moves are usually announced months in advance.'

Fiona looked at Tracy. 'We leak like a sieve.'

'Horgan or O'Reilly?' Tracy asked.

'Take your pick.'

Byrne opened his satchel. 'I managed to get hold of the class photos we took during the period Mangan terrorised us.' He tipped out a large batch of A4 sized photos onto the table. I didn't teach all the boys myself so you may have to depend on the class photos. Many of these are not my personal copies, and I might be accused of theft by the school if they learn that I've taken them.'

'Once we identify the boys you can return them,' Fiona said.

'There are six classes over a ten-year period so there are sixty photos in all,' Byrne said. 'There is at least one photo of each boy who attended the college during Mangan's reign of terror. Some of the boys will, of course, appear in several of the photos.'

'We'll set up Mangan's photos and we'll run through them.' She nodded at Tracy who brought up the first photo.

Byrne recoiled when he saw the image.

'Just write down the name of the boy and the number of the photograph. If you don't know the name, just put *don't know* and the number of the photo.'

Byrne stared at the first photo and wrote a name on the pad Fiona had provided. He brought up the second photo, stared at it for a while and wrote a name. Fiona noticed that he was tearing up and the first drops had already exited his right eye. He waved them away with his hand.

'Would you prefer if we left you alone?' Fiona asked.

'Yes please.' He removed a handkerchief from his pocket and dabbed at his eyes.

Fiona stood. 'We'll come back in an hour.' She nodded at Tracy and Brophy and all three left the room.

'Poor bastard,' Brophy said. 'To realise that it happened right under their noses, and they knew nothing about it.'

'I wouldn't go as far as that,' Fiona said as they entered the squad room. 'I think one or two were in the know but they didn't say anything as long as nobody squealed.' She went to her desk and sat. 'Tea and biscuits time.' She looked at Brophy. 'Your shout.'

'Tartare Cafe on Dominick Street,' Tracy said. 'And forget the biscuits, bring back a cake, we could be here a while.'

HORGAN SAT FACING O'Reilly in the latter's office. Neither man looked happy and on the scale of unhappiness, O'Reilly was way ahead.

'I thought I could trust you, George.' O'Reilly leaned forward. 'Instead, you dumped us into the biggest fuck-up of my career. I made promises to certain people that we had the situation under control, but it's anything but under control. I fear to think what Madden is up to while we're sitting here. The plan was to run the ritual murder theory into the ground. Do you want to tell me where it all went pear-shaped?'

'Madden is good at her job.' Horgan sat back in his chair.

'You should have known that once she oversaw the investigation it could go anywhere.'

'Then Madden shouldn't have been running the investigation. The upshot is that a murder case that could have been swept under the carpet is going to lead to the closure of a college and recriminations for the staff and the order that operates it. Not to speak of the loss of revenue. We're entering a veritable shitstorm. You put us there, George, how do you intend to get us out?'

'I don't know. There are people in the Park who are aware of what's going on. The genie is out of the bottle, and we can't get him back inside. We've reached the top of the rollercoaster and the only way out is to buckle up.'

'Buckle up my arse.' O'Reilly was on his feet and stalking around the room. 'I'm not about to let a skinny little lesbian hole my career. I'm supposed to go up in the organisation. Promises have been made.'

Horgan watched as his superior started to mumble incoherently. 'Calm down. It's not the end of the world. She doesn't even have a prime suspect, so a court case is miles down the track. The press cycle is getting shorter and shorter. There'll be a brouhaha for a week or two and then it'll be forgotten.'

O'Reilly suddenly stopped walking and mumbling. 'There are people who won't forget. And it's you and I that they won't be forgetting.'

CHAPTER FORTY-FIVE

Byrne looked up from the laptop when Fiona entered the conference room. She noticed that his eyes were red and assumed that the few tears they had witnessed had turned into a flood as soon as they left. It was a shit job, but someone had to do it and Byrne had put himself on the line when he left the note on Fiona's bike. But that didn't mean that she didn't pity him. She realised that she didn't know much about him. 'Why don't you take a short break. Can we get you tea or coffee?'

'No thanks.' He closed the laptop and sat back. 'I'm going to have a stiff drink when I get home, but I don't think there's enough alcohol in the world to erase the images I've just seen. I don't know how you guys do your jobs.'

She sat down beside him and saw that there was already a long list of names. 'Most coppers never have to deal with the crap side of the job. They might have the odd domestic but serious crime is the shit end of the stick.'

'Then why do you do it?'

It was a question she asked herself all the time. 'I'm good at it and Tracy's good at it. You must believe that you're doing something useful, and you must like dealing with details. It's not like the cop shows on TV. There's a lot of checking of alibis, poring over witness statements, examining financial documents, and an endless parade of interviews. To be honest, a lot of what we do would bore the pants off the normal citizen.' She smiled. 'And the money's not great.'

He returned her smile.' It's a bit like teaching. You must be dedicated. I always think of it as a calling rather than a profession. We get young minds, and we have the chance to form them.'

'Do you have children of your own?' she asked

'Two, an eight-year-old boy and a five-year-old girl. And no, my boy will not be going to a boarding school.'

'This is an aberration. It's probably your first contact with a serious crime and if you're lucky it might be your last.'

He picked up the list and looked at it. 'I taught all these boys and I never for one moment knew what was going on in their lives.' He handed the list to Fiona. 'I'm finished. There are two boys that I didn't recognise. You'll have to use the class photos to identify them.'

Fiona looked down the list and read the names off to herself – none rang a bell. 'Have you any idea what happened to these boys?'

'No, you'll have to check the files from the college. I think I'd like to leave now. Let me have the class photos back when you're finished with them.' He closed his satchel.

'You've been a great help,' Fiona said. 'There's little chance that we'll find Mangan's killer among this lot but it's a line of enquiry.'

He stood. 'The knowledge that I might have assisted in identifying one of these abused boys as a killer doesn't please me. There's a part of me that wants Mangan's killer to get away. And like I said in Maggie May's, if you do find the murderer, thank him for me.'

She walked him to the reception area. 'With a bit of luck, we won't need to call on you again. Don't beat yourself up because you didn't know what was going on at the college.

Just keep doing your job and helping form those young minds.'

He held out his hand. 'You know I think that in a perverse way this experience will help me become a better teacher. I'm glad to have met you.'

She took his hand. 'Likewise.' She watched him as he walked out of the door, a concerned citizen who realised that he had a role to play in the criminal justice system. He'd never be the same again.

TRACY AND BROPHY were the only occupants in the squad room when Fiona returned with the laptop, the class photos and the list in her hand. 'Tomorrow is another day.' She handed Tracy the laptop. 'He couldn't recognise two of the boys so tomorrow you'll go through the class photos and see if you can find them.' She held out the list to Brophy. 'I don't recognise any of the names, but I want to know where all these boys ended up. Then I want to match them with the names we took of the passengers leaving Inis Mór on the morning the body was discovered. This list stays between us three. That means if it gets leaked, I'll know who leaked it. And none of the names go on the whiteboard.'

Tracy locked up the laptop and saluted. 'Yes, boss, have a good evening.'

Brophy locked away the list and followed Tracy to the door. 'Night, boss,' he called back.

'Night,' Fiona said. She opened her computer and checked her emails, the usual crap. The word boss in Copland was reserved for detective inspectors. She had told Tracy and Brophy to refer to her as sarge principally because people like Horgan might be miffed with her being elevated by members of his team. There was a very good chance that she had reached her level when she had been promoted to sergeant. Moving up would require a mentor and she didn't see anyone rushing to fill the position. She decided to give herself the same advice she had given Byrne, not to beat herself up. She loved her job and promotion would only increase the administrative workload. She was shocked at how easy it was to convince herself to accept her place in the Garda Síochána. She looked around the room. Was this all there was? Had she really topped out at thirty-five?

She switched off her computer and contemplated a drink. It was Aisling's early day and she would already be at home. She smiled when she realised that she had no one to call. She had no friends but then again, few police officers had. As soon as you told someone you worked for the police you could see the light go out of their eyes. The Kawasaki was parked in the yard and the nearest drink was in her cottage in Furbo.

THE SMELL from the kitchen was instantly recognisable as she opened the door. Aisling was doing her famous roast lamb with all the trimmings and Fiona's stomach juices were already anticipating the coming treat. The table was already set, and she began to think that she had forgotten an event like Aisling's birthday or their anniversary. She looked quickly at the calendar on the wall and saw that there were no pencil markings on the date. Something was up and she would learn what it was in due course.

'You're home.' Aisling wore her cook's apron over her best black linen pants and a white blouse. She hugged Fiona and planted a kiss on her lips.

Fiona stood back. 'Okay, let's get it over with now. What did I forget?'

'You haven't forgotten anything.'

'The lamb and you cooking up a storm, that's not an everyday event.'

'We're having a guest for dinner. I invited your mother to join us.'

'Shouldn't we have discussed this first?'

'I can't invite someone for dinner without discussing it with you first?'

'Of course, you can invite who you like, just not my mother.'

'Have a shower and I'll have a glass of wine ready when you're done. Maire is due to arrive any minute.'

'Maire,' Fiona mumbled as she went to the bathroom.

When Fiona exited the bedroom, Aisling and Maire Madden were sitting close together on the couch. She hesitated before picking up a glass of white wine from the coffee table and sitting in an easy chair facing them.

'I was just thanking Aisling for inviting me to dinner,' Maire said.

'Slainte.' Fiona raised her glass in a toast before taking more than a sip. 'How did you get here?'

'I got a lift with Father Flanagan; he has business in Galway.'

'I would love to have been a fly in that car,' Fiona said. 'I bet the discussion centred on your wayward husband.'

'Father Flanagan promised me a lift to Shannon, that is if you're not intending to go.'

'I've had a shit day at work,' Fiona said. 'Can we have a drink, eat the nice food that Aisling cooked and discuss the weather before we get on to the unsavoury subject of the impending arrival of the man formerly known as my father.' She downed her wine and refilled her glass while ignoring Aisling's disapproving look.

'I'm sorry,' Maire said. 'I know your work is difficult. I don't mean to upset you.' She looked at Aisling. 'I think I should leave.'

'Not after I spent the afternoon cooking,' Aisling said. 'And I think it would be better for all concerned if we cleared up the issue of whether Fiona is going to support her mother by accompanying her to Shannon.' She stared at Fiona. 'Your mother needs you.'

'There was a time I needed her. It's a pity you weren't around then to bring us together. My mother preferred to listen to Father Flanagan.'

'I've said I'm sorry.' Maire dabbed at the tears running down her cheeks. 'Can't you ever forgive me?'

'I can forgive but I'm afraid I can't forget. But you're my mother and if you need me then I suppose I should respond. I don't want to meet that man again, but it looks like I'm going to have to. The lamb must be ready by now and it would be a shame to ruin it by overcooking.'

'You two sit here and chat.' Aisling finished her wine and stood. 'Dinner will be on the table in two minutes.' She smiled at Fiona as she passed her on the way to the kitchen.

DAY SEVEN

CHAPTER FORTY-SIX

F iona stood under the shower at the dojo and turned up the hot tap until she couldn't bear it before turning on the cold water. Every muscle in her body ached and the visiting Japanese sensei had worked her harder than she could have imagined. If she needed a lesson in how much more she had to learn, she had just received it. The workout had lasted an hour and she hadn't thought about the Mangan investigation for one second. When they finished, they bowed, and the sensei congratulated her for her effort. She might not make it as a top cop but at least she was appreciated by her peers in the martial arts field. As she soaped up, she came back to earth and wondered if they would have a prime suspect or would the whole issue of the boys in the photos be a bust.

She deposited takeaway coffees on Brophy's and Tracy's desks before taking her place at her computer. She was still enjoying her brew when Horgan stormed into the squad room and tossed a copy of the *Irish Post* onto her desk.

'What the fuck is going on?' Horgan shouted. 'Who is leaking this stuff?'

Fiona looked at the front page. The headline screamed *RITUAL MURDER MAN MAY HAVE BEEN PART OF*

PORNO RING. The byline indicated the article was by Ginny Hinds. 'I have no idea where she's getting this stuff, boss.' She took out her mobile phone and brought up the email Hinds had sent her showing a photo of the whiteboard containing details of the Mangan investigation. 'Maybe you should look at this.'

Tracy arrived, picked up his coffee and stood beside Fiona's desk.

Horgan took the mobile and stared at the picture. 'She sent this to you.'

'I think she was trying to make a point. She was telling me that she had a contact in the station. That photo was taken in this room. I learned yesterday evening that they're cleaning house at St Cormac's. The president has been sent to Coventry. Well not exactly but a metaphorical Coventry where we can't get hold of him. I bet a load of files went along with him. There are a lot of questions that need answering about who knew what and when. But the evidence might be difficult to locate. Maybe Hinds' inside man tipped off St Cormac's as well.'

Horgan handed back the phone.

'As soon as we finish with Mangan,' Fiona said, 'I'm going to find out who leaked to Hinds and he's going to be missing a set of balls.'

Horgan wandered over to the whiteboard. 'Nothing new on the horizon.'

'Nothing that we're prepared to put on the whiteboard. Let's just say that our enquiries are proceeding.'

Horgan walked to Fiona's desk, put his hands on the front and leaned forward into her face. 'Do I get the impression that I'm not to be trusted?'

Fiona could smell an extra strong mint on his breath, and she wondered if he took an early morning snifter. 'No, boss.' She lifted the newspaper and held it with the headline facing him. 'But given the level of leakage in this investigation, I think it's wise to keep our progress to ourselves. We may have a prime suspect by the end of the day, but I can't promise.'

'I want you in my office before close of play this evening and I want to know exactly what you're up to.' He stormed out of the squad room.

Tracy finished his coffee and lobbed the cardboard cup into his wastebasket. 'You think Horgan is the leaker.'

'No, but I'm sure that O'Reilly leaked to St Cormac's. His allegiance to the Garda Síochána is somewhat less than his allegiance to the people who put him in his job. Get to work on identifying the two boys that Byrne didn't know. Start at the oldest class photos.' She turned around and saw that Brophy was busy on his computer.

FIONA GOT BORED WATCHING TRACY, magnifying glass in hand, playing Sherlock Holmes with the class photos. She downloaded a batch of administrative notices and worked through them quickly. It was necessary to convince the hierarchy that she was serious about aspects of the job other than solving crimes. After an hour Brophy came and sat in her visitor's chair.

'I've done a cheap and cheerful search on the ten names on the list. They range in age from twenty-one to twenty-four so there isn't a lot of information on them.' He handed her a page from a pad where he had handwritten notes. 'One of them is studying in Canada so you can probably rule him out. One works for an adventure company and is currently leading a trip around South America. The other eight are gainfully employed in Ireland.'

'Do you have addresses and telephone numbers for them?'

'I'm working on that.'

'I checked the housing register but there's no sign of them. That's not unexpected for men that young. Neither Tracy nor

I own a property. I don't want to ring up their employers to ask for the information.'

'What about their parents? Check if they're working in the same locality as a parent. There's a good chance that they live at home.'

Brophy returned to his desk.

Fiona wondered whether she had put all her eggs in one basket. What if the murderer was one of the boys' fathers? Or an uncle or a grandfather? Every time the pool of suspects appeared to get smaller it became larger. She picked up the page that Brophy had left behind then searched on her desk for the lists that had been drawn up by the Aran Ferry staff. She went through them, name by name, and tried to match them with the names on the list. She almost jumped in her chair when she found the first one. Alan Gibbons was on the list and was also on the ferry the morning the body was discovered. She continued her search and located a second name that matched: Theo O'Grady. She continued to the last name on the list, but they were the only two names that matched. It could be a coincidence, but she didn't believe in coincidences. She went to Brophy's desk. 'Forget the global search. I want everything you have on Alan Gibbons and Theo O'Grady, and I want it before lunch.' She felt her heart racing. It looked like she'd called it right. She returned to her desk and looked at the ID photos of the two young men then at the photos Tracy had taken on the quay. Neither Tracy nor she had circled the two fresh-faced men. 'I've got them,' she said to Tracy. 'There were two people on the list who were on the ferry the morning we arrived.'

'Could be a coincidence,' Tracy said. 'Two guys on holiday.'

'Yeah, two guys on holiday standing at opposite ends of the group on the quay. I don't think so. Any advance on the last two boys?'

'It's like looking for a needle in a haystack. The photos are packed with kids, and they all look alike.'

'We need those last two boys' names. Keep at it.'

Fiona looked at the photographs of the two young men. They didn't look like killers but neither did Ted Bundy. What does a killer look like? In Fiona's experience, they came in all shapes and sizes; some looked like thugs and others like choir boys. She felt that she had the motive and she had at least two of the participants in the murder. The only bugbear was that she didn't have any proof. Aside from one or both cracking under interrogation and confessing, she had nothing that placed either Gibbons or O'Grady at the crime scene. Somewhere in the mass of evidence collected by Foley and O'Malley, there had to be a drop of blood, a hair, a blob of saliva, some damn thing that might put either or both men at the keep. But the scene at Dun Aengus was not sanitary. People had been traipsing through the fort during the day and there was no cleaning crew. They could have deposited their DNA at any time including but not limited to the hours the murder was committed. Perhaps she should keep her excitement under control. Identifying possible suspects was one thing, getting the cuffs on them was another. Foley had mentioned something about mitochondrial DNA, but she'd never heard of it. She needed to talk to him before she tackled either of the potential suspects. She punched in the number of the Technical Bureau in Phoenix Park. Foley was out on a case. She asked his colleague to pass him a message that she needed to speak with him urgently. It was coming together but not at the pace that Fiona would have liked.

'I've found one,' Tracy called over. 'Frank Kearney.'

Fiona repeated the name to herself, but it meant nothing to her. She went back to the Aran Ferry sheets and looked for Kearney. There was no sign of him. It was down to Gibbons and O'Grady.

CHAPTER FORTY-SEVEN

Fiona's stomach rumbled. She'd turned down an invitation from Tracy for lunch and instead sat by the phone waiting for Foley's return call. Brophy had dropped a note on her desk before he left. The information on Gibbons and O'Grady was scant. They had both finished school, attended university and were gainfully employed. He checked the families, and it looked like both were resident in the Galway/Mayo area. For her part, she had Googled mitochondrial DNA and read a couple of articles and watched a video, but she was still none the wiser. The problem with DNA and other genomic techniques was that the technology developed so fast that the layman couldn't keep up with it. The only information she understood from her research was that such techniques existed and were being employed in difficult forensic areas.

Tracy returned, dropped a coffee and a tuna sandwich on her desk and picked up his magnifying glass.

'Thanks.' She took the lid off the coffee and unwrapped the sandwich.

'Did Foley call?'

'No, I spent the lunch hour reading up on mitochondrial DNA.'

Tracy looked impressed. 'Not a subject for the faint-hearted. I suppose you're an expert now.'

'Are you joking? It's your total boffin subject. I watched a video and the professor looked like he stepped off the Star Ship Enterprise. The guy was a total nerd, and I don't think he could have explained it in layman's terms if he tried.' She took a bite of her sandwich and began to chew, then her phone rang. She dropped the sandwich and picked up the phone. 'Detective Sergeant Madden.' That's what she intended to say but much of her name was muffled by the chunk of bread in her mouth.

'What's wrong with your speech? Are you having a stroke?' Foley sounded alarmed.

She swallowed the bread. 'No, late lunch. I'd just bitten off a chunk of a tuna sandwich.'

'Happened to me before,' Foley said. 'I was speaking with a colleague when suddenly he started talking gobbledygook. He was having what they call a TIA. According to him, he was speaking normally. I thought the same thing was happening to you. Seems like you needed to speak urgently.'

'I've got a couple of live suspects. They were in Mangan's photos, and they left on the ferry the morning the corpse was discovered. The problem is that I can't put them at the murder scene.'

'Dun Aengus isn't a room in a house. It's a large expanse of rock and grass open to the air and walked over by hundreds of people. Placing them at the murder scene is more than likely beyond my skill.'

'I've been looking into the mitochondrial DNA that you told me about.'

Foley laughed. 'And what did you learn?'

'That it's a bloody difficult subject populated by nerds of the highest level. The way I read it we might need DNA from the killer's mother.'

'That's one way to make a match. I sent the dagger to the

guys at the DNA lab we use. They're at the cutting edge of the technology. They can work wonders with very small amounts of skin cells.'

'Yeah, I remember.'

'It's up to them to work their magic.'

'What if the murderer cleaned the knife with ammonia or something that removes DNA?'

'If it doesn't get into the grooves, you have a chance.'

'What if he didn't handle the knife?'

'Then you can forget it.'

'You mean I have a live prospect for a murder, and I have no forensic evidence.'

'That's pretty much it. I'll have news soon on the mito-chondrial. You may have a DNA profile of someone who handled the knife. Sorry, that's the way the ball bounces.'

'Call me.'

'I will.'

She went to Brophy's desk. 'I want to know where we can pick up Gibbons and O'Grady. I want them in the station tomorrow morning.'

'Still working on it, boss.'

'Just do it.'

When Fiona went back to her desk, Tracy put down his magnifying glass. 'We're all trying our best.'

'I know. We've come so far on a nearly impossible case.' She brought the thumb and forefinger of her right hand almost together. 'And we're this close. I can feel it. Gibbons and O'Grady were in Inis Mór to kill the man who abused them. I'm going to sweat them until one of them cracks.'

'You're getting too involved in this case. You're always telling me not to take things so seriously. Sometimes I think you should listen to your own advice. Is there something about this case that strikes a chord with you?'

'I've got a shrink at home; I don't need one at work.'

'Something is eating you. Maybe if you shared.'

'There's nothing personal and I have nothing to share. I just don't like to lose.'

He picked up the magnifying glass. 'We're not going to lose.'

She went to the ladies' room and splashed water on her face. There isn't a police officer alive who is totally detached or who doesn't have something on their mind. That's why so many coppers are in therapy. Aisling didn't talk about her outside clients, but Fiona would bet that most of them led less stressful lives than the average murder detective. She took a paper towel from the dispenser. 'They'll crack,' she said to the mirror. She wished she had the confidence.

FIONA WAS ABOUT to sit when Tracy stopped her. 'Horgan called while you were communing with nature. He mentioned that it was almost the end of play.'

She cursed and turned on her heel. What she didn't need right now was a dose of Horgan, but beggars can't be choosers.

Horgan's desk had been cleared and he was ready to head home. 'You were supposed to brief me on the investigation. O'Reilly has been missing all afternoon and he didn't tell his secretary where he was going.'

'It's a toss-up between the Park and the Bishop's Palace. I have two suspects that I think were involved in the murder. There was no ritual killing. The motive appears to be revenge associated with child abuse. There are going to be repercussions way beyond this office when the whole story comes out. One sick individual is going to bring a lot of people down with him. But some of them deserve it because they probably knew what he was up to and did nothing to stop him.'

'You're sure you can get them?'

'There's no forensics and so far, the case against them is circumstantial. But they were involved.'

'You're good, Madden. I don't say it often enough, but you are good. It wasn't me that leaked by the way.'

'I didn't think you did,' she lied.

FIONA AND TRACY were alone in the squad room. Tracy was still searching for the last boy and Fiona was planning for the following day. Brophy had managed to locate Gibbons and O'Grady and arranged to have both attend for interview at the station the following morning. It was past knocking off time, but she wasn't tired. The case was coming together but there was no chance of a conviction and the DPP would laugh at the evidence she had. She was about to call it a day when Tracy turned to her and smiled.

He wrote on a notepad and passed the page to her. 'The last boy.'

She looked at the name on the page and her face saddened. She recognised the name. 'Looks like we're heading back to Inis Mór.'

DAY EIGHT

CHAPTER FORTY-EIGHT

F iona was too excited to sleep. She watched an inane comedy show until past midnight and then crawled into bed beside Aisling. When she woke, the clock on her bedside table showed five minutes past four. She was wide awake, so she slipped out of bed, dressed quickly and silently and went into the living room. It was pitch black outside. Her muscles were still taut from the previous day's exertion, and she wondered if a run would help loosen them, but she didn't feel like exercise. She contemplated putting her favourite old movie into the DVD player but decided instead to put on her fleece and get some air. She walked down the short road that led to the rocky shore of Galway Bay. She sat on *her* rock. Her grandfather had christened it *Fiona's rock* when she was a little girl and that had become a family story. The ocean had been encroaching for the past twenty years. But her rock still stood proudly against the waves although she knew that in time it too would disappear. But that morning with the first streaks of light appearing over her shoulder she stared out to sea and watched a mind movie of all the happy days she'd had as a child. She missed her grandfather terribly; he had been her real rock. He'd stood with her through thick and thin and she was glad he had lived to see her pass out of Templemore a fully-fledged police officer. She couldn't say the same for her father. She had cried for weeks after he had left and she realised that he wouldn't be coming back. It was like a death without a funeral, but the grief was the same. Someone she loved wasn't there and wouldn't be returning. Except he was coming back. Aisling was continually asking her how she felt about that. She didn't answer because she didn't know how she felt. He was coming back to die. This time there would be a funeral, and she could grieve properly. This time it might be different, this time she wouldn't have to love him. She felt a tear leave her eye and trace a line along her cheek until she wiped it away. She would have to steel herself for the days ahead. She would put three young men through the wringer, men who, in a better world, she might never have met. She wasn't looking forward to being the person trying to inflict more pain on them. In her opinion, they had suffered enough. The light from the east was casting golden beams across the ocean bringing the Aran Islands into stark relief. She stayed staring out into the bay while the scene in front of her was illuminated like a fabulous diorama. She loved this place. It had its ghosts but there was a serenity and a closeness to nature. Her feeling for Connemara was almost religious. She had no idea how long she had spent sitting watching the earth wake up. Perhaps this had been her Gethsemane.

WHEN FIONA and Tracy entered the interview room at the station, Alan Gibbons was staring at the table. He raised his head slowly and looked at them.

Fiona put a buff-coloured file on the table and sat facing Gibbons, Tracy beside her. She was surprised that Gibbons showed no fear. People at their first police interview are generally a bundle of nerves. Gibbons was the exception that proves the rule. He was fair-haired with good features and a pleasant face. He was dressed casually in an open-neck shirt and a cotton blazer. 'I'm Detective Sergeant Madden and my colleague is Detective Garda Tracy. We are investigating the murder of James Mangan on Inis Mór eight days ago.'

'Am I under arrest? Gibbons asked.

'No,' Fiona said. 'This is a preliminary interview.'

'Should I have legal representation?'

'If you wish.'

'I think I'd like that. My solicitor is outside in his car.'

'Call him.'

Gibbons made the call.

'Would you like something to drink? Tea or coffee?'

'I hear the beverages in these places are crap, but I'll try your coffee.'

Five minutes later there was a knock on the door and a short squat man wearing a pin-striped suit and carrying a brief-case entered the room and sat beside Gibbons. He produced two business cards and pushed them across the table. 'Gerard Fahy.' He removed a pad and pen from his briefcase and asked Fiona and Tracy for their names before writing them into his notepad. 'Please continue.'

Fiona began. 'I am the senior investigating officer looking into the death of James Mangan on Inis Mór. You may have heard about it.'

'Yes,' Gibbons said. 'Ritual killing, satanists, like that *Wickerman* film.' He sipped the station coffee, didn't look too pleased, and pushed the cup aside.

'That was newspaper talk,' Fiona said. 'James Mangan was murdered.'

'What has that got to do with my client?' Fahy asked.

'That's what we're here to establish,' Fiona said. 'You were a pupil at St Cormac's College for a period?'

'Yes,' Gibbons said. 'From the age of ten until seventeen.'

'And during that period, you got to know James Mangan?'

Gibbons looked at his solicitor who nodded. 'I wouldn't say

that I got to know him. He was my form master for one year and he taught me English for several years.'

'You didn't know him very well?'

'Not really.'

She opened her file, removed a photo and laid it on the table.

'Do you recognise the boy in this photo?'

Gibbons smiled as he lifted the photo. 'Yes, it's me.'

'What age would you say you are?'

'Eleven or twelve.'

'Did you consent to James Mangan taking this photo of you?'

'I've never seen this photo before today. I didn't even know it existed. It could be Photoshopped for all I know.'

'Did James Mangan sexually abuse you?'

'What! Are you kidding me? He was my teacher full stop.'

Fiona and Tracy looked at each other. She took another photo out of her file and put it on the table. 'This is a photo taken on the quay at Kilronan on the morning that the body of James Mangan was discovered. Would you please look at the man circled? Is that you?'

Gibbons picked up the photo and looked at it. 'Yes, I was in Kilronan last week.'

Fiona took out another photo and placed it on the table. 'Do you know the man circled in this photo?'

Gibbons examined the photo. 'Never saw him before in my life.'

'Would it surprise you if I told you he also attended St Cormac's College?'

'He wasn't in my year, or I would have known him. If he's younger or older than me I might have met him, but we weren't friends.'

Fahy dropped his pen and looked at Fiona. 'I'm sorry for interrupting you, detective sergeant, but where are you going with these questions? My client was a student of Mr Mangan and yes, he was in Inis Mór when Mr Mangan was killed. If you have evidence of my client's involvement in the death of James Mangan other than what we've already seen, I suggest you put it on the table. Otherwise, I am going to advise my client to terminate this interview by leaving. You're fishing and my client isn't biting.' He packed away his notepad and pen and closed his briefcase.

Fiona stared at Gibbons. 'We know that Mangan was a child abuser and despite your protestations, I think he did abuse you and that you were part of a conspiracy to murder him.'

'Really, detective sergeant.' Fahy was on his feet. 'I am surprised that you would slander my client with baseless accusations. When you have evidence of his involvement in such a conspiracy, you can give my office a call.' He tapped Gibbons on the shoulder and the young man rose. Gibbons picked up the coffee cup. 'Nice try, I'll wash it in the bathroom and leave it there for Garda Tracy.' He smiled as he and his solicitor left the room.

'Clever bastard,' Fiona said.

'That went well,' Tracy said, putting away his pen.

Fiona put the photos back in her file. 'The minute I saw how relaxed he was when we entered the room, I was afraid we were in trouble. Breaking them might prove more difficult than I thought. I hope to God Foley comes through for us.'

'What about O'Grady?'

'Let's look at him. Maybe he isn't made of the same stern stuff as Gibbons.'

CHAPTER FORTY-NINE

F iona had an hour to kill before O'Grady was due to
arrive. Her first port of call was Brophy. She told him
what had happened in the Gibbons' interview and that it
would probably be repeated with O'Grady. If she was going to
make a conspiracy charge stick, she would have to provide
some proof. Conspirators needed to contact each other. She
wanted Brophy to get warrants for their phones and their
emails.

'That's heavy duty, boss,' Brophy said. 'Think about the
O'Dwyer case. They had him bang to rights on the mobile
phone data and the stuff on his computer. Then he goes and
brings a case against the use of that data conflicting with Irish
law and wins. We might end up in the same boat. I'll prepare
the warrants but getting them signed will be another matter.
Maybe you should take them upstairs yourself.'

Brophy had a point. The O'Dwyer case would screw up
police work until the lawyers straightened out the legal issues
regarding data ownership. There wasn't a dog's chance that
Horgan or O'Reilly would put themselves on the line. The
college boys weren't going to roll over. They had taken their
time in planning the murder and they were careful not to leave

any evidence at the crime scene. She knew they were involved but she might not be the one to collar them. An hour dragged by until Tracy tapped her on the shoulder. 'O'Grady is downstairs.'

She picked up the file and followed him to the interview room.

When Fiona and Tracy entered the room, O'Grady was sitting back in his chair. He eyed them suspiciously as they took their places facing him.

Fiona began by introducing herself and Tracy. As she was speaking, she stared at O'Grady. He was red-haired and she hoped more temperamental than the phlegmatic Gibbons. He was a good-looking young man and like Gibbons, he was dressed casually in a stylish jacket over an open-necked shirt. He came across as cool and confident. It looked like St Cormac's was worth the five thousand a term after all. She finished her spiel by pointing out that they were investigating the death of James Mangan. O'Grady didn't bat an eyelid.

O'Grady looked at his watch. 'I had a busy morning planned, detective sergeant. I'd really like to help you, but I know nothing about James Mangan's death. I hope we can get this over quickly.'

Fiona smiled. Brophy's profile had mentioned that O'Grady had finished top of his class in law at Trinity College in Dublin. He would not be asking for a solicitor.

'Sorry for messing up your agenda. Can we offer you something to drink, tea or coffee?'

'No thank you.'

'We would just like to explore a few issues with you.'

'Of course, since I haven't been cautioned and there's no recording equipment, I assume I am here simply as a citizen who might have relevant information.'

'That's the situation. You knew James Mangan?'

'Every pupil who attended St Cormac's knew James

Mangan. He was my English teacher and my form master for one year.'

'What did you think of him?'

'As a teacher, he certainly knew his subject and he was good at getting the information across.'

'As a man?'

'He was charismatic, a bit aloof, and a hard taskmaster.'

'Did you like him?'

'Not particularly.'

Fiona removed a photo from her file. 'Do you recognise this boy?'

O'Grady took a quick look at the photo and frowned. 'It's me.'

'The photo was taken by James Mangan, does that surprise you?'

'A little.'

'Why are you not wearing clothes in the photo?'

'I have no recollection of this photo being taken, so I can't answer that question.'

Fiona decided she would have to go hard. 'Mangan has been selling this and other photos on the Internet to paedophiles. Does that bother you?'

'There's very little I can do about it. I'd be more worried if my current girlfriend released a sex tape without my knowledge. I was a child when that photo was taken.'

'Did Mangan sexually abuse you?'

'Not to my knowledge.' The answer was delivered in a calm confident voice.

Fiona placed the photograph of the crowd on the quay at Kilronan on the table. 'Do you recognise the man whose face is circled?'

'It's me.'

'This photo was taken on the morning that James Mangan's body was discovered. You were on Inis Mór at that time.'

'I was certainly on Inis Mór when that photo was taken. I have no idea when Mangan was murdered.'

She produced a photo of Gibbons. 'Do you know this man?'

O'Grady looked at the photo. 'No.'

'He was also a pupil at St Cormac's. Your paths never crossed?'

'I don't think so. One stuck to one's form. I may have played football against him, but I really have no idea.'

'Strange, two boys from the same school where Mangan taught and abused boys being on the island where he was murdered at the same time.'

'A coincidence certainly.' He looked at his watch. 'I'm sorry but I really must leave. Unless, of course, you wish to show me evidence that can link me to Mangan's murder.' He waited a beat. 'I didn't think so.' He stood and left the room.

'I hope you took note of that interview,' Fiona said. 'The questions were answered in the minimum number of words. He gave no additional information. We're going to need more than a couple of photos and a lot of conjecture to break O'Grady.'

THE MOOD WAS sombre as the three detectives reviewed the morning's interviews. 'We still have one more ex-pupil to inter-view but these boys have been clever and I've no reason to believe that we'll make progress without physical evidence to back up our theory.' Fiona had used the word *we* advisedly. She was the one who was driving the theory that the boys from St Cormac's had been involved in Mangan's murder. She had been the one who had rejected the ritual murder hypothesis and she was the one who had rejected Tracy's *scorned woman* theory. If the investigation came to nothing, she would be the one that carried the can. 'How are the warrants coming along?'

'They'll be ready this afternoon,' Brophy said.

'What's the problem?' Tracy asked.

Fiona explained the situation regarding the O'Dwyer case. 'Horgan definitely won't sign the warrants and I suppose neither will O'Reilly.'

'So, where are we?' Tracy said.

'Garda Brophy will continue to look into the backgrounds of Gibbons and O'Grady. I know that they were involved but I doubt if I'll ever be able to prove it. We would certainly need physical evidence that they were present at the crime scene and we're not going to get that. Even if their DNA was found at the site, we have no proof it was deposited at the time of the murder. We need someone to confess and that's not going to happen.'

'What about Foley?'

'He has the DNA boys working on trying to extract skin cells from the decorations on the handle of the dagger. Apparently, it'll be a minor miracle if they succeed.'

'And in the meantime?'

'We keep plugging away and we pray.'

CHAPTER FIFTY

F iona generally thought of herself as a nice person but
sometimes she came up with ideas that she was
genuinely ashamed of. She had lunched with Aisling and they
had discussed the case and how she should approach the interview with the last boy on the following day. She had liked
Charlie Grealish when she had met him on Inis Mór. More
than that she felt a level of kinship with him. Now she was
going to demean herself to prove him a murderer.

'We're going out,' she said to Tracy as soon as she returned
to the station. She picked up the file that Brophy had made on
Grealish.

'Where are we going?'

'Kinvara, a small seaport village to the southwest of
Galway.'

'And what's in Kinvara.'

'Margaret Grealish lives there.'

'I didn't think you had it in you.'

'That just shows you how desperate I am. Let's give her a
call and see if she'll entertain us this afternoon.'

. . .

MARGARET GREALISH LIVED in a large two-storey detached house just off the main road into Kinvara. Tracy pulled into the wide area at the front of the house and parked beside a Range Rover. 'How do we play it?' he said as he turned off the engine.

'It's about Mangan not about her or her son, and I want her DNA.'

'You are a sneaky so-and-so.'

'Needs must when the devil drives.'

When Tracy knocked, the door was opened by a well-dressed and groomed middle-aged lady. She looked the way Fiona hoped she would look in her fifties. She was slim and wore a loose sweater over a narrow paisley skirt. Her grey hair was cut short exposing a face with high cheekbones and piercing blue eyes. Tracy held out his warrant card for her perusal and she opened the door wide to permit him and Fiona to enter.

She closed the door, led them into the living room and invited them to sit. 'Can I offer you tea? I've just baked a lemon drizzle cake.'

'That would be lovely,' Fiona sat on a couch and Tracy joined her. 'Detective Garda Tracy is very fond of lemon drizzle cake.' She looked around the living room, the paintings smelled of money, a display case was full of silver and there were Persian carpets underfoot. Beyond the bay window was an expansive view of Galway Bay.

'She's not short of a few shillings,' Tracy remarked. 'Hardwood flooring, solid teak by the look of it.'

Grealish re-entered the room carrying a tray with three cups, a teapot, milk jug and sugar bowl and a plate with three slices of cake. Tracy rose to assist her, but she waved him off. She put the tray on a coffee table situated in front of the detectives. She poured their tea and invited them to milk and sugar themselves.

She sat facing them. 'I was a bit confused by the purpose

of your visit.'

'We are currently investigating the death of James Mangan,' Fiona said. 'You possibly read about it in the papers.'

'Yes, I think I have, something about satanism.'

'He was a teacher at St Cormac's where your son Charles was one of his pupils.'

Grealish sipped her tea. 'I didn't know that.'

'We've discovered that Mangan had taken lewd photos of several of the boys, and we've located one of Charles. We won't upset you by showing you the photo, but we wondered whether you or your husband knew about this.' Fiona put milk and sugar in her tea.

'You mean did Charles ever mention an episode involving this man Mangan?'

'Yes.'

'I'm afraid not. When did this occur?'

'Charles would have been about eleven or twelve. Perhaps he said something to your husband.'

'My husband was rarely around. He was totally dedicated to his business, and it finally killed him; massive heart attack.' She sat silently for a moment.

'I'm sorry,' Fiona said.

'Long time ago. I was thinking more about Charles. This business with Mangan could explain a lot. Charles was a wonderful boy growing up, even accounting for the fact that his father didn't have much time for him. He suddenly changed. He started having night fears and became depressed. His schoolwork dropped off a cliff and he withdrew from his friends. He was quite sporting, but he quit sport completely. Have you spoken to Charles?'

'No, perhaps he has suppressed memories about that period of his life.'

Grealish's brow furrowed, and she absentmindedly put her cup on the edge of the coffee table. 'He had quite a rocky period when he left school. There were issues with drugs and then his father died. He was left some money and by a miracle, he pulled his life together. He put his money into helping rehabilitate young drug addicts. What are you going to do about Mangan?'

'I'm afraid he's beyond the law but we will be looking into whether he could have been stopped at an earlier date.'

'What a dreadful business. Was Charles the only boy photographed?'

'I'm afraid not.'

Tracy leaned over the coffee table and managed to knock Grealish's teacup onto the hardwood floor where it broke in two.

Grealish jumped up and headed into the kitchen and returned with a brush and pan. She looked at the ground, but the cup was gone. She turned to Tracy and saw he held it in his hand.

'I'll replace the cup,' he said.

'Don't be ridiculous.' Grealish held out her hand. 'Give it here.'

'He feels bad about breaking it,' Fiona said. 'Let him try to replace it.' She stood up. 'Thank you for agreeing to meet us. You've been very helpful.'

Grealish looked confused. 'Did I really help you?'

'Every piece of information we collect is important.' Fiona extended her hand.

Grealish put down the brush and pan and shook Fiona's hand. She led the two detectives to the door and waved them goodbye.

'You are one sneaky you-know-what.' Tracy removed the cup from his pocket and dropped it into a plastic evidence bag. That's the thing about you, boss. The odd person talks about going the whole nine yards. You actually do it.'

'We need to get the sample back to the station as quickly as possible.'

· · ·

'You FOLLOWED up on our little talk at lunch.' Aisling and Fiona were cleaning the dinner dishes. 'And it's left you feeling unhappy.'

'Everything about this case makes me feel unhappy. A group of boys were abused, and I'm sure people knew about it. If they didn't exactly know about it, they suspected and they did nothing. Boys suffered major trauma at a young age and from what I've seen they've come out of it. But that's just what they're showing me. The trauma was so deep that they harboured the desire to murder their abuser. And when they got the chance to act, they took it. One person plunged the knife into Mangan but others were involved. And they've been clever about it. The murder scene was carefully chosen, and the murder arranged to fit Mangan's obsession with the occult. If we'd gone down the road they wanted us to follow, the crime would never have been solved.'

Aisling stacked the plates on a shelf. 'Don't count your chickens on that one. Most people who suffer that kind of trauma only recover when they receive an apology from the person who abused them. With Mangan dead that avenue has been cut off. If Mangan went the whole way with his abuse, those boys may carry that trauma to the grave. They should all receive therapy paid for by that damn school. You're going to Inis Mór tomorrow to interview the last boy?'

'Yes.'

'You think he was involved?'

'I think maybe he was the major player. I don't want him to be. I like him and I relate to him. I knew a young girl just like him.'

'Maybe that will colour what happens.'

'I can't allow that.'

'Then I don't envy you. Empathy is one of God's great gifts to man but unfortunately, we don't use it often enough. Movie and bed?'

'Movie and bed'

DAY NINE

CHAPTER FIFTY-ONE

Fiona leaned over the rail at the bow of the ferry. The weather was clear and crisp when they left Rossaveal which made the islands that lay ahead feel close enough to touch. Outside the bay, there was a chop on the sea and as they ploughed ahead a spray of briny water rose in the air from the prow and smacked into her face. The spray stung and she found pleasure in the pain. She had been a reluctant riser and Aisling had to push her out of the door when Tracy had arrived at the cottage. It was the final day of the investigation into the murder of James Mangan.

'You're taking a bit of punishment.' Tracy joined her at the rail as the ferry hit a wave and spray covered them both. 'I think your mate on the bridge is in a hurry. Maybe we should move back like most of the clever passengers.'

Fiona looked around and saw that they were the only ones at the bow.

Tracy leaned towards her. 'You'll be soaked by the time we get to Inis Mór but from the look on your face I don't think it would matter much to you.'

She left the rail and moved back to a point that the spray failed to hit. If all went to plan today, she was going to unmask a murderer and put him in jail. She should have been happy. She and Tracy had done their jobs and there should be congratulations all round. But there probably wouldn't be. It would be one of those cases where a lot of people would be happier if they hadn't done their jobs so well.

'What about a cup of tea?' he asked.

She looked at him and smiled. He was turning out to be a real find. 'You think your constitution could take what passes for tea.'

'I like it better when you smile.'

'There's not much to smile about.'

'Horgan can be a bit of an arsehole but amid all the bull-shit there's the occasional pearl of wisdom. Our job is to inves-tigate the crime and bring the culprit to book. We do our part, and the legal and penal system does the rest. We can't be the investigators and the judge and jury.'

'We're almost there but Brophy was proved right. Neither Horgan nor O'Reilly would sign the warrants. I got the impres-sion that they didn't exactly wish us well.' She looked over his shoulder and could clearly see the village of Kilronan ahead. It was a place that had held pleasant memories for her, but the memories of this day would not be among them.

They were the last passengers off the ferry. Clarke was at the end of the quay smoking and chatting with O'Flaherty. Tracy had convinced her to let Clarke away with his indiscre-tion. She supposed it was a case of letting him with no sin cast the first stone. Still, she would never trust the guy.

While they were walking along the quay, Fiona's phone rang, and she stopped to answer it. She moved to the shelter of the quay wall and listened. 'Thanks, I'll be in touch.'

'Who was that?'

'Later.' She marched towards Clarke and O'Flaherty.

'Will you be needing the van?' O'Flaherty smiled as they approached.

'No,' Fiona said. 'You're free to pick a sucker from among our fellow passengers.'

The smile died on O'Flaherty's face. 'I thought I was a member of the team.'

'Not anymore,' Fiona said. 'You've been dumped.'

'She only joking,' Tracy said quickly. 'When we're finished, we'll give you a bell and we'll have a farewell drink.'

'You've finished your investigation?' Clarke dr/opped his cigarette and crushed it under his shoe.

'More or less,' Fiona said. 'No thanks to you.'

Clarke reddened.

'Don't worry, just thank Tracy for interceding on your behalf. Send me the receipt from the charity for the five hundred euros.'

'Do you need me?' Clarke asked.

'No, but I'll need the station for the rest of the day. Just stay out of the way.' She began to stride away in the direction of the station. 'We may need your official vehicle.'

Tracy held out his hand for the keys.

Clarke fished the station key and the car key from the pocket of his tunic before dropping them into Tracy's hand. 'What's with her today?'

'None of your business.' Tracy put the keys into his pocket. 'Just stay out of her way.' He jogged after her.

Tracy opened the station door. 'How do you want to play it?'

She moved beyond the reception area into the rear. 'We'll use Clarke's office.'

'Are we going to caution him?'

'It's a preliminary interview.'

'A legal adviser might disagree.'

'We need to give him a chance to explain. If he doesn't, we'll arrest him and take him back to Galway. I've arranged for transport.'

'What kind of transport?'

'The kind that bobs around on the ocean like a cork.' She moved to the door. 'Let's get the shitshow on the road.'

Tracy settled himself behind the wheel of Clarke's Ford and started to cough. 'I thought we weren't supposed to smoke in these cars.'

'The car, like Clarke, is clapped out. Both will soon be heading to the knacker's yard.'

'God, but you're harsh today.' Tracy started the car, and the engine made a clunking sound before catching.

Tracy turned off the main road and pulled in at Grealish's cottages. The young people in the field stopped working and looked as the two detectives descended.

Fiona marched up to the door of the main cottage and rapped on it.

Charlie Grealish opened the door. 'DS Madden, back again.'

'Last visit, Mr Grealish. We'd like you to accompany us to the station. We have questions we'd like answered.'

'Sounds serious.' Grealish closed the door behind him.

'Murder usually is.'

Tracy opened the rear door of the car and ushered Grealish in. They drove in silence to the station where Tracy opened the front door and they moved to Clarke's office where Fiona had set two chairs behind the desk with one facing.

'Is this an official interview?' Grealish said when he was seated.

'Do you want us to make it official?' Fiona asked. 'Then we'll move the circus to Galway straightaway.'

Grealish thought for a moment. 'I've done nothing wrong so I've nothing to fear.'

'Good,' Fiona said. 'Then we should be able to get through this quickly.' She introduced Tracy, produced a file from her messenger bag and laid it on the table. She stared at Grealish, and he returned her stare until he broke it off. 'When I spoke to you several days ago, you told me that you didn't know the man we knew at that time as Sebastian Dangerfield. Do you still maintain that position?'

'Yes.'

He had been prepped and was keeping his answers short and sweet. 'You've been interviewed by the police before?' Fiona said.

'Once or twice.'

'I thought so.' She opened the file and put a picture of Mangan on the table. 'Do you recognise this man?'

'He resembles someone who was once my teacher.'

'His name was James Mangan, and he was living on Inis Mór as Sebastian Dangerfield but, of course, you knew that already.'

Grealish sat up straight. 'No, I didn't.'

'You mean that in the year he spent on this tiny island you never ran across the man you knew as James Mangan and who taught you every day of your school life.'

'I never met him.'

'I didn't say that. Did you ever see him?'

'Not enough to recognise him.'

'There's only one way that you are going to get out of the hole you're in and that's to tell us the truth. You knew James Mangan was on the island?'

Grealish didn't reply.

'I was thinking about Mrs Diranne's evidence of your charges always being around Mangan's place,' Fiona said. 'They were keeping an eye on him for you.'

'I don't know what you're talking about.'

'I'm going to drag every one of them in for questioning. I presume that you really care about those young people and I'm sure you don't want them facing a conspiracy charge. I'll leave you to dwell on that.' She opened the file, took out a photo and laid it on the desk. 'Do you recognise this boy?'

Grealish stared at the photo.

She saw his eyes soften and then go hard. He'd never seen the photo before and he was incensed.

'It's me.'

'This photo was found on a laptop that was the property of James Mangan. It was one of many we retrieved. We are currently investigating whether this photo and others are widely available on the Internet. We believe, but we have not yet established, that Mangan was selling these photos to paedophiles.' She stared into Grealish's eyes and thought she saw him suppressing a tear.

'We know that Mangan was abusing the boys at St Cormac's.'

'I've never seen this photo and I have no recollection of it having been taken.'

He was sticking to the line already established by Gibbons and O'Grady. They had all been prepped probably by O'Grady. She took two more photos from the file and placed them beside Grealish's. 'These are similar photos to yours which were taken of your schoolmates Alan Gibbons and Theo O'Grady. I have interviewed both young men and they used the same language when presented with the photos.' She paused for a moment. 'Why don't you tell me about what Mangan did to you and your friends?'

'I don't remember Mangan doing anything to me.'

'Tracy and I spoke to your mother. She told us how you changed in your early teenage years. You became withdrawn, gave up your sporting activities, you were anxious, slept badly and had night fevers.' She looked down at his arms. 'And you self-harmed. These are classic responses to child abuse. You were a victim, Charlie.' She searched his face; he was stoic. 'Tell us about Mangan. What did he do to you?'

'I really have no idea what you're talking about.'

Fiona sighed. She took another photo from the file and placed it on the table. 'This photo was taken by Detective Garda Tracy at Kilronan Quay the morning Mangan's body was discovered. Do you recognise the two young men whose faces have been circled in red?'

Grealish stared at the photo. 'No.'

'They're your friends Gibbons and O'Grady. It's a coincidence that they were also victims of Mangan's abuse, and they were present on the island when he was murdered.'

'They're not my friends.'

'You're a college boy tutored by the Jesuits. Remember during Jesus' agony what he said to Peter? *Before the cock crows you will deny me thrice.* You intend to deny your friends?'

'I told you, they're not my friends.'

Fiona removed a third photo from her file and placed it on the desk on top of the others. 'Have you ever seen this dagger before?'

Grealish stared at the photo. 'Never.'

'It's the dagger that was found embedded in the victim's chest. It was owned by a famous occultist and purchased by Mangan along with other occult paraphernalia.' She placed a blow-up of the handle of the dagger on the desk. 'The handle is heavily decorated with deep grooves. Have you ever heard of mitochondrial DNA?'

'No.' Grealish shifted uneasily in his chair.

'Neither had I before this case,' Fiona said. 'I'm not sure that I fully understand it, but Tracy here has a degree in something or other, so I asked him to look into it.'

Tracy had been writing and he put down his pen. 'Normal DNA analysis is based on having a sample taken directly from the donor. This allows the forensic scientist to develop a full DNA sequence. Mitochondrial DNA is the small circular chromosome found inside mitochondria which are organelles found in cells that are the sites of energy production. The microconidia, and thus mitochondrial DNA, are passed from mother to offspring. That's the science and its major use is in forensic testing. Unfortunately, the criminal at many crime scenes tries not to leave any DNA behind so mtDNA has been developed by forensic scientists to deal with small or in some cases minuscule traces of DNA. A full sequence can be developed from as few as eight or ten skin cells. For example, a murderer might attempt to clean the murder weapon with bleach but if the handle of a knife has grooves it might be possible to retrieve enough skin cells to develop an mtDNA sample and then a full DNA sequence. Luckily, this technique is well-proven and is accepted as the equivalent of full DNA. The druid's dagger used to murder Mangan proved very effective in providing a decent mtDNA sample.' He looked at Grealish. 'Did you get that?'

'I still don't get it,' Fiona said. 'But the nerds working for the Garda Technical Bureau certainly do. We have an mtDNA sample of the last person who held the knife.'

'That wasn't me. I suppose you'd need a sample to compare it to and I don't intend to give you my DNA.'

'We visited your mother yesterday,' Fiona said. 'To get background details on your teenage problem. She had no idea about the photo or any aspect of your dealings with Mangan. Tracy is a competent detective but he's a clumsy bugger. He managed to knock your mother's teacup off the coffee table but he took it away so he could buy her another.'

Grealish slumped in his chair.

'We're going to confirm that the mtDNA on the knife handle is a match to your mother which means that you were the last person to wield the knife.'

Grealish remained silent.

'I'm going to put a hypothesis to you,' Fiona said. 'You, Gibbons and O'Grady were abused by Mangan, possibly even sexually abused. I'm sure that you three are not the only ones but you came out to one another, and you formed a little group of the abused. I think the basis of the group was that if you ever got the chance for revenge, you'd take it. You'd gotten on with your life and found a niche where you could be helpful to people who had been injured like you as teenagers and who turned to drugs. Everything was going fine until Mangan decided to spend his year's *sabbatical* on Inis Mór. You recognised him probably on the street and I doubt if the recognition was mutual. You told your pals and you realised that no one had done anything about the man who had ruined your lives. You planned to kill Mangan. And like I said, it involved your charges keeping an eye on him. Diranne is a busybody, so she spotted the activity. You told me she was mistaken, and I didn't form that impression of her. You needed to make sure that he wouldn't leave as quickly as he arrived. That was the first time I thought you might be involved somewhere along the line. But I had no idea that you might be the ringleader. I think you went to the cottage possibly with your friends and drugged him. He had no idea who you were. You have a dramatic touch about you, so you took the knife and the goat-head mask as props for your little charade at the fort. It was a solid plan. The three of you carried him up the hill, stripped him and laid him out on the stone platform. Then you plunged the dagger into his heart, eviscerated him and placed the knife back in the original stab hole. You used spray paint to draw the pentagram. There was no pagan ritual but because of Mangan's interest in the occult, you wanted us to believe that's how he died. And we almost bought it. How am I doing?'

Grealish looked straight ahead.

Fiona looked at Tracy. 'Will you do the necessary with Mr Grealish?'

Tracy stood. 'Please stand, Mr Grealish.'

Grealish stood.

'Charles Grealish, under Article 3 of the Criminal Justice Act of 1990, I am arresting you on suspicion of the murder of James Mangan at Inis Mór. You do not have to say anything but anything that you do say will be written down and used in evidence against you.'

'Call Brophy and tell him we'll need the transport,' Fiona said. 'I want Mr Grealish in Mill Street as soon as possible.'

Tracy took out his phone.

'Do it outside,' Fiona said.

Tracy's eyebrows rose but he headed for the door.

Fiona waited until Tracy was out of the room. She stood and locked the door before retaking her seat. 'When we last met you said that you recognised me as someone who'd had the same experience as you. How did you know?'

Grealish smiled. 'As I said, I'm an expert at spotting fellow travellers. It's in the way you carry yourself, the way you walk, the way you talk and the way you lug your aggression around with you. It's become a part of you. You were sexually abused; you did the drugs and led a degrading lifestyle. You've turned it around, but the mark is still on you. There's no reset button. You sometimes think of your abuser, and you want to kill him. You only require the opportunity. That's why you understand me. We'll probably be victims until we die.'

Fiona leaned forward. 'Tell me what happened. You'll tell it all eventually. Concentrate on the extenuating circumstances. The man was abusing children. He was a paedophile who could and should have been stopped.'

The door handle rattled and there was a knock on the door.

'Let him in,' Grealish said. 'I want to make a statement.'

Fiona opened the door.

Tracy stared at her before taking his place. 'The rib will be here in an hour. A rib is an open boat, right.'

Fiona smiled. 'They'll kit us out.'

Grealish looked at Tracy. 'Take out your phone and record my statement.'

Tracy set his phone up and put it on the table in front of him.

'My name is Charles Grealish and I murdered James Mangan. I acted alone. I recognised Mangan as a man who abused me when I was twelve years old. On the night of the murder, I went to his cottage and told him I was a member of a satanist group and there was going to be a pagan ritual at Dun Aengus. I said I could arrange for him to take part. I knew his proclivities, so I knew which button to push. I convinced him to take along his dagger and goat mask. He was as excited as a child on Christmas morning. I had a flask containing brandy and a couple of GBH tablets picked up from one of my old contacts in Galway. Nothing was happening when we got to the fort, so I offered him a drink while we were waiting. The flask was two ended. He drank from the top end, and I drank from the bottom which contained only brandy. He fell asleep and became comatose. I thought that I'd gone too far and killed him, but I could feel a pulse. I undressed him, laid him on the platform and stabbed him. Then I collected his clothes and the goat-head mask, drew the pentagram and left. I burned the clothes and the goat-head mask.'

'How did you lay him on the platform without help, he was a large man?'

'By the time he fell unconscious we were sitting on the platform. I just tilted him back, laid him out and undressed him. Then I waited for his eyes to open. I was wearing his goat-head mask and brandishing his dagger. He could see but couldn't move. He was hallucinating. The scenario I had set up was playing in his mind. I wanted to scare the shit out of him, and I think I managed.' He smiled at the thought. 'When I stood above him with the dagger poised, I had a mental picture of what he did to me in his cottage when I was drugged. I plunged the knife in then withdrew it an...' His speech tailed off

'You did all this alone? You carried the goat head and the clothes back to your cottage?'

'We don't have a refuse collection, so we burn non-compostable waste in a burn pit. The clothes and the goat head were ashes the next morning.'

Tracy's phone rang, and he took the call. 'The boat is on the way,' he said. 'We'll be back in Galway by lunchtime. Horgan wants to speak to you.'

'Do you have a solicitor?' she asked Grealish.

'Yes.'

'Then you'd better call him and tell him to meet us at Mill Street.'

She turned to Tracy. 'Make Charlie a cup of tea.'

CHAPTER FIFTY-TWO

F iona sat on the stool in the reception area of the Garda station. She'd known it was going to be a shit day, but it was exceeding her expectations. The problem was that it resonated with her. She picked up her phone.

'Well?' Horgan's tone was brusque.

'He did it. Alone he says.'

'But you don't believe him?'

'No, I think his two friends helped but he was the one who wielded the knife. We have the mtDNA that'll put him behind bars, but Gibbons and O'Grady will skate for lack of evidence and there's no chance Grealish is going to implicate them.'

'Will he plead guilty?'

'You mean will all the crap come out?'

'You know what I mean.'

'If it were me, I wouldn't but I have no idea what he'll do.'

'We're not talking about a hard-arse like you, Madden.'

'No, we're not. He's a nice young man whose life has been ruined by a teacher who abused his position. Someone knew about it and did nothing. He'll play well with the jury and the press, and someone will eventually apologise but they'll be crucified just the same. And they deserve to be crucified.'

'What's next?'

'We'll bring him back to Galway, charge him and take his statement. Then he's yours and the DPP's. Given the circumstances, I'm sure a deal will be in the offing. The big question is whether he'll take it or not.'

'Is his solicitor informed?'

'He'll be in Mill Street when we arrive.' There was no sign of a *well done, Madden*. She hadn't really expected one, but it would have been nice. 'I don't suppose there'll be a celebratory drink.'

There was a silence on the line. 'It's traditional but I think in this case we might forgo the pleasure,' Horgan eventually said. 'I have a feeling that a lot of shit is going to be flying about when this goes public. I hope that you and Tracy have enough paper to cover my arse.'

Fiona suppressed a laugh. 'I'll leave the paperwork to Tracy.'

'You always get there in the end, Madden.'

He couldn't go the full distance to well done but she supposed it was in lieu of actual congratulations. 'It's a real pleasure to be a public servant in the new Ireland.' She terminated the call.

CHAPTER FIFTY-THREE

They didn't wait for five o'clock before hitting Taaffes. If there wasn't going to be a traditional drink to celebrate their success, they would have their own celebration. They sat at the end of the bar reminiscing about the case. The trip to Rossaveal in an open-air rib was an adventure. The chop was still on the water and the gear provided by the skipper just sufficient to keep the spray and the chill out. Grealish was handed over to two uniforms at the quay and Fiona and Tracy followed the police car to Mill Street. The duty sergeant read Grealish the charge sheet and he was put in a room to meet with his solicitor who had already informed Horgan that there would be no more interviews and a statement from his client would be forthcoming.

Tracy fished around in his jacket pocket. 'I bought you a present. Something to remember the case by.' He handed her a DVD.

She looked at the cover. 'The Wickerman.' She was touched by Tracy's kindness.

'The original, made in 1972 starring Edward Woodward and Christopher Lee.'

'Thanks.' She put the DVD in her bag. 'Do you have a date tonight?' she asked.

'No.' Tracy sipped his pint. 'Cliona is away on a shoot.'

'Good, because I intend to get shit-faced, and I might need someone to take care of me.' Fiona smiled when she saw the effect of her words on Tracy. He took out his phone and she guessed a call to Aisling was imminent. 'Don't worry, I called her earlier.' She finished her pint of Guinness and called for another round. 'She'll be here when she's finished work.'

'Working with you is a barrel of monkeys.' Tracy laughed. 'I never know what to expect next.'

'Maybe you'd prefer to work with someone like Ginny Hinds, all made-up, dressed like a mannequin and up on six-inch heels. She has a nice pair of legs though, don't you think.'

'I hadn't noticed.'

The drinks arrived although Tracy was only halfway through his. Fiona paid then turned back to him. 'Liar,' she said. 'I saw you ogling her.'

They both burst out laughing.

Fiona looked up. Aisling was standing at the door watching them. Fiona beckoned to her.

Aisling dropped her bag on the ground and sat on a free stool. 'If I didn't know better, I would have thought that you two were lovers.'

The smiles disappeared from their faces and they both blushed.

'Our superior refused to stick with the tradition of a celebratory drink,' Fiona said. 'Tracy and I decided to have our own celebration. Turning us into lovers might be a step too far.'

Tracy's cheeks were returning to their normal pale colour. 'And I have a girlfriend that I happen to love.'

'Relax.' Aisling sat and ordered a juice. 'I think it's nice that you get on so well together.' She looked at Fiona. 'But I wouldn't blame you fancying a handsome lad like Tracy.'

Tracy reddened again and Fiona and Aisling laughed.

'She said she wants to get shit-faced,' Tracy said. 'And I don't want to be around for that.'

'Nobody's getting shit-faced tonight,' Aisling said. 'We're up at the crack of dawn tomorrow to pick up her mother and the three of us are off to Shannon to collect her father.'

'What do you mean *we*?' Fiona was on the edge of her seat. 'I thought Flanagan was going to drive.'

'Don't play coy. You know that plan was shelved long ago. It would have been too easy for you to skip out.'

'You're devious,' Fiona said. 'I didn't think you had it in you.'

'Thanks be to God,' Tracy said. 'One more round and we'll call it a celebration.'

'What will happen to the young man you arrested?' Aisling asked.

'The jury will probably shed a tear before finding him guilty,' Fiona said. 'That is if it ever comes to trial. There are a lot of vested interests who will be working hard to keep this affair under wraps.'

Tracy's round arrived.

Fiona finished her pint and put the empty glass on the bar. 'I wish we'd been putting Mangan in jail rather than Grealish. But murder is murder, and our job is to bring the culprits to justice. What happens to them after that is not our business. That's what Horgan told us.'

'But that's not the way you'd like it to be.'

'He's guilty of murder and he should stand trial for that. But there are a lot of other guilty people who will walk free. He was vulnerable and no one protected him. I'm afraid that there are parts of his story that are going to be hushed up.'

'But you did your job,' Aisling said.

'Is that enough?'

Tracy stood and disappeared in the direction of the toilets.

'Have you thought about how you're going to react tomorrow?' Aisling asked.

'You mean have I decided to kill the bastard on the spot.'

'It's important that you visualise what meeting a father you haven't seen in more than twenty years will be like for you. It could be traumatic.'

'I don't do traumatic.' She'd run through a couple of scenarios but none of them would probably happen. There certainly wouldn't be a rush-into-each-others-arms scene. Just as there wouldn't be an acrimonious scene that people would want to catch on their mobile phones.'

'Have you thought about what you're going to say?'

'I've been a bit busy.'

'It's no joke. You have a lot of resentment; it may come out despite your best efforts to control it.'

Tracy was wending his way back to them.

'I'll do my best to be a good girl. Now, let's get this drink down us. I'm tired and a bit emotional. Charlie Grealish got to me in ways I hadn't expected.'

'He reminded you of yourself at a point in your life.'

'Yes, I could just as easily be standing where he is today.'

'This is a sombre looking party.' Tracy picked up his pint from the bar. 'Here's to the best crime-fighting duo since Batman and Robin.'

CHAPTER FIFTY-FOUR

They rose at four o'clock in the morning, had a quick coffee and went to pick up Fiona's mother. Shannon Airport is ninety kilometres from Galway city and most of the journey can be accomplished on a new motorway. They arrived at the airport parking exactly on time at six o'clock. The journey had been made in silence.

Aisling helped Maire out of the rear and turned to Fiona. 'Ready?'

'Ready.' Before going to bed, Fiona had retrieved the cardboard box from underneath her bed and looked again at the photographs of her father. She'd removed a sepia photo of him carrying her on his shoulders. To a little girl, he had appeared big and strong. She stared at the photo committing his face to memory. She was conflicted about meeting him. She was his flesh and blood, and he was an integral part of her past even if it wasn't a particularly pleasant part. As far as she remembered, he had been loving and he'd never struck her. She had been too young to know who he really was and then he was gone. A part of her wished that they had never heard from him again. He had helped create her and take care of her but had then betrayed her. But she was the fruit of his loins. She would carry his DNA to the grave. She noticed that Aisling and her mother were already at the entrance to the airport while she was still standing in the car park. She hurried to catch up with them. When she entered the concourse, she saw them standing under a large TV screen indicating the flight arrivals.

Aisling turned to face her. 'It landed early, more than thirty minutes ago. He's probably already through immigration and customs. Let's take a turn around the airport and see if we can spot him.'

They walked around the concourse looking at those seated in the waiting areas and cafes.

'Maybe he changed his mind,' Maire said when they had gone from one end of the concourse to the other.

'Chance would be a fine thing.' Fiona scanned the area at the end of the concourse. There was no sign of her father.

'Perhaps,' Aisling said. 'Let's give it one more tour.'

They turned and walked back the way they'd come. Halfway along the concourse a strangled voice called 'Maire, is that you?'

Fiona looked in the direction of the voice. There was a small, emaciated man sitting on a seat in the waiting area, a large kitbag at his feet. He was wearing a heavy jacket and jeans and a tuft of curly grey hair shot out from under a flat cap. The skin was loose about a face that bore no resemblance to the man in the photographs she'd examined the previous evening. Her father was in his late fifties. The man who appeared to have spoken looked thirty years older and stood uneasily.

Maire Madden approached him. There was a shocked look on her face. 'Is it you, Conor?'

'It is.'

Fiona joined her mother.

'Welcome.' Maire made no move towards the man.

Fiona bent and picked up the bag. She looked at the man she'd spent twenty years hating. It had been a wasted emotion.

If it had been her wish to reduce him to a shambling wreck, life had done her work for her. 'You look tired. Why don't we get you home?'

'Is this Fiona?' her father said. 'You've grown into a fine woman.'

Fiona wanted to say *no thanks to you,* but the words wouldn't come. She took his arm. 'Let's get you to the car.'

Maire linked her ex-husband's arm as she led him out of the airport building and into the car park. Fiona dumped the kitbag into the trunk.

'You're handling it well,' Aisling said after settling the older couple in the rear.

'If that's my father,' Fiona said. 'He's suffered enough for what he did to us.'

'You'll have to reconnect with him quickly. He doesn't look like he has long to live.'

Fiona nodded.

'Ready?'

'I need to make a quick call.' Fiona moved away from the car, took out her mobile and a card from her pocket then dialled a number. The call went to voicemail 'Hi, Ginny, it's Fiona Madden, I'd like to meet for a drink. I think there are a few things you should know.'

AFTERWORD

Author's Plea

I hope that you enjoyed this book. As an indie author, I very much depend on your feedback to see where my writing is going. I would be very grateful if you would take the time to pen a short review. This will not only help me but will also indicate to others your feelings, positive or negative, on the work. Writing is a lonely profession, and this is especially true for indie authors who don't have the backup of traditional publishers.

Please check out my other books , and if you have time visit my web site (derekfee.com) and sign up to receive additional materials, competitions for signed books and announcements of new book launches.

You can contact me at derekfee.com

HAVE YOU READ THE WILSON SERIES?

If not, you can get the first two books in the series FREE by signing up at: https://www.derekfee.com

ABOUT THE AUTHOR

Derek Fee is a former oil company executive and EU Ambassador. He is the author of seven non-fiction books and sixteen novels. Derek can be contacted at https://www.derekfee.com.

HAVE YOU READ THE WILSON SERIES?

If not, you can get the first two books in the series FREE by signing up at: https://www.derekfee.com

ALSO BY DEREK FEE

The Wilson Series

Nothing but Memories

Shadow Sins

Death to Pay

Dark Circles

Boxful of Darkness

Yield up the Dead

Death on the Line

A Licence to Murder

Dead Rat

Cold in the Soul

Border Badlands

Mortal Blow

Moira McElvaney

The Marlboro Man

A Convenient Death

Fiona Madden

Connemara Girl

Murder in Clifden

Standalone

Cartel

Saudi Takedown

The Monsignor's Son

Crash Course

Dreamhunter